*To all those who strive
for equality and freedom*

Palms and Pomegranates

A Novel

L.S. CSIDA

Artempo Publishing
© 2020 L.S. Csida
All rights reserved.

Book cover and interior design by Monkey C Media
Edited by Adrienne Moch

Pomegranate image: Freepik.com

First Edition
Printed in the United States of America

978-1-7347458-0-1 (trade paperback)
978-1-7347458-1-8 (eBook)

Library of Congress Control Number: 2020910429

Palms

Symbolism:
Victory, triumph, paradise, protection, divine inspiration, justice, supply, respite and hospitality.

Flower Essence:
Represents flexibility, immense strength and the ability to endure even in the midst of extreme wind and weather. Palm essence will help you to stand true in your truth.

Pomegranates

Symbolism:
Fertility, unity of diversity of cultures, abundance of God's love, bloody death, prosperity, hope.

Flower Essence:
Represents all feminine issues and has always declared itself to be about freedom of choice in women's lives. It is useful for helping women resolve how they want to use their creative life force energy, free of cultural, tribal or religious bias.

Quoted, with permission, from *A Guide to Green Hope Farm Flower Essences* by Molly Sheehan.

"It is God who sends rain from the sky, bringing forth buds and green leaves on every plant. The rain causes the grain to swell, the palm trees to yield clusters of dates, the vines to yield grapes, and the olive trees to bear olives; it brings forth all manner of pomegranates. Look at the fruit as it ripens! Surely this is a sign for true believers."

—Qur'an, Al-An'am, Surah 6:99

Thursday Ritual

There may be sweet pleasures for the body in this world.
But anything other than love for Him, whose beauty is unmatched,
is agony to the soul. What is agony of the soul? It is to advance towards death
without being sustained by the water of life. —Rumi

Everything always went the way Perin wanted and she had no reason to believe this day would be any different. After a half day at work on Thursday, she looked forward to the weekend ritual that began at the ancient baths tucked deep within the Casbah that clung to the hills above the Mediterranean city of whitewashed houses.

She passed under the citadel's arched gateway and adjusted her headscarf before ascending the incline. At the top, she encountered a barefoot child in a ragged dress, rummaging through a pile of trash, a jute bag slung over her left shoulder. The girl dislodged a plastic bottle from a mound of sticks, broken glass, leaves, and orange peels, and stashed it in her bag, her eyes locking on Perin. Half tempted to give the girl a few coins, Perin reconsidered as her father's words rang in her head: *Only give if they're selling something you want to buy, or doing a job. If they think begging pays, it will do them, and society, no good.*

She clutched her bag under her arm and followed the maze of passageways toward the center of the walled fortress, reminding herself that her mother's warning was not idle; petty thieves, gangs, drug users, and dealers had always hidden here, away from the prying eyes of police who were often hesitant to enter. But tempering this caution were her childhood memories of spending time here with her father, a time when this inner city was a source of wonder, an escape to a foreign land, a place she could explore and satisfy her curiosity about other ways of life, and people different from the city folk she knew.

Her pulse quickened as she continued up a narrow lane devoid of sunlight, past crumbling walls and worn wooden doors, their once-intricate carvings now only faint shadows. At a tiled public fountain, women—most in Western dress and a few in *abayas* or with headscarves—collected water and washed dishes and clothes. Near them sat two Berber women from the Atlas Mountains with tattooed chins and cheeks, surrounded by their ripped-open burlap bags, heaped with vegetables and herbs they brought down weekly on their pack animals.

Away from prying eyes, she took off her headscarf and draped it around her neck as she neared the candy section, where she sought out her favorite shop. The owner, in a white pillbox hat and smock, sat in his usual spot amid mounds of nougat in various colors, while behind him flies licked the nectar of the hard candies that hung like stalactites from the ceiling. An overhead fluorescent light illuminated him like a portrait encased in a frame of sweets. She bought her favorite white nougat with pistachios.

Purchase in tow, she made her way to the centuries-old mosque adjacent to the main square, where she sat on a nearby bench and began writing a note. A disheveled man emerged from a group idling nearby and came toward her. She instinctively tensed up and turned away, keeping him in her peripheral vision until he was out of sight. She chided herself for being so jittery, but the years away had eroded her visceral memory, and her body needed time to settle in again. Was she letting the stories about the dangers of the Casbah get to her? It was more than that. The air smelled different now. Since coming home, the quarter seemed seedier and more cramped than what she remembered.

She reminded herself that she had always been safe here. And, didn't Huda say that if you think something negative, then something negative will be attracted to you and come your way? Huda was always right.

Under the suspicious eyes of the local denizens, Perin completed her wish: *In Your infinite wisdom, show me I made the correct decision and let my career path be fulfilling. I am but Your servant.* She folded the note in half, wrapped some money around it, and dropped it into the slot in the bronze plaque built into the facade of the mosque.

Sitting back down, she noticed a tall, thin black man in a Texas A&M t-shirt coming her way, his head shaved bald like the American basketball players. He stopped in front of the mosque, looked up at the ancient structure, and then read from his Fodor's guidebook to North Africa, repeating the sequence several times. A small boy, leaning against the mosque's stone façade, walked up to him and offered him a roughly carved camel trinket. The man took the carving, thanked him, and started to reach into his front pocket.

"He doesn't want money. It's a gift," Perin said, placing her scarf back on her head. The man turned and looked at her. "Put your hand on your heart," she told him, her eyes gravitating to his black Levi boot-cut jeans and black cowboy boots with inserts of beige cactus.

The man did as she instructed, hand over heart, and the child did the same before running away.

"Hey, you speak English," he said, coming closer. "You from here?" He had a broad smile and perfect teeth; people here always joked that you could tell Americans by their straight teeth. Before she could answer, one of the men standing nearby yelled at the man, "Are you Muslim or a heathen?"

Perin jumped. She clutched her handbag and nougats against her stomach.

The American smiled at the men, nodded, and asked Perin to translate.

"They want to know if you're a believer." She turned to the men and said in Arabic, "He believes in one God, like you do." She explained to the American what she said, adding, "I don't know if that's true, but—"

"Yeah, cool." He placed a foot on the bench, rested his arm on his knee, and bent forward. Feeling the men's eyes on her, Perin leaned away and then stood up. "I must go. I have to meet someone. Enjoy your stay."

"Wait, can't you have a coffee with me, tell me the best places to go?" he called after her.

She shook her head and ducked under a carpet strung between wooden poles. As she walked away, she chastised herself for not staying to talk to the man, and letting a group of locals intimidate her, making her feel as if she was doing something wrong. But yet her instincts told her to leave; people here had a way of misinterpreting things.

Only three months ago, she had been in New York. She missed the relaxed company of Americans and the ability to be anonymous, to go anywhere and do as you like without eyes following you and casting judgment. It would have been interesting to know what enticed the man to visit and hear his impressions of her county. Next time, she would hold her ground—what could they do, yell at her, call her names? She could handle that. She'd experienced similar things in Woodside while conducting interviews for school—people who did not want their names in the paper, people who resented an interloper inquiring about their lives, people who were just nasty. It had frightened her at first, making her stomach roil and palms sweat, but she gradually gained confidence, and she did what Huda told her to do—visualize herself surrounded by a white light of protection whenever she felt insecure.

"*Balek! Balek!*" rang out the familiar trill of a delivery boy. Perin sidestepped the chunks of meat that butchers had draped over hooks and pressed herself against the wall. A teenager dodged among the people crowding the walkway, a tray of coffee and glasses held aloft as if it was a prop in a dance.

Traversing the main square, the aroma of apple-scented tobacco wafted around her as she passed the outside cafes where men played backgammon and smoked hookahs. She waited until a group of donkeys laden with powdered milk and bags of vegetables passed, and then headed to the small alley that led to the eighteenth century *hammam*. After walking a few meters, she sensed someone was following her. She turned around. The men from the mosque were pointing their fingers at her and calling out, "Prostitute. Get her." One man had a switch in his hand.

Panic constricted her throat and her heart raced. Unable to speak or scream, she felt her legs get weak. There was no one else in the alleyway and she was still a hundred meters from the baths. She started running, but the men quickly closed in around her. Fists pounded on her back and she felt stings of a switch as one of them swatted her torso, legs, and arms. Shielding her face with her hands, she tried to break away, but one man clasped her arm in a painful grip. Everything was happening so quickly that she could barely process it. As the sound of her heartbeat thrashed in her ears, images of her lying beaten and bloody on the cobblestones flashed through her mind. Then she heard women's voices screaming at the men to stop. As the men's attention was diverted by the bags and oranges the women flung at them, Perin forced her way between two of the men and ran inside the women's entrance to the baths.

Gasping for breath, she threw herself flush against the wall and clutched the top of her tunic, tears welling in her eyes. She was safe now; no men were allowed in the women's section. Slowly she sank to the floor, her face in her hands. How could this have happened to her—*to her*? She had done nothing but say a few words to a stranger. She pulled up her pant legs; they had not broken the skin, but red, swollen welts were visible and her back stung. But what hurt the most was that she felt afraid and vulnerable, crushing her self-image of being capable to manage anything.

She wondered about the women who helped her and hoped none of them were injured. They were the brave ones and she should have stayed to help them ward off her attackers. But she was their target—she had to get away.

Ashamed to find herself engaging in self-pity, she pulled herself up and made her way to the heavyset woman commandeering the entrance to the baths. She paid the fee and went into the disrobing chamber, where an attendant handed her a wrap. Perin forced a smile and shook her head; she disliked how the knee-length elasticized sheaths dug into her armpits and she never wore one. But then she hesitated—a wrap might hide some of the welts on her upper legs, and it, along with the bath's thick steam, would hopefully make it difficult for anyone to notice marks.

After locking her clothes and undergarments in a cupboard, she slipped on the *wrap* and wooden sandals, took a towel and a cap for her hair, and went to the entrance to the pools. Gradually, the intricate periwinkle and cerulean blue-tiled walls and Corinthian columns took shape, and like desert mirages, the faint images of women of all ages appeared in the large thermal pool. Most wore wraps or underpants and a few were nude, as she usually liked to be when she took the baths. Skin tones of toast, almond, mocha, and olive glistened and glowed with sweat, earth-toned skins that seemed more sensual than the women she'd seen in the saunas and steam rooms at gyms in New York—stark white bodies, some covered with freckles or red blotches from the heat, others with veins showing through parchment-like skin.

Wearing the towel like a shawl, Perin clung to the perimeter of the room, passing a corner where the melodic strains of a newborn purification ceremony filled the air. Still engulfed in disbelief, she watched, without seeing, while friends and family surrounded the mother and infant, flickering white candles in their hands. A special attendant recited a blessing as she spread henna on the walls and the marble water font before covering the mother and baby with the brown paste. "Water is the source of all that lives. The Qur'an says that without bodily cleanliness, prayer is of no value in the eyes of God. May the baths prepare you for your life, save you from evil, and heal you."

The woman rubbed the child with salt, the symbol of long life; he whimpered as the coarse grains ground against his delicate skin.

Perin's newborn initiation ceremony had also taken place here at these ancient baths, and this was where, one day, she wanted her children to be purified, carrying on the long thread of tradition that linked one generation to another. She had always been made to believe that it was her path in life to continue to populate the land of her ancestors. But she made certain her family knew she would do it only after she had established her career and found the ideal companion; she announced at a young age that she would not necessarily accept their designated mate, should they even so much as think of an arranged marriage.

Shaky and anxious, Perin stopped before a marble scallop shell-shaped washbasin and filled her cupped hands with cool water, splashing it over her face and arms. She needed to sit; her knees felt weak again. She scooted onto the end of a bench, next to two women, and gently stroked the welts on her thigh. As she watched streaks of light from the domed ceiling's skylight strike the sunken pool, she mulled over the attack. What bad timing that she was at the mosque when the American came by, and the men were idling nearby. Once again, doubt about her decision to return home reared its nagging head. She quickly rejected the thought, needing to convince herself that she'd made the right decision. Her attack was a fluke and nothing more. Next time she would be more cautious, and her family must never know this happened or they would try to curtail her activities.

"My husband's going to want sex tonight," one of the women next to her said. "He's coming back from Europe. Those women there argue with men and he gets excited."

"Lucky you," said her companion. "My husband says his arthritis and gout give him too much pain to have sex."

"Divorce him. The Qur'an says you can, if he can't satisfy you."

"Who would I find at my age? I satisfy myself."

Perin had closed her eyes and leaned toward the women to better hear what they were saying when she felt a light tap on her shoulder. She opened her eyes to see her friend, Shereen.

"Why are you wearing *that*?" a nude Shereen said, drawing out the last word like toffee as she sat down next to Perin and kissed her on both cheeks.

Perin brushed a strand of Shereen's curly hair away from her face and then readjusted the towel over her knees. "You shaped your brows. I like it. It opens up your face."

The two women beside Perin went into the pool and another woman took their place, sitting close to Perin. She moved closer to Shereen and frowned at the stranger; the woman's eyes met hers and bore into Perin.

"You didn't answer me," Shereen said. "Why the *wrap*?"

Perin gave a dismissive wave and shook her head.

"What's that on your leg?" Shereen started to move the towel.

"Please. Don't," Perin said, holding it in place and debating whether she should tell Shereen. Realizing she needed to talk to someone about the attack, if only to relieve some angst, and certain her friend would be sympathetic, she told Shereen what happened.

Instead, Shereen whispered, "Are you mad? You can't talk to strange men in public—especially a foreigner. And better not walk alone."

"I don't want people dictating how I live. I did nothing wrong. And I like to wander alone here ... it gives me time to think."

"You can't think anywhere else?" Shereen nudged Perin. "Know what I think? Living abroad made you believe that you can do here, what you did there."

"Maybe." Perin put her hand on Shereen's arm. "Let's talk about something else."

"Being away didn't change your avoidance techniques, I see," Shereen said with a wink. "All right, how's work going?"

"Fine," Perin said through clenched teeth.

"I've thought more about it and I'm glad you didn't get that job with *The Gazette*. Of course, it would have been nice if your first choice had hired you, but I think it's much better you're at *The Daily*—oh, don't give me that look. I only mean that this job is less taxing and you'll have more time to spend with me. You were away too long."

Perin rested her head against Shereen's shoulder. "I missed you, too." Sitting upright, she continued, "Maybe it is better to start with a small paper and make my mistakes there. But honestly, Shereen, the women's section is not what I thought I would be writing about." Perin looked off into space and smiled. "There's one positive aspect—the editor is rather charming. I like the way he runs the newsroom and includes all of us in the weekly meetings. Do you know anything about him, Ali Zayer?"

"I've seen him at the club. Seems a bit on the quiet side. I remember my father saying that his father came from abroad to work in oil here. Married a local woman and stayed." Shereen pulled her hair back and twisted it into a knot. "I always hoped you and Kamal would end up together so we can be true sisters. Wouldn't that be nice?"

Perin smiled. "I thought he was seeing a German girl."

"It means nothing. When he settles down, it will be with someone from here. Well, now he's busy with the business and the ranch, so he isn't thinking of much else."

"You forgot his cars and the cycling club," Perin added. "I'd like to see all he's done with the ranch."

"Come out this week before Leila's wedding." Shereen said. "Listen to this, for her wedding her parents bought her an apartment, on the eleventh floor in one of the new buildings in colonial town, and they gave her one of the family maids to take care of it." Shereen let out a chuckle. "The maid spent one day at the apartment and came back and told Leila's mother she couldn't work there—she said she got altitude sickness."

Perin shook her head and laughed, momentarily forgetting the men from the mosque, who kept invading her mind.

"Remember Leila's brother," Shereen asked, "the one who looks like he has plums stuck in his cheeks? Well, he's decided that the only way he'll find a proper wife is to have his parents arrange a marriage with a daughter of a family friend—but she can't be over twelve—and she is to be promised to him when she turns eighteen. He thinks he's *so* irresistible."

"Don't they all," Perin said as she watched a mother brush her daughter's hair in the pool. "Do you realize we'll be the last two of our group not married?"

Shereen looked down and smiled.

"Is there something I don't know?" Perin said.

"Remember when Hakim and his family were here from Cairo and I told you we got along so well, and he called me every night after he returned home?" Perin nodded. "We discovered we want the same things out of life—we get along so well. Perin, we're in love and a few days ago he asked me to marry him. I was waiting to tell you today."

"Really? Oh, goodness, I'm ... I'm ... I'm so happy for you." Perin hugged her friend and wondered how marriage would change things between them, hoping Hakim would not place too many boundaries around Shereen, and she would not give in to his every demand.

"We're thinking October. My parents are excited. They're friends with his parents."

An attendant asked Perin and Shereen if they were ready to be scrubbed. Perin went to the water basin first, requesting that the woman be gentle on her back and legs, explaining she'd had a horseback riding accident. The woman, her hand encased in a glove-like loofah, made circular movements on Perin's back and worked up a lather of sandalwood-scented soap. As the coarse mitt rubbed her buttocks, Perin turned to Shereen. "What about your plan to work at the Finance Ministry?"

"Too many economists looking for work and entry-level jobs are boring."

Perin knew Shereen did not have to work, but she wondered why she so quickly abandoned all her goals—maybe love did that to a woman, but she was certain she would never give up a career for a man.

Shereen talked about Hakim while the attendant scrubbed her back—how considerate and courteous he was, how his eyes shut out the world when he looked at her, how they could talk about everything, and he made her laugh. Seeing her friend so happy, Perin felt a tinge of jealousy. She'd had admirers over the years, but she'd never felt any major stirring of what she imagined love must be like; she considered the men she knew to be merely friends. While studying abroad in Paris and later in New York, she mostly went out with groups of friends from school, really dating only once—an American named Kris, a sensitive writer from South Carolina who was willing to respect her wishes to not go beyond kissing and fondling.

A masseuse led Perin and Shereen down a corridor with doors fanning out on each side and ushered each of them into a room. Supine on a padded table scattered with rose petals, Perin read the labels on the cobalt blue oil bottles lined up on the metal cabinet across from her: relaxation, invigorating, sensual, inspiration, rejuvenation. She chose rejuvenation.

After the massage, Perin waited for Shereen in the courtyard. As she watched children play tag around the fountain, her thoughts wandered first to the baby being purified, then to the mother combing her daughter's hair in the pool, and then to the girl rooting in the garbage—until the men from the mosque hijacked her thoughts. She shivered and felt her body grow rigid; she placed a clenched fist to her mouth. It was still difficult to accept what had happened to her.

"Excuse me," a middle-aged woman in a business suit said as she sat down next to Perin. "I was there earlier. I saw you get lashed."

"Were you one of the women—"

"You probably did nothing wrong, but you must have done something stupid because they obviously thought it was not in keeping with Allah's wishes—they get riled up at the smallest thing."

Perin felt the blood rise to her face. "Excuse me."

"Why else would you have been attacked?"

Her no-nonsense attitude annoyed Perin. "How can you judge me without the facts?"

"I *was* one of the women who came to your rescue—you ran away before I had a chance to see if you were all right. Are you okay?" She scrutinized Perin without a hint of compassion.

"Yes, nothing serious ... I, yes, I'm fine. I ... I ... thank you for helping me."

"Women should help each other. I hope you will repay it in some way. In the baths I overheard you say you're a journalist at *The Daily*."

Perin closed her eyes and nodded, tempted to tell her it was none of her business. But the woman had helped her and she was curious why she was asking.

"Where else have you worked?"

Perin scanned the woman's square face for a hint of who she was. Her dark auburn hair hung straight to her shoulders, and her wide-set eyes gazed at Perin so fervently that Perin felt she was being hypnotized. Focusing on the woman's thick eyebrows, she said, "My local beat in journalism school—I mean the area I reported on; I studied in America."

The woman hesitated. "Hmm, well, I could tell you a lot. But not here." Steeliness inflected her voice. "There's a lot at stake— there are things that need to be told. And you need to learn to work in covert ways." She thrust a business card at Perin: Zahara Massi, M.D., Department of Psychiatry, University Hospital.

"What exactly—"

"Call me. It might help your career." The doctor stood up and started to walk away.

"Wait a minute," Perin called out, but the woman did not look back.

Perin wondered what was at stake and she had to know more before she called. Whatever it was, it sounded like the doctor had a vested interest in it. As she turned the business card around in her hand, she remembered the woman who'd sat on the bench next to her and Shereen. But she'd said very little about her job at *The Daily*.

An attendant placed a dish of figs, nuts, and dates and a pot of tea on the table in front of Perin just as Shereen joined her. "My driver will be here in ten minutes," Shereen said, placing her mobile in her bag. Perin nodded and watched the birds pecking at the stale water in the fountain. She leaned back and closed her eyes, feeling the sun's nourishing rays on her skin. She forced thoughts of the doctor and the attack out of her mind, and tried to focus on the chirping birds, and the broadcast of prayers coming from the transistor radio the ticket taker had in her booth. There was no need to think right now or to utter a sound; she only needed to feel safe in this refuge, sitting next to her childhood friend, their familiarity a comfort.

Family Night

*Love alone cuts argument short, for it alone comes to the rescue
when you cry for help against disputes. Eloquence is dumbfounded by
Love: it dares not wrangle; for the love fears that, if he answers back,
the pearl of inner experience might fall out of his mouth.* —Rumi

Late afternoon sun filtered through the shutters, forming a stepladder pattern across the Persian carpet as Perin entered her room after her day at the *hammam* and hairdresser. The sound of gurgling water from the fountain drifted up from the courtyard. Everything was familiar, just as she'd left it years ago, and yet the room seemed much smaller since her return.

She flung open the shutters. The blue morning glories and the violet irises were in full bloom, and the grass was still acid green from the spring rains. It would be weeks before the summer heat, stroked by the southern sirocco winds, scorched the earth, leaving dry brown patches in its wake. A breeze fluttered the fronds of the palm tree outside her window, rattling them against the open shutter, a sound she loved listening to when she lay in her bed late at night or early in the morning. Now, she willed the sound to sweep over her, helping to fade the memory of the men.

In a shaded area of the courtyard, Arabia, the family's saluki, lazed, his long legs spread out nearly the length of the table behind him. Perin remember how her brother Nabil had insisted on getting the sleek animal; he wanted to take him on hunts in the desert as befitted the breed. Huda and their housekeeper Nadira had protested at first—dogs were impure, they'd said. But her father explained that nowhere in the Qur'an does it say man should not associate with dogs and this *hadith* was probably not something the Prophet said, but was most likely written by a follower who didn't like dogs. Finally, the staff acquiesced and Arabia became a beloved member of the family.

While she was dressing for dinner, her mother, Assia, came into her room, wearing an aquamarine caftan embroidered with a gold, pink, green, and purple design that lit up her face. "How were the baths today, *habibti*?"

Perin quickly finished putting on the khaki pants she had chosen to wear to hide her legs. "Is that new?" Perin said, ignoring her question and pointing to the large turquoise necklace that accented her mother's long neck.

"It's lovely, isn't it? Iranian turquoise, the best, your father says. What took you so long today?"

"Mother, it wasn't that long. We had to wait at the hairdresser and Shereen had to tell me about her engagement."

"I spoke to her mother while you were at the baths and she said he's a lovely boy from a good family. We should all be so fortunate to have such stellar prospects for our children. I hope you and your brothers will find partners as wonderful."

Perin nodded as she adjusted the billowy, long-sleeved white-and-khaki floral print peasant blouse on her shoulders; she hoped it wouldn't press against her back where she was struck. Her arms and legs were still hurting; it would take a while for the arnica gel to speed the healing.

Assia cast a critical glance over Perin. "That's very casual. Don't you have something else to put on?"

"It's just family tonight." Perin slipped into open-toed leopard-print heels and held her peridot earrings near her face; she liked how they brought out the green in her hazel eyes, but they seemed too delicate for her outfit. She decided on the rose-quartz chandelier earrings she bought in New York's East Village one day with her friend from university, Eva.

"Don't take too long," Assia said. "Huda made a special dinner for you again tonight. She's eager for you to see it, so act surprised."

Perin glanced in the mirror one last time to ensure none of the red blotches were visible. Satisfied, she was about to go downstairs when she heard voices coming from her younger brother Rashid's bedroom. Lingering at his doorway, she watched her brothers play a basketball video game. Nabil sensed her presence first. "Hey, racy earrings for our budding journalist," he said in his silky voice, his eyelids half closed. It was the look she'd seen him use on their mother and Huda when he wanted something, or when he was just being cocky.

"We call journalists 'dead reporters,'" she said, rubbing an earring.

"Yeah, that applies here," Rashid said, "they get killed if they write something against the clerics." Perin noticed the acne scars on his nose and cheeks had faded; at twenty, maturity was starting to chisel angular lines onto his face.

"That's not what it means. Journalists are the ones who have established careers, have made a—"

"Mother thinks you should teach," Nabil said. "More respected job, more prestigious than being a journalist—oh, excuse me, a *reporter*."

The sarcasm dripping off his words floored Perin. Let it go, she told herself; she didn't want to start a row before dinner.

"I thought *reporters* want to be where the power is," Nabil continued. "Have to say, I'm still surprised you weren't seduced by all the opportunities there, now that you have your *big important American degree?*"

Perin shuffled back a step. Surely Nabil didn't feel intimidated because he hadn't studied abroad—but it was common here for people to confer prestige on those who studied in the States. Nabil came over and pinched her cheek; she swatted his arm away and said, "Don't be late for mezze."

Leaving the room, Perin wondered about her brother's snide remarks. One year between them, they'd been inseparable growing up, the best of friends. Besides her father, he'd been her greatest supporter, even taking her side when Assia objected to her studying in the States. Nabil's arrogance was nothing new, but maybe being away from it for a while made her notice it more.

At the bottom of the stairs, faint strains of a jazz rendition of "The Man I Love" filtered from the study, where her father, Fuad, was rifling through papers on the credenza. "An apropos song," Perin said, entering. After kissing her father on both cheeks, and then on the hand, she couldn't help noticing again how the creases running from his nostrils to the corners of his mouth seemed more pronounced, and his eyes seemed to sink deeper into the folds of skin under his eyes.

"I missed that when you were away." Fuad held her hands to his chest for a moment, before pushing out a chair for her.

She sat down and pointed to a vial of pills on a silver tray. "What's that for?"

"Nothing, really. Blood pressure was a little high at my last checkup and Dr. Kareem thought I should get it under control. Just a precaution, nothing to worry about."

"Are you sure?"

"You know doctors. It's their job to imagine the worst."

The incident in the Casbah pierced Perin's thoughts. Her parents must never know what happened. If they did, it could be detrimental to their health.

Assia came into the study and Rashid soon followed, leaning against the door frame, one hip thrust out. "Don't slouch. That's not a recliner," Assia said. Rashid gave a little smirk before complying.

"Your Mother has on her necklace," Fuad said. He took a box from a desk drawer and handed it to Perin. Inside was another necklace, simpler and daintier than the one Assia wore but made of the same Iranian turquoise.

"Oh, it's beautiful. I love it." Perin held up her hair as her father clasped it around her neck. She ran her fingers over the polished stones. "I'll never take it off."

"Ha, you'll change it as often as you change your shoes," Rashid said. "Come on, mezze's ready and I'm hungry."

Fuad grabbed his jacket from the back of his chair and playfully shoved Rashid out of the room. They'd only gone a few steps when someone pounded on the front door. Fuad turned to Assia and Perin and told them to wait in the study. Unable to make out what the muffled voices were saying, Perin popped her head out of the room. Assia grabbed her blouse and pulled her back. In spite of Assia's grip, Perin managed to get a glimpse of her father, arms crossed, shoulders raised toward his ears. Visible on each side of him were the gray robes of two mullahs. As soon as she heard the door close, she rushed out of the study and asked what they wanted.

"Donations for one of their *madrassas*," Fuad said, his voice low and his smile forced.

"They come to houses now?" Perin said.

Fuad told Assia to go into the living room and he led Perin back to his study and sat facing her.

"I haven't wanted to say too much and have you regret returning home, but I think it's time to make it personal." Fuad looked down and exhaled. "I know you know a lot about what's going on, and even if you're hearing and reading about things, I sense they haven't sunk in, or you haven't come to terms with them. Maybe it's just you've been busy seeing friends and getting used to your job. But I want to tell you a few stories that you might not know about." He rubbed his hands together. "A few months ago, the guerrillas were coming down from the hills every morning to get bread at a bakery over by the old mosque on the southeastern edge of town. The baker realized who they were and reported them to the authorities. The next day a squad of soldiers lay in wait and arrested them. A few nights later, their comrades hid behind the bakery and in the morning, when the baker had the fires roaring, the men barged in and threw him into the ovens—alive." Perin gasped and her hand flew up over her mouth. "When they say Allah is on their side, it makes people scared to go against them. Even the police."

Perin shook her head. "Things like that happen in the provinces, not here in the capital ... not here." She faced the wall, the image of the baker searing into her mind, followed by that of the men in the Casbah encircling her; her breath grew rapid. "Did they prosecute the men?" Fuad shook his head. "So, they made them seem more powerful than they really are. Humph, I doubt Allah would approve of their brand of Islam."

"What's maniacal to us is sacred to them." He leaned forward and took Perin's hand. "It's best we keep a low profile and be careful. If they come to the door, I greet them and give them a nominal gift."

"But you always told us that if we saw something unjust and didn't act or protest, we were just as guilty."

"Times are different. I have to think of the family … and my workers. I can't risk agitators finding an excuse to take away the factories. Remember the man with the cement company?" Perin nodded. "He refused to hire some of their supporters and they shot one of his managers in front of the company." Perin clasped her throat. "The fundamentalists told him that if he didn't do what they wanted, they'd burn down his buildings or kill him next." Fuad rubbed the nape of his neck. "I'm telling you all this because we all need to be careful"

She tried to keep her voice steady as her mind played tricks, supplanting her father for the fallen manager. "Can't the government do more to stop these atrocities? Is anyone documenting what they're doing?"

"The moderates in the coalition government are trying to persuade them to issue a decree prohibiting such killings. And rumor has it that some of the military officers are talking of a coup." Fuad extended his arm. "Come. Mother's waiting for us." Perin snuggled up against her father's arm as he escorted her into the living room; she felt sheltered, something she needed at the moment.

Mezze was laid out on the wooden coffee table that ran half the length of the wall sofas—baba ghannouj, tabbouleh, goat cheese, olives, roasted peppers.

"Where's Nabil?" Fuad asked as he poured a glass of currant juice.

"He said he had to run out for a few minutes," Rashid said, scooping up hummus with a slice of toasted pita bread.

Perin leveled her plate to keep from spilling food on the carpet. She thought Nabil had changed only toward her, but here he was disrespecting their father by not excusing himself, something she'd never seen him do before.

Assia stroked her neck, eyes glued on Fuad, who stared at the floor.

Rashid gave Perin a smirk that seemed to say *I told you so* before popping a fried kibbeh ball into his mouth, and she remembered what he'd said to her about Nabil last winter when the family visited her in New York—how Nabil expected everyone to cater to him, how he constantly criticized Rashid and lectured him about wasting time playing with computers and hanging out with his "crowd of loafers." Nabil only invited him places when he needed help, like when his soccer team was a player short.

"Let's have some music." Fuad turned on his old stereo and strains of "That's a Plenty" filled the room. "My father used to say this is the song they played during silent movies—"

"When the posse chased the bandits," Perin and Rashid said in unison before breaking out into laughter.

"Good to know you were paying attention."

Huda beamed as Perin complimented everything she had prepared for dinner: a cucumber and green pepper salad; mint-dappled *labneh*; baby eggplant stuffed with ground lamb and pine nuts; and a favorite of Perin's, chicken smothered with walnuts and pomegranate juice.

"Please tell me you made my favorite for dessert," Perin said to Huda, her mouth watering as she thought of the phyllo dough treat filled with a mixture of ground almonds, sugar, and cinnamon, and sprinkled with honey-vanilla syrup.

"You'll find out," Huda said, pride puffing up her words.

A short time later, the front door opened and slammed shut. The silence at the table made the footsteps on the tile floor sound like shutters hitting the side of the house during a storm. Nabil entered as if nothing was amiss and sat next to his father, across from Perin. He had changed into a tailored gray Italian suit and a light caramel shirt, accented with a burnt-gold silk tie. His dark hair was slicked back with gel; light from the chandelier bounced off the top strands.

"Where were you?" Fuad asked, his eyebrows knit together.

"The fiber salesmen, remember?" Nabil placed a yellow cotton napkin on his lap. "I told you they want to raise prices because their raw material and labor costs increased, and I told them our clients won't accept increases and we'll lose market share." Nabil glanced around the table and raked his fingers through his hair. "I didn't finish negotiating so I'm meeting them later at the club."

Fuad's face burned red. "It's Thursday, family dinner night. You can negotiate by phone. Call them and cancel."

Perin stared at the eggplant and chicken on her plate, focusing on their every word.

"They fly back to Germany tomorrow and it's better to do it in person—to gauge their reactions," Nabil said.

Perin looked up and saw Rashid smiling at her. She rubbed the scar in the palm of her hand, the one Nabil had given her when they were children playing pirate.

"Father, I am not trying to go against you, but you want me to take responsibility for the business and I have, and I believe that this is the best way to keep us profitable."

The tension in the room bore down on Perin, pinning her to her seat. She was angered that Nabil would speak to their father this way.

"He said they're waiting," Assia said. "And you did put him in charge. Can't he go this once?"

Perin whipped her head around and looked at her mother, unable to believe she'd taken Nabil's side. She tried not to brood, but her hopes of being close to her brother again were evaporating like the wisps of smoke rising from the candles on the table.

Fuad peered over his eyeglasses at Assia. He twisted his watchband around his wrist and silently nodded his agreement.

As Nabil served himself salad, Perin remembered her father's pills. Worried the tension might elevate his blood pressure, and trying to keep her bitterness at bay, she told her brother to leave.

"What are you saying, mother said—"

"*Min fádlak*," she said with averted eyes. "Please."

Silence reigned again after Nabil left the room. In the quiet, Perin fought back her tears as she thought of how nothing was turning out as she imagined. What had happened to the idyllic family life she remembered and had hoped would envelop her again? Now she had to wonder if it ever really existed. Had she pushed all memories of discord out of her mind and created the perfect life? No, it had been a wonderful and happy life.

Fuad's mouth quivered for a moment and then he began to talk about the improvements they'd made at the family's textile factories. Perin smiled and nodded but the sting she felt upon Nabil's departure still weighed on her, as well as the beating, both pushing her emotions to the surface. She wanted to get away, hide in her room, but she couldn't, especially after Nabil's departure.

Before joining her parents and Rashid in a game of cards after dinner, she went into the kitchen to thank Huda for the meal.

As she neared the kitchen, she heard the plaintive wails of Umm Kalthoum emanating from the radio. Memories rushed at her. She was a child again, sitting at the table with Huda, who tried to teach her to memorize the legendary Egyptian singer's songs of love, nature, and classical Arabic poems. Daily, she'd listened to Huda's stories: how her parents gave her in marriage to a distant cousin at thirteen, how she'd worked every day since childhood, and how her husband couldn't keep a job.

She sat at the table and gazed through the metal-grated windows at the date palm that stood sentinel over the kitchen, absentmindedly fiddling with the silverware drying on a dishcloth.

Hearing the clinks, Huda turned around. "What's that face about?"

"Huda, Nabil—"

"Aiyee, he just wants attention. He's used to being the big man. Remember what I've always told you—there's only love and fear and it's not hard to figure out which one he's acting out of."

Huda stopped short as Assia walked into the room and she resumed wiping down the counters.

Assia sat down next to Perin. "You're upset about Nabil." Eyes cast down, Perin shrugged.

"I had to stop it or your father would have gotten angrier and Nabil wouldn't have given in." She stroked Perin's hand. "It's too bad he gets this way."

"You made him this way. The eldest son. He gets preference. He can do whatever he wants," Perin said, with more bitterness than she had intended.

Huda glanced over her shoulder and frowned at Perin.

"We've tried to give you all the same opportunities, you got to study in Paris and New York, and he didn't go abroad because he had responsibilities here." Assia gazed out the window and was quiet for a few moments. "We thought we could help shape your personalities and characters, but temperaments are predestined."

"Forget it," Perin said, standing up. "Let's go beat father and Rashid at Ronda."

On the way out of the kitchen, she turned to Huda, "If there's any dessert left, save it for me."

"Remember," Huda called out, "the best memory is that which forgets nothing but unfairness. Write kindness in marble and unfairness in dust."

Perin turned her back and winced.

French Lace and Tourists

If you wish for light, be ready to receive light. Nourish your ego and be deprived of light. If you wish to find a way out of this prison, do not turn away; bow down in worship and draw near. —Rumi

Friday morning, Perin sat next to Shereen and rested her head against the marble façade of the thirteenth century mosque. Gazing through the arabesque arches toward the center fountain, she watched her father and brothers perform their ritual ablutions alongside men in polyester slacks and dusty flip-flops, while soft chants of *In the name of Allah* mingled with the sounds of flowing water. As Islam taught, the men splashed it on their faces, and over their heads, arms, and feet to cleanse their bodies, as well as their thoughts. The murmuring voices of other women sitting nearby mixed in with this symphony of sound.

An elderly custodian, a lean man with an eyepatch and white stubble, sat at the entrance, as was his habit when not sweeping the floor of the mosque or cleaning the courtyard. He ripped the frayed black piping from the edge of his cloak and watched the men to ensure they performed the purification rite properly.

Surrounded by tradition, the outside world almost slipped away from Perin, but it remained difficult to keep at bay the memories of the men who beat her and the flareup at dinner last night—and then there was Dr. Massi. Curious, she'd made up her mind to contact her the next day.

"I can't believe your mother called my mother to see where we were," Shereen said as she picked at imaginary pieces of lint on her long jacket. "We weren't gone that long."

Perin tilted her head and shrugged. "She's always worrying about me—she forgets I lived in New York and I did just fine."

"It's different when you're at home," Shereen said.

Ablutions finished, the men milled around the fountain, or sat on the ground with their backs propped against its marble inlay, waiting for Friday services to begin.

Kamal stood in a far corner of the courtyard, talking in rapid cadence with Nabil and a group of well-dressed men in tailored jackets and polished shoes. His gesticulating hands stopped only to stroke his curly hair, or adjust his shirt collar or watchband.

Over the years, Perin had frequently seen Kamal when he stopped over to visit Nabil, or when she was staying at Shereen's. She'd even had a crush on him when she was fourteen. He was still rather good-looking, in a rugged way, perhaps stockier than what she remembered, but always the natty dresser, today in an impeccable gray tailored suit. Even though she didn't like the way Kamal often dismissed Shereen, and thought some of his remarks were tasteless, there was still something about him that intrigued her, in that attractive bad-boy way.

Two stray dogs entered the courtyard and wandered near Kamal and the men. They grimaced and stepped away from the mangy animals. One of the men kicked at the dogs to shoo them away. The caretaker stood up and told them not to touch them, or they'd have to cleanse themselves again.

"Poor things. They're not unclean. A misinterpreted *hadith*," Perin said, as she thought of how well the family cared for Arabia. "In the States dogs are members of the family, have their own birthday parties. There's even a Miss Doggy America beauty pageant and dog psychics."

"You're joking," Shereen said, pushing her gold bracelets higher on her arm. "I do know the pet business is recession-proof."

"Our little economist." Perin rested her elbows on her knees and cupped her chin in her hands. She looked down at the worn, smooth pavement stones before her eyes drifted to Shereen's foot, peeking out from her long skirt. "Fishnets?" Perin asked with raised eyebrows.

"My head's covered." Shereen inched up a corner of her skirt. "A little undercover subversion does me good."

Perin pulled out the scoop neck of her tunic. "French bra, red and black lace."

Shereen waggled her finger. "Shame, shame."

Perin checked to see if the caretaker had overheard or seen them, but the old man was busy winding his turban around his head; the light spilling through the arches accented the lines in his weathered face.

Perin leaned toward Shereen. "In New York, I bladed to mosque in my shorts and tank top. I'd stop a block away, sit on the stoop of a brownstone and exchange my skates for shoes, and put on my black tunic and scarf." She gazed toward a corner of the courtyard, her eyes smiling. "I'd sit with elegant women from sub-Saharan Africa in these beautiful embroidered dresses and matching veils in colors like ginger, lemon, almond, and lime." She let out a laugh. "I felt like the lone licorice gummy in a bowl of jelly beans."

A local guide, his official badge prominently pinned on his shirt, escorted two Western women into the courtyard. He pointed out the five minarets and the gilded onion-shaped dome, and directed them toward the vaulted passageway that ran underneath the arches and surrounded the courtyard.

Perin was trying to make out what the guide was saying in French—something about the architecture representing the authority and principles of the traditional society—when a man yelled out to the guide, saying he had touched one of the women. "It's forbidden." He turned to the other men around him. "He touched her arm."

"Not true. I did not touch her," the guide screamed, straining his voice.

"Foreigners out," another man said, raising his fist and beating the air.

A third man joined in. "Non-believers, not allowed."

The tourists asked the guide something. He ignored them and continued to refute the charge. The men began to throw pebbles at the visitors. The women put their arms over their faces and tried to hide behind the guide. A stone hit the cheek of one woman. She yelped and put her hand to her face, while the other woman grimaced and rubbed her arm to ease the stings from the gravel missiles.

Perin shot to her feet. Shereen grabbed her arm and yanked her back down. "What are you doing? Did you forget what happened yesterday?" Shereen shook her head. "Amazing how you can push things out of your mind."

A woman on the bench next to theirs yelled out, "I was watching. He didn't touch her."

Silence draped the scene.

As the stone-throwers turned their attention to the other woman and began screaming at her, the guide rushed the tourists out of the courtyard.

"You're no better than a heathen."

"You're too impure to be here," a man said as he picked up more stones.

Perin and Shereen rushed behind a column.

Fuad stepped away from the fountain and lowered the arm of one of the men. He motioned for the others to do the same as the *muezzin* called from the minaret.

Perin wobbled and nearly tripped as she put her shoes in one of the wooden cubicles outside the women's entry to the mosque. Entering, she silently recited the saying, *When Friday comes, the angels are standing at the door of the mosque.* She sat next to Shereen in the front row of the mezzanine, at the back of the mosque, and let her eyes trace the calligraphic sayings from the Qur'an scripted on the glazed tiles around the bottom of the dome: *Allah is your Protector; sufficient is He, the greatest of helpers.*

She thought about what happened in the courtyard. She, too, had been watching and the guide did not touch the woman. She felt ashamed she hadn't spoken up like the other woman did when they accused the man, especially after yesterday when she was unjustly condemned. She was letting fear control her life, but how could she dare confront the men with her father and brothers watching? They would have been enraged, especially her father, after telling her to keep a low profile—not to mention her mother, who worried every time she left the house. She glanced up at the *mihrab*, illuminated with rows of small electric lights strung with wire so thin that they appeared suspended in space. *Please, don't let any harm come to the woman who tried to help*, she prayed, *and all those who aren't afraid to stand up to injustice.*

The service began. An imam in a beige robe and black turban walked up the *minbar*. The ancient pulpit creaked as he trudged his heavy frame up its intricately carved wooden steps. He began the *khatib*, Friday's most important moral sermon. "In the name of Allah, the Benevolent, the Compassionate."

Perin tried to listen to what he was saying, but the scene outside replayed in her head, mixed in with thoughts of her beating that she'd been unable to dispel. It was only when she heard the word "West" that she concentrated on his sermon.

"We are the protectors of the Qur'an, our sacred book," he intoned. "It is even more important today that we let its holy words guide us because we are under attack by the West. Our repression comes from the West. The West tries to impose its culture on us. Look at how our young people are infatuated with Western ideas."

The imam slammed his fist on the pulpit. "They do not understand that the world seeks to corrupt them. Western society lacks morals and it has no respect for women who are our diamonds to be protected."

Perin tried to gauge people's reactions to the sermon, wondering how many of the followers believed what the imam was saying. Had this vitriolic talk become so rife over the past year that it didn't register with anyone any longer? Or did it fire them up and make them want to go out and convert, or attack, non-believers?

Below, on a jumble of Berber, Iranian, and Moroccan carpets, Perin saw her father kneeling between Nabil and Rashid, their bodies facing the direction of Mecca.

How did her father, who Perin felt represented the best of what it meant to be Muslim, reconcile this in his heart? She had to believe that he and others still adhered to the integral part of Islam that taught that God was merciful and compassionate to all, even to non-believers. Then she remembered that in the courtyard her father had only asked the men not to throw rocks. He hadn't really stood up to them and defended the tourists— nor had her brothers.

"We must rid our lands of infidels. We will have a Holy War to banish them from our holy places. If one dies for the cause, he will get eternal life. World domination is the only way we can achieve salvation."

After the service, no one spoke as Nabil drove off down a busy side street. The absence of her family's voices seemed unnatural and Perin burst out, "He didn't touch her."

"They see what they want to see," Fuad said, his gaze fixed on the road ahead. "If they pass the Family Code—and my guess is they will with the help of the moderates—the morals police just might enforce it more stringently than it's written. They'll look for the least infraction."

Perin felt her chest tighten. She couldn't bear to think that every time she went out, her every action would be scrutinized and subject to interpretation.

"They're not thinking of Sharia law, are they?" Rashid said.

"I don't think so. It's too extreme," Fuad said. "And remember, much of Sharia is man-made." Fuad wiped his brow with his handkerchief. "They'll do things little by little so people won't notice much, things they think they can get away with, like ban makeup and music. And they'll make it easier for men to divorce their wives and keep the children and property."

"It makes me angry. Women are always the first victims— the battlegrounds for their ideology," Perin said. "Just like the Taliban and—"

"Oh, please, men were affected, too," Nabil said.

"You're right," she said. "And if they make us live under seventh century laws, you won't be able to drink, you'll have to—"

"I don't like it when you taunt each other this way," Fuad said.

"Terrorists," Perin muttered, "weak people with a little bit of power."

"They want to instill fear," Fuad said.

"What if things get really bad?" Rashid asked. "Do we leave?"

Fuad shook his head. "This is our home."

"We can't abandon our property and investments," Nabil said. "You want to be a refugee like those you see on television? No one wants refugees."

When they reached home, Fuad said, "For your own safety, and the safety of the family, I want each of you to be careful. I don't want any of you to speak out in public like that woman did. If anyone asks you what you think about a new law, or what certain clerics preach, tell them you know nothing about it." After a pause he added, "Don't mention any of this to your mother."

When Fuad turned back around, Perin saw his head droop. She'd comply with his wishes, except she'd already decided to contact Dr. Massi. One telephone call wouldn't hurt anyone.

The Daily

The object of search is never withheld from the seeker. Thus, the sun is paired with heat and the cloud with water. This present world is the Creator's prison. You chose to invite punishment, so suffer punishment! God said, "To whom We bestowed a particular disposition, We also sent the appropriate provision." —Rumi

Before work the next morning, Perin rang up Dr. Massi, who wanted to meet in Satellite Village, an area that sprang up in the 1950s to house low-skilled workers during the government's building boom. A sore appendage cut off from the pulse of the city, it had one of the highest crime rates. She was to come with someone she trusted.

"Wait," Perin said. "I need some assurances—"

"Don't tell anyone else where you're going."

"But you've got to give me something."

"When you're here."

Perin's stomach knotted up as she tried to think of another way to find out what the doctor wanted. When nothing came to mind, she pushed aside her apprehension and agreed.

"Call again when you arrange a way to come. Then I'll give you the address."

There was a click and the line went dead.

Perin stared at the phone. Intrigued, she couldn't help wondering if she might get a good article from the visit, one that could help her get noticed. Stop it, she told herself, for all she knew it could be nothing.

Her parents could not know she was venturing into that part of town, so she couldn't ask the family driver, Mohammed, to take her. Nabil would never agree. She'd have to ask Rashid. But first she had to devise a plan of what to tell him about her having to go there.

Perin entered the stately white granite building that was once the private home of a French colonial administrator, and now housed the offices of *The Daily*. She passed the armed sentry who stood outside the massive brass-studded wooden doors, and nodded to the concierge, an older man in a white crocheted skullcap, sitting on a rickety metal chair, hugging his knee to his chest, his prayer beads dangling in front of him. Squinting, he scrutinized her, as was his want, revealing several gold-capped teeth.

Entering the paper's reception area, the familiar din of clacking computer keys, ringing phones, and chattering voices filtered out and siphoned into Perin, rekindling the same euphoric feeling she experienced when she was in newsrooms in New York.

This was where she'd waited before her first interview with Ali Zayer—a tall, nice-looking, bespectacled man in shirtsleeves who she'd describe as, "distinguished-looking, serious, quiet authority."

When he told her about the open position, her heart sank: staff writer for the women's page, in the features section, three to four articles a day, a combination of household and beauty tips, children and education, latest fashion. She tempered her disappointment by rationalizing that her Columbia degree did not assure her a coveted position, and what did she expect? For here, this was a very good job—just not the one she wanted.

A few minutes later there was another disappointment—it was a shared desk; the beat wouldn't be totally hers. She tried to rationalize that three to four articles a day would be too much for her to handle alone at first, and maybe, just maybe, she might be able to outshine the other reporter, a woman named Andrea, and advance.

Mr. Zayer said some staff members thought the position was a lot of grunt work, day in and day out, and he was concerned she'd get bored and leave after a few months.

She couldn't tell him that this was her last chance, something she found difficult to admit even to herself, and so she told him if he hired her, she'd be totally committed, she'd always been able to make things challenging, and researching diverse subjects each week would make it interesting. She tried to give her answer an eagerness that belied the pretense.

She wanted to ask Mr. Zayer if she'd be able to do research for major reporters and co-report, but decided it should wait until she proved herself—provided she got the job. And even though she debated making her next statement, she decided it was better to find out. She mentioned that she'd been hearing—without saying she had direct experience—that some places did not want to hire women. When he told her he wanted a woman's perspective and women had contributed much to the paper, she knew he was an editor she could work for.

Reminiscing about the interview, Perin remembered her father saying that sometimes you only arrive at your destination by taking a circuitous route—or by going in the opposite direction.

During the weekly staff meetings, Perin enjoyed watching the group dynamics and she felt like a cat—quiet, no movement, eyes darting from side to side, taking everything in. Ali's quiet command over the proceedings and the staff impressed her—strength combined with gentleness, just like her father.

The managing editor Ghazi spoke. "We'll continue coverage on the pending decrees as we always have, first to state them in detail and then analyze—"

"I'm not comfortable with critique and analyses," said Qabil, the features editor. "It could rile up the clerics and then they'll scrutinize everything the paper does. They might even close us down."

Ghazi bent his heavyset body over the table and stared directly at Qabil. "We can't abdicate our responsibilities, no matter what we think could happen. We can't just list the decrees. We need editorials and commentary."

Perin watched Ali, expecting him to say something. But he let them go on.

"You want to compare us to other countries with bans," Qabil said. "It's premature. It could turn out differently here."

Ghazi slammed his fist on the table. "We have to give the why's—why it happened there, why it's happening here, who's behind their rise to power. We have to look at why the fundamentalists have done more for the people than the government. If it weren't for them, there'd be no schools in some villages." Ghazi shook his head at Ali.

"I agree with Ghazi," Ali said. "We need to give perspective. But the three of us can discuss it later. We have other sections to get through."

Perin liked that Ali let the staff air their points of view, and also that he was not afraid to be critical of the government. Ali looked over at Perin after the discussion, and she wanted to believe it was purposeful, as if he wanted her to know that he'd stand up for what he thought was right. She let her eyes respond for her, encouraging, but careful not to give off any impression she might have an inkling that he had singled her out.

After the sports editor and his reporters went over their proposed stories and layouts, Andrea outlined their articles for the coming week. "We plan a piece on planting herb gardens, and because it's early summer and many flowers are in bloom, detailed instructions on how to make potpourri. For our third article…."

Perin barely listened as Andrea went over the rest of the list. Even though she knew dealing with innocuous topics came with the job, hearing them read aloud made her wonder if she could write about such trivia week after week. It was nice of Andrea to say *we and our*, but surely the others knew she hadn't prepared the list. She'd have to wait longer before trying to get what she considered to be more interesting articles on the agenda.

Ali gave his full attention to Andrea as if this was one of the paper's most prestigious pages. He had a relaxed elegance about him—left arm slung over the back of his chair, right elbow on the arm of the chair, his face resting against his fingertips. His burgundy suspenders stood out against his light blue shirt. For a second, she wondered what it would be like to see him outside of work. She told herself to stop being foolish, and besides, she couldn't get involved with someone she worked for.

Back at their cubicles, Andrea gave Perin several of the pieces to work on, emphasizing that she wanted to review them when Perin finished. Perin silently fumed, careful to hide her displeasure at Andrea's telling her what to do. She wasn't Perin's boss—it was a shared desk. But Ali had implied that Andrea would oversee her work for several months.

After Andrea went to get tea, Perin looked over her assignments. After the high from being around Ali, she felt deflated, skeptical she could make interesting the selection and care of fish for home aquariums.

She jumped when someone came up alongside her. Her eyes met Ali's and she felt her face flush. Then something Eva told her in New York popped into her mind: *Sit up straight and make those breasts work for you. No sagging.* She inched her shoulders back slowly so as not to be noticeable.

"Just checking how everything's going and wanted to say it's nice having you with us."

"Thank you for saying that. Everything's fine."

"Good. I'll let you get back to work."

As he turned to walk away, she stood up. "I want to ask you something." Ali stepped back and waited. "I'd like to write about the country—excursions families could take to know our land better—a visit to the Roman ruins, coastal trips, a day in the desert." She let out a nervous laugh. "There are so many possible topics on the desert alone that we could dedicate a week to it— the habitat's animal and flora, how the people eke out a living, the danger of sunstroke, the geology."

It seemed to take Ali forever to say something. "What's the angle? The hook?"

Keeping her shoulders back, her voice grew animated, "The importance of documenting and maintaining the ecosystem, how all life is interconnected." She stood still, barely breathing, waiting.

Ali tilted his head to the right and looked down at the floor, his face a mask. She started to doubt her boldness while relatively new, and chided herself for not waiting longer. She also worried he might think her eager to make an impression, to show him she could come up with more than just recipes.

"It needs more focus. Discuss it with Andrea. If she agrees, pitch it to me next week."

Perin sat down and cradled her face in her hands, savoring the conversation. *But he said to discuss it with Andrea.* Did he think I overstepped my position? She resented having to pass everything through Andrea. She had attended an Ivy League school and Andrea only had a degree from the local university, and she hadn't traveled as much as Perin, or experienced as much by living in different cultures.

"What did Ali want?" Andrea asked.

Perin shot up straight as the scent of cinnamon tea wafted over her. Andrea's seemingly casual question, fraught with possible hidden meaning, resonated in her head. Andrea took a sip of tea, her gaze steadfast. *No time for reflection. I have to tell her everything.*

"A whole week? What makes you think our readers are interested in the desert?" Andrea shook her head. "You can't change the format from one week to the next."

"He said it was your decision," Perin said, hating her submissive tone. She watched the dust motes dance in the shafts of light coming through the windows and waited for Andrea to say something. But she didn't. "I hope you're not upset."

"Why would you think that?" It was impossible to miss the sarcasm in Andrea's tone. "This is your first job . . ." Andrea's tone shifted. "Well, who knows, I might have done the same thing ... if I had your audacity." Perin preferred to call it tenacity. "Maybe one week we can do one or two—as long as they're entertaining and not didactic. But finish this week's articles first and we can discuss later."

Had Andrea really agreed or was she being polite? Perin still felt uneasy. She should have realized that going behind Andrea could alienate her, and Andrea was someone she wanted on her side.

She'd have to worry about it later. Now she had to work on her articles so she could leave on time to get to Aunt Safina's for dinner. There, she planned to corner Rashid to ask him to take her to Satellite Village.

Dinner at Aunt Safina's

Whoever is sitting with friends is in the midst of a flower garden,
though he may be in the fire. Whoever sits with an enemy is in the fire,
even though he is in the midst of a garden. —Rumi

From the terrace of Aunt Safina's villa, Perin gazed down at the Mediterranean coastline's sandy bays and rocky headlands. Dina, her aunt's fine-featured Ethiopian maid, rolled out a cart with a pitcher of lemonade, bottles of ale, and a bottle of champagne in an ice bucket. The tang from the smoldering braziers drifted past Perin as Safina called out from inside the house, "My darlings, we're coming."

Perin felt almost giddy hearing her lilting voice. Safina was more than an aunt; she was the sister Perin never had, the one who had listened to her dreams and concerns since she was a young girl, always encouraging her. She was the family member who felt it her duty to make everyone happy, and keep her own suffering and problems inside.

Safina glided in, swooshing one side of her white caftan embroidered with gold peony blossoms. "You're all here. My world is complete."

Following her was Uncle Omer, Safina's portly, urbane husband, a minister in the Cabinet of Foreign Affairs. Behind him came their nineteen-year-old son Tariq, whose spiky gelled hair made Perin do a double take.

Safina kissed Perin and complimented her on her floral print dress before whisking around to greet the others, the threads in her caftan glowing like flickering fireflies as she passed the lit wall sconces.

"She's still over the moon you're home," Omer said to Perin in his gentle voice. His face had filled out and jowls were forming.

"Omer darling, let's start with the champagne," Safina said, smoothing her hair piled high on her head to accent her gold and pearl necklace and earrings. Perin always wished she had some of her aunt's talent for playing to an audience.

"How was your trip, Omer?" Assia asked.

He was about to answer when Safina cut in, "Fantastic. We even had dinner with a Bedouin family in Petra—we all sat on the floor around the plates and ate with our hands."

"I'm surprised you're not replicating it tonight," Nabil said under his breath.

Perin swatted his arm.

"Was the food good?" Rashid asked.

"Very tasty. They made their own flatbread in an oven in the patio of their home. They live in one of the concrete houses the government built for them so they would move out of the caves." Safina stopped and looked around. "Omer darling, please use the new flutes."

Dina came out from the kitchen with a plate of marinated fish and pita bread, and placed it on the coffee table in front of Fuad and Assia.

Safina asked Perin how her job was going and Nabil, with a sarcastic edge said, "Oh, the women's column. She never does anything at home so I don't know how she expects to write about such things."

"At least she doesn't have to write about unpleasant things," Assia said.

"Educated here and in Paris and New York—a world perspective," Safina said. "And you're so creative—you take after our side of the family." Fuad and Omer looked at each other and smiled. "Omer knows Ali Zayer," Safina continued. "He can put in a word for you."

"Father already did. That's why she got the interview," Nabil said. Fuad frowned at Nabil. "Just stating the facts."

"But I got the job on my own." Perin felt her face get warm. It was true her father had contacted Ali and asked him to see her. At first it had upset her that she hadn't landed the interview herself, but here connections were everything.

"Zayer's a good man," Omer said. "I've had dealings with him at the Ministry. He's balanced and he's been fair when writing about us."

"Your mother and I can give you ideas," Safina said. "I'd like to see articles on travel. And just remember it doesn't matter how you do the job, but that you look good doing it."

Nabil looked up at the terrace overhang and shook his head.

Perin smiled. Even if she disagreed with her aunt, she couldn't help but adore her.

Moonlight seeped into the crevices in the rocks below, beckoning squawking sea gulls to shelter for the night. A breeze wafted up from the shore and rippled the sea's blue expanse. Assia wrapped her arms around herself and asked Nabil to get her shawl.

"What else besides work have you been doing since you got home?" Omer asked Perin.

"Arguing a lot," Nabil said with a smile, as he handed his mother her black wool wrap with embroidered crimson and tangerine flowers.

"Because I question things?"

"It's been a bit of an adjustment," Fuad said before taking a sip of champagne. He came over and rested his hand on Perin's shoulder. "We've seen the changes gradually and she's seeing them all at once. It takes a while to fully understand all the nuances of what's going on."

"She thinks she's immune." Nabil flashed Perin a grin. She resisted the urge to tell him she didn't need his opinions.

"Unfortunately, the clerics now think that politics is part of their religious domain," Omer said. "The way to determine what's right and lawful." Omer took a paper from his pocket. "You'll hear about this in a day or two, but I'll give you an overview now."

Omer read about how the clerics criticized the West and its secular political system that gave them great wealth, power, and technological advances, but at the expense of lost values, vulgarity, and taking advantage of other countries. They stated there must be an Islamic state that conducts its affairs in accordance with the teachings of Islam.

"Great," Nabil said, "other countries will turn their backs on us, hiding behind the 'sovereign state' rhetoric and let us destroy ourselves. Some countries may even be glad—business could shift to them because they think it is too dangerous here."

"You're jumping too far ahead," Fuad said, "with your worse-case scenario."

Dina entered. No one spoke while she cleared away dishes and poured more champagne. After she left, Fuad continued, "We have to be vigilant, but we can't lose hope."

"They'll soon announce new decrees," Omer said. "They want *hijabs* for men—it will be forbidden for men to wear earrings and gold. And no smoked-lens sunglasses or pearl-diver style watches—those large watches with many dials."

"As if the style of watch or sunglasses means you're good," Rashid said with a sneer.

Omer continued. "They'll say that if one sees these things, one must report them to the proper authorities. But there's one major edict: All schools will be segregated and girls will be placed in their own schools, from primary to university. And they plan to post morals police outside schools for girls and padlock the doors while school is in session."

"Treating young girls like criminals," Safina said, shaking her head. "Terrible."

"Humph, again putting the burden on girls and women," Perin said. "They should lock up men."

Safina and Omer stared at each other, their eyes communicating silently. "Before we left the Ministry today," Omer started, "someone found—"

"Please, darling. Not now," Safina said. "We've heard enough."

"It'll leak out—it's best they hear it from me." Everyone stopped talking and waited for Omer to continue. "Only the top four or five of us at the Ministry know about this … someone planted a bomb at our offices. We got the bomb squad there before it went off."

"No. Why the Ministry?" Assia moved to the edge of the sofa.

"Some people don't like how it's conducting foreign policy," Nabil said.

Perin wondered if newspapers were also on the hit list. If dailies thought they were vulnerable, what precautions would they take with reporters, especially women reporters?

"What do you think about it, Uncle?" Perin asked.

"I've been a bureaucrat all my life. I'm used to shifting with whatever party is in power. We've been threatened before, but never been direct targets."

"I want to tell our renters in Paris that we need the apartment," Safina said, "in case we have to leave, but Omer—"

"What do you mean, leave?" Assia cried out.

"We don't want to," Safina said, "but if Omer's life is in dang—"

"We need people like Uncle to protect our interests here and abroad," Nabil said. "Like I said, other countries won't want to deal with us."

Perin nodded. At least she and Nabil agreed on something.

"May we be excused?" Tariq said. "I want Rashid to listen to my new CDs." Safina nodded.

The conversation stopped after the cousins left and Perin stared down at the coastline. Shrouded in shadows, two boys in tattered shirts and pants walked around the rocks, hunting for washed-up trash they could salvage and sell. As she was gazing out to sea, Dr. Massi popped into her mind. She excused herself and went upstairs.

Strains of "La même" filtered out from Tariq's room. Perin knocked and entered. Tariq was on his mobile phone. She motioned for Rashid to follow her into their uncle's study. With the door closed, she started to tell him about the doctor and then hesitated. It was one thing to put herself in danger, and another to endanger her brother. But her options were limited.

"Well, will you take me?"

"Satellite? Can't you meet her in town?" Rashid fiddled with the chain on the desk lamp.

"I have to go where the story is. She was glad I'm a reporter."

Rashid let out a laugh. "Right. Woodside, Queens? Women's things?"

"Woodside was a real beat, even if it was for school. Stop acting like Nabil. Will you just listen?"

Rashid slid his hand in front of his face like a curtain coming down between acts of a play, and his tone went from mocking to serious. He asked who the woman was and Perin explained she was a doctor who worked at University Hospital.

"You sure? She could be an impostor sent by clerics to lure you into their lair. Aren't you a little suspicious?"

Perin said she had looked her up on the internet and had called the hospital. The doctor was certified and had a good reputation as a psychiatrist, with published papers on obsessive-compulsive disorder. She found nothing strange in her background.

"That you know of. I'm not convinced. What else?" Rashid waved his hand near Perin's mouth in a come-hither motion as if to coax out her words.

"I told you everything. If you won't do it, I'll, well, I'll ask … Tariq."

"Wait a minute." Rashid held his hand in front of Perin's face. "Okay, but you have to promise to tell me everything. You owe me that, if I'm going to stick out my neck for who knows what."

Perin knew he'd have no way of knowing if she was telling him the truth. "Fine. I'll tell you everything."

Satellite Village

*Water said to the defiled, "Hurry come to me." The defiled replied,
"But I feel ashamed before the water." Water said, "But without me how will
you wash your shame? How will your filth be removed?" Shame hinders
the faith of the tainted who hide from the water. —Rumi*

Rashid honked and waved at the cars in the inside lane to make room for him.

"Stop driving like Nabil," Perin said. "I don't want us to have an accident."

"Have you figured out why this doctor wants to talk to you?"

"Why does anyone want to talk to a reporter? Maybe publicity for herself, for her work."

"Yeah, right. If it's about her work, it wouldn't be so secretive." Rashid smirked and raised his eyebrows. "Why so snippy?"

Perin told herself not to harp on him. He could tell her to forget Satellite. The thought of him not taking her there made her realize how much she wanted to see this through. Apart from her curiosity, the information the doctor wanted to pass along could well be her chance to get an exclusive, provided she'd find something newsworthy. If it couldn't be published in *The Daily*, maybe Eva or her former advisor at Columbia could help her get it published.

Rashid followed a circuitous route into a drab neighborhood with rundown buildings interspersed with carpentry shops, ironworks, and stalls that made sandals out of old tire treads. People stared as they passed. No one smiled. Etched on their faces was only cynicism, wary of all who ventured into their territory. Perin put her purse on the floor of the car and placed her feet on top of it. "Not very welcoming here."

"Their sixth sense kicks in when a stranger's around. You lived in New York; you should be used to strange neighborhoods."

"Parts of the Bronx were dicey. But I only went there in the daytime." She had to admit she was nervous, but only because she didn't know what to expect. And she had to hide her fear from Rashid or else he might insist they turn around and go home.

A policeman stopped them at an intersection to let an oxcart and cross traffic go through. Aqueous air simmered off the asphalt surfaces of the roads, creating a mirage. Sweat ran down the small of Perin's back. As she pulled the back of her tunic away from her skin, something thumped on her window. She jumped. A grimy man in rags with a wild halo of gray hair around his head banged again, leaving grease marks on the pane. She leaned into Rashid.

"You're like a cat on a one-inch ledge," Rashid said, motioning for the man to come around to his side of the car. He grabbed a few coins from the ashtray and placed them in the man's dirt-encrusted palm.

"May Allah bless you, good sir."

"You shouldn't. Father —"

"The poor man. Where can he find work, tell me?"

Perin wasn't about to argue with him. She kept an eye out for other creatures who might be lurking in the alleyways, ready to pop out and pounce. She had to make the meeting quick so they could leave before dusk. She wasn't about to fall prey to the shadows.

She disliked being on guard and feeling surrounded by invisible walls. But with the potentially violent political scene, her memory of the beating, and her parents' fear that something might happen to her, it was natural that she waged a battle with herself about how far she could go. Rashid had a point; why hadn't she insisted on meeting Dr. Massi in town?

Rashid crept up the narrow street a few more blocks and then leaned over the steering wheel and pointed to a plain building with crumbling eaves. Tiny rusted balconies with bent ironwork dotted its chipped façade. As he idled in front of the building, Perin picked up her purse and adjusted her headscarf. "Courage," Rashid said in French as she left the car.

It was nearly dinnertime and a pungent smell of onions and potatoes with a hint of cinnamon tumbled out onto the front steps. Perin made her way down the dark hallway where one burnt-out bulb dangled off a wire. There were two doors on each side and behind them she heard people talking and arguing, children playing, and a radio blaring music. It sounded like several generations of a family lived together in each apartment.

She reached the stairs in the back and started climbing, testing for creaks before putting down the full force of her weight. She was to go up three flights of stairs, to apartment 3B, at the back and to the right. She knocked on the door, keeping an eye out for any movement. No one answered. She knocked louder.

"Who's there?"

She pressed her cheek against the door. "Is Dr. Massi here?" The doctor opened the door, stuck out her head, and glanced down the hallway before motioning Perin into the living room. The windows were covered with gauze-like strips of red and blue batik fabric from India that cast a faint purplish tint in the room.

On a low sofa and pillows placed on the floor were three women, all expressionless, like actors on a stage who'd forgotten their lines. Only when one of them languidly reached out for a dish of dates did the tableau come to life. It struck Perin as odd that Dr. Massi didn't formally introduce her before whisking her down a hallway. The doctor could have told them beforehand who she was, or perhaps only that she was expecting someone, but people of all social classes here prided themselves on their unbridled hospitality and courtesy to guests, two of the signatures of her culture she loved.

The doctor led Perin into a room with two small pane-glass windows that faced east, but the view was obscured by heavy drapes. Only a small desk light was on, but the room was stifling and Perin felt moisture tickling under her arms.

"Would you like a tea?"

"No, I'm fine, thank you. What is this place? Who are those women?"

"A safe place for women who've been thrown out of their homes, or escaped. Some were rejected because their families considered them a burden, or they thought they had somehow disgraced the honor of the family."

Perin took in the doctor's lined face that made her seem old before her years and asked where she'd found the women. She explained she'd seen a few of them at the hospital, the ones who weren't afraid of the stigma of seeing a psychiatrist, and some came through word of mouth. She added now she finds many in the streets, ever since the clerics declared a man only had to say, "I divorce you" three times to end his marriage.

"There have always been, unfortunately, stories about abused and abandoned women. Why is this place so secret?" Perin couldn't help but wonder if she was only brought here for a group of women who had problems.

"As much as I try to protect the women, it doesn't always work. Before we came here, I had another apartment, but I had to move because the husband of one of the women found out where his wife was. He broke in and started beating her. The other women said he demanded she go back to their village to take care of his mother. She resisted—the mother tortured her worse than he did. We never saw her again."

The desk lamp went out and the doctor tapped it a few times before it came back on. She stretched her arms across the desk and leaned forward. "You can help us expose the hypocrisy. We have to stand up to this patriarchal society and the clerics who say they're for the people and religion's the only salvation. Now we have more destitute people than before and everyone turns a blind eye to these women, negating their existence. And what'll happen if, or I should say when, they reduce the marriageable age for girls from eighteen to twelve as they say they will?"

"Heaven forbid." Perin looked down at the scuff and ink marks on the floor. This was not the news-breaking story she'd hoped for and she wasn't certain she wanted to be involved with these women. But there had to be a reason she was here. She thought back to what her professor said about thinking about a story from a fresh perspective, what the unanswered questions are, and how one can bring something new to it. And weren't the best stories those that disturbed us or made us feel threatened? In the back of her mind she remembered someone saying the test of a good article is if people want to argue about it.

"The way to write about this is from a human-interest angle," Perin finally said. "You'd have to tell your story and the women would have to tell theirs. But if it's published here, it could expose you to danger."

"I'll only be an anonymous source. Strictly off the record." The doctor straightened the tassels on her worry beads while gazing steadfastly at Perin.

Her authoritative tone peeved Perin. But more than that, without someone on the record, she could be vulnerable to charges that she made up the story. "Someone has to go on the record."

"You want the human side. Come with me." Dr. Massi directed Perin back into the living room and introduced her to the women. She pointed to one with a drawn and deeply lined face, her hands and feet thick with calluses. "Camilia's thirty-three years old. Lived here in Satellite. Her husband threw her out like a sack of rubbish with no financial means to take care of herself. He said he needed a younger wife to have more children for Allah."

Perin looked closer at the woman, trying to find a trace of her relative youth. She'd have estimated her to be at least fifty.

The doctor touched the shoulder of an older woman crippled from what appeared to be arthritis. Her legs extended straight out in front of her and she had no defined ankles; the skin around her toes and lower legs was taut with fluid. The woman reached out to take the doctor's hand, her swollen red fingers twisted into odd shapes, like the trunks of olive trees.

"This is Ummee. Her husband died and her daughters' husbands didn't want her around because she was unable to work and bring in money. And this is Karima. Her brother abused her."

Perin looked at the young woman with a complexion the color of honey. Her long dark hair fell before her oval face like a curtain hiding belongings in an untidy room. She felt a pang in her chest and tried to imagine what it would be like to have a brother who didn't protect and care for you, a brother who was your enemy, your every hour fraught with tension. "Did she report him?"

"How could she? He was her brother, a son—a privileged and esteemed position in the family. She knew he would refute her testimony and her family would cast her aside, accusing her of bringing dishonor to them."

All her life, Perin had been taught that the Qur'an stresses the sanctity of every single life, which encompasses not only the physical body, but also the mental, emotional, and spiritual, and that a woman has rights and is to be respected and protected, no matter if she is a Muslim or not. And yet in practice this wasn't the case, especially when it came to women.

"There are two other women in the back bedrooms I want you to meet."

"It's been a pleasure to meet you," Perin said to the women, realizing how absurd such pleasantries were in the face of all that had happened to them. She followed Dr. Massi down the hallway.

Before the doctor opened the door to a room that faced the alley, she said, "Her name's Imene—she's still fragile."

"What happened to her?"

Dr. Massi put up her hand before opening the door.

Perin saw a small figure quickly angle herself in the corner of the room. She clasped her hands to her chest and folded up tight, returning Perin's glance before deflecting her eyes, her antennae on high alert.

"Imene, this is Perin. She's a friend who wants to help you and the others."

Standing slightly pigeon-toed, Imene kept her eyes averted. Perin made no effort to engage her, like one would do with a small child wary of an unfamiliar adult.

"How are you feeling? Do you need anything?" the doctor asked, her words soothing, not piercing as if prying.

In a hushed tone like the wind off the sea, Imene whispered that she was fine. She lifted her heavy fringe of eyelashes and looked at Perin, drawing her in with a sweet gaze. Perin felt an instant connection and wanted to reach out and protect this shy beauty, seemingly as delicate as a blown-glass Roman vessel, and as private as an unsung song. Before Perin could say something that would let the young woman know she wanted to help, Dr. Massi escorted her out of the room.

In the hallway, Perin asked, "Why is she so frightened?"

"She was kidnapped. She's eighteen years old."

The doctor opened the door to the room across the hall that faced the street. Curtains the color of claret wine covered the windows. In the right corner was a single cot. A woman curled up in a fetal position was lying on it, her back to the door. She didn't move when they entered. Dr. Massi sat beside her and stroked the woman's dark hair, which fell from her shoulders and spread out like a fan on the bed. The doctor lifted her under her ribcage and coaxed her to a sitting position.

Perin nearly gasped when she saw the woman's face. The entire right side was a mass of hideous scar tissue. Pink and red bundles of puckered skin formed ridges and zigzags from her forehead to her chin. Her right eye was hidden in shriveled up flesh that extended past her nose, exposing a nostril.

Perin felt nausea rising, but she willed herself to look the woman straight in the face. She'll be watching to see how you react, Perin said to herself. But the woman kept her head down and stared at the floor, her shoulders slumping.

"Fatma was home one day with her two-year-old daughter and got distracted. The girl ran out onto a busy street and Fatma ran after her, not taking time to put on a scarf—the child could have been hit by a car. Men in her village saw her and yelled that she was a whore because she was not covered like a proper Muslim woman. Later that night, the same men barged into her home and threw acid in her face. They said it would be a lesson for all the women in the village who dared to go out uncovered."

Perin shivered and felt goose bumps rise on her arms. She silently cursed the men who had taken away Fatma's identity—a stranger even to herself, forced to endure this unavoidable daily reminder of her attackers. She wondered if she could encourage Fatma to talk about her experience. And then she recalled how difficult it was for even her to talk about her attack—one that paled in comparison to what Fatma had endured.

The doctor went on to say that the village elders decided no crime was committed and it was Fatma's fault for not obeying the law. Her family didn't want her—they were afraid that if she stayed, they'd be ostracized. A friend brought her to the hospital one night and dropped her off. A plastic surgeon on staff tried to minimize the scarring, but it was too late. "I saw her the next day. You can imagine the psychological effect on her. An object of horror to herself as well as to others."

Back in the small room, Dr. Massi called her office, Perin grappled with all she'd seen and heard, and thinking she had to say something, muttered, "Thank goodness for people like you who have the compassion and courage to help."

"How many of us really have it? Most do lip service but rarely act. But I can see the torment in your eyes, so maybe you'll get the courage and compassion to help." The doctor moved a notebook to the other side of the desk. "Everyone focuses on the big political story and forgets ordinary people."

A thought rippled through Perin's mind—helping these women might mitigate her previous lack of courage. She looked down at her bag on the floor and hesitated. It could also put her at personal risk, and thinking of being attacked again made her want to get up and leave. But she hadn't committed to anything. She pulled a small tape recorder out of her bag. "Would Fatma, Imene, and the others cooperate in interviews? Give me quotes? I need firsthand details if they're going to be anonymous sources."

"You can't tape them. But I'll see that the women give you what you need."

"What if someone finds out you're the source?"

"Would my punishment be any worse than what they've been through?"

"Neighbors haven't reported you?"

"There's a code among those who live in this area. Most are escapees in one sense or another, whether it be from poverty or the law."

Perin nodded. "How many women live here?"

"Seven. Two have part-time jobs with friends of mine, doing housework, babysitting—they're not here now. I hope to train them all in sewing, or jewelry-making, and then start a cooperative to help them become financially independent."

Perin looked away for a few seconds. "How do you do this every day?"

"In medical school, we were taught the value of equanimity. I've tried to make it a guiding principle in my life." She picked up her prayer beads. "Do you think you can help?"

The clacking of the doctor's beads ticked off the seconds before Perin redirected her gaze at Dr. Massi. Writing about the women would not generate accolades for her, or further her career, but Imene, she just might be able to help Imene.

"I could possibly feed articles to my professor and a former classmate in the States and they might be able to get them published, either on the internet or in journals. But why me? What makes you think I can help, Dr. Massi?"

"Call me Zahara." The doctor looked up at the ceiling for a moment and hesitated. "I sense we need each other, and that we can accomplish something together. Remember, 'A gentle hand may lead an elephant with a single hair.'"

Perin got in the car and stared straight ahead.

"Well, was it worth it? The big mystery solved?"

"She's helping these women—one's face was destroyed by acid. It was ghastly. It hurt to imagine what she must feel. And then there was this other one—tiny and brittle—like a harsh word would shatter her." She told Rashid what she knew about each of the other women, and that Zahara wanted her to write about their abuses.

"Forget it. The clerics will find out it's you writing the stuff and they'll target you."

Perin nodded, not letting on that she had already committed herself to do something, any little thing, to help Zahara and Imene. But she hadn't helped the women fend off her own attackers, and she hadn't joined the woman at the mosque in denouncing the men making the false accusations. What made her think she could show some backbone now?

"Remember," Rashid said, "a donkey went seeking horns and lost its ears."

In the days following her visit to Satellite Village, the women, especially Fatma and Imene, would pop up like demons in the night and ransack Perin's mind. Intermingled with these thoughts were the Prophet's words: *Those who care for widows and the poor are equal to those who follow Allah, and to those who pray all night and fast all day.*

The Bonds that Weave

If you wish to shine like the daylight, burn up the night of self-importance.
Dissolve the self like copper in the elixir; dissolve in Him who fosters all existence.
But you are bound by the discord of "I" and "We." The cause of your
ruin is this sad dualism. —Rumi

The next day, Perin turned in her work assignments early and told Andrea she had a family matter to tend to. The weight of her decision to help Zahara made it difficult concentrate on work and she needed to talk to her father. Maybe he would understand her desire to help and give her some perspective. She was uneasy about telling him, but her need for reassurance overrode her fear.

She found Mohammed outside polishing her mother's Mercedes and asked him to take her to the factory. He hurriedly placed his rags and tin of wax by the edge of the driveway and opened the car door for her. As he started the car, he mumbled *Tawakilt Ala Allah*, as was his custom, and then headed down the tree-lined street of the residential district of large homes and embassies perched on the hill like overseers, keeping a watch on the city and the sea.

As they reached the intersection where the old town joined the colonial part of the city, the muezzin call for prayer rang out from the central mosque. Men came out of stores, video arcades, and pizza parlors and unfurled their prayer rugs, faced Mecca, and knelt down. Mohammed bowed his head and moved his lips in prayer.

Perin considered herself a devout Muslim, like the rest of her family, but she did not pray five times a day. Her grandfather, a university professor, had always said that religion was a way of life, not a ritual, and the Qur'an their guide. Her father and brothers attended Friday prayer services as did most men, and she often accompanied them, but more often she attended mosque with her mother on women's day.

At the port, a small encampment of trucks with tailgates down, lined up on the grassy knoll near the boardwalk. Men peddled oranges, shoes, sunglasses, and clothing from their flatbeds. Mohammed stopped behind a diesel bus that had *My father is the Prophet* finger-written on its soot-covered back. A boy holding a cone filled with melon seeds tapped on Perin's window; she shook her head and the child scurried to the car behind them.

Mohammed squeezed between a car and a cement mixer in the next lane. On a construction site's temporary wall, two boys were plastering posters of a mullah. Perin asked what Mohammed thought of the decrees everyone was talking about.

"Oh, Miss, I don't know nothing about those things."

"You used to love politics. I listened to you complain to Huda about all the corruption—how the government made money selling natural gas and still kept raising prices. And the bureaucratic paperwork. Remember how you had to stand in line for a day each time one of your sons was born, just to register them?"

"Things are confusing now. A poor man like me can't understand. I just mind my own business."

Watching this gentle and loyal Berber adjust the saying that dangled from the rearview mirror, *Allah is your Protector. He is the greatest of Helpers.* Perin wondered if anything specific had happened that made him hesitant to speak his mind, or if he was just cautious. Or perhaps her father had spoken to him, too.

He parked in front of the textile mill's modern steel-and-glass offices nestled on the hillside, and walked her to the entrance.

The day had a luminous quality to it. She looked out at the Mediterranean shimmering in the sun, and breathed in the briny air scented with jasmine, while saying a short prayer. *Please angels and djinns, let Father understand and help me.*

For Perin, visiting the family's mill was like an excursion to see old friends; she'd spent countless hours here as a child, accompanying Fuad on his inspections, trudging up and down the rows of looms on her little legs. Or she'd pretend to be her father as she sat at his massive mahogany desk—the one he inherited from his grandfather, who started the factory in the 1920s—shifting from one side of the overstuffed chair to the other until her back made contact with the soft leather.

As she walked into the vestibule, the attendant Boulus bowed his head. She greeted him, her eyes dipping down to the food stains on his tie and on the lapels of his battered suit. He opened the door to the administrative offices and within moments, employees from the sales and accounting offices surrounded her. After catching up on their latest news, she located her father in the main weaving room. A worker handed her a pair of wax plugs, which she placed in her ears to dim the clacking of the loom shuttles as they hit the boards.

Fuad's face lit up when he saw Perin and he led her to a back row of machines. "The new looms for novelties and jacquards. Have a total of 1,500 looms now."

Even with all the noise, it was impossible to miss the pride in her father's voice. Perin watched the yarn-dyed shirtings being woven and nodded to the workers. Many had been there for decades, often following in the footsteps of their parents and grandparents. Fuad considered them extended family and no matter concerning them was too small for his attention. He'd help them get building permits for new homes, find the right doctor for serious ailments, and write letters of recommendation so their children could attend better schools. The workers returned the favors with their loyalty; staff turnover was low.

It pained Perin now to think that forces beyond their control could destroy all the family had built.

Back in her father's office, the hunched-over porter in his white smock and cap wobbled in and put a silver tray with beverages on the credenza near the desk. The man placed a napkin embroidered with birds in front of Perin, and set a gold-rimmed glass of tea on top of it. Daylight streamed in from the blinds and bounced off the napkin's flaxen edge, creating a miniature aurora borealis around the glass. The scent of mint drifted upward. After giving Fuad his tea, the man shuffled out and back into his little room, where he would wait for beckoning buzzers. Perin liked the centuries-old tradition that created a refuge for these older men, saving many from a life of poverty.

Perin pointed toward the credenza to a photo of her and her father at a puppet show when she was three. "You still keep that here."

"Do you remember the marionette troupes we took you to?"

"Yes, and I loved the stories. My favorite was the one of the old king who dies and his daughter tries to reach the sun and bring it into the kingdom."

"Just like you brought the sun into our home when you returned."

"Thank you, Father. It means so much to hear you say that."

"And I'll tell you a secret. I don't like to say it in front of the others, but I enjoy reading your column. See, you've broadened the readership—at least by one."

Perin felt her heart swell. "You mean you like reading about meal planning and how to make children's party hats? You're just prejudiced."

She fiddled with the pens and pencils in the inlaid box, debating how to tell her father about Zahara, but the words remained trapped in her throat. After finishing her tea, she said, "Well, I just wanted to stop by and see you. I'll let you get back to work."

"I'm glad you came by."

As she cut through one of the smaller weaving rooms on her way back to the front of the building, she saw Nabil. She stood near a post and watched as he handed the floor supervisor a loom punch card. Ramrod straight, he strutted from loom to loom. His little fiefdom, she thought, in spite of knowing he treated the employees well—their father wouldn't tolerate anything less.

Nabil spotted Perin before she had a chance to duck behind the pillar. Still peeved at his recent remarks, she steeled herself to speak to him, remembering a saying of the Prophet: *Even the smallest act is important, only if it's greeting your brother with a happy face.*

He kissed her on the cheek; his breath smelled of café au lait. With eyes full of affection, he said, "I know I've been picking on you and I want to make it up to you. Come to the club tonight with Kamal and me."

He sounded contrite, yet she was wary. Did he really want her to join him, or had one of their parents said something to him about his behavior?

"Did you see the changes I've made?" he asked, sweeping his hand around the room. "New computerized looms, spinning machines for finer yarns."

"Father made those changes."

"I suggested them. You know how he is. He thinks everything is running smoothly and we should leave it as is."

"That's not true. He's always upgrading."

"But not innovating. Have to keep up with the competition."

"Are you saying the mill would languish without you?"

"I wouldn't expect you to understand—"

"The mill is what it is today because of Father. I'm not saying you don't contribute."

"I don't want to argue about this."

Perin nodded and kept quiet. She wanted their relationship to get back on the right footing. "Okay, I'll go. Tell Kamal to have Shereen come, too."

Perin and Nabil walked up the marble stairs of the three-story French colonial building that housed the Sailing and Sports

Club. A chilly breeze wafted up from the bay, rustling the fronds of nearby palm trees, and flapping the navy and white awning. She turned toward the water and let her eyes follow the concave coastline laid out like a necklace of twinkling diamonds within the black velvet box of the evening sky.

They passed the armed sentry cradling a semiautomatic rifle and entered the main foyer, where flecks of light that emanated from the archway's brass lantern's cutout design swirled around them. A fashionably dressed crowd sat at small groupings of sofas and chairs arranged around low tables. In spite of the chill, most of the women wore low-cut caftans or lightweight dresses with ruffles. Perin worried she was dressed too conservatively, in black slacks, white blouse, and black jacket with gold embroidery. Nabil led her to a seat that afforded a view of the entrance.

Waitresses from Thailand and the Philippines rushed around with large trays of food and drink. Nabil called one over and ordered cider and stuffed grape leaf appetizers.

"When did the guard at the door start carrying a heavy weapon?" Perin asked, remembering that on her last visit they had only pistols.

"After they set off bombs in the shoe factories and at the Ministry of Economy."

Perin had read about the incidents, along with the shooting of one of the economic ministers. "Have you heard more about Uncle's Ministry?" Nabil shook his head. "Are you worried about our factories?"

"Of course. Workers in other companies have complained to the clerics to get back at bosses because they didn't like something, or to settle scores. The government didn't investigate their stories and before the owners could fight the charges, the officials fined them or froze their bank accounts. A few had to close because they couldn't access cash and loans to finance operations. Later, when the government found out there was no basis to the complaints, it was too late. The owners had lost everything.

"The workers love Father," she said. "They'd never do that."

Nabil stood up and waved at Kamal as his friend squeezed through a group of young women holding silver balloons and presents wrapped in metallic paper. Kamal said something to them and they parted like a chorus of admirers welcoming home a triumphant hero. Like aged cognac, there was a hint of smoothness in the way his feet glided across the floor, with each shoulder moving in tandem with the opposite hip.

"Of course, I had to enter when that blasted group did." He kissed Nabil on both cheeks and smiled at Perin, his ebony eyes roaming the length of her body. She dropped the drink menu she had in her hands. Kamal picked it up and handed it to her.

"Where's Shereen?" she said as she took it from him. "I asked Nabil—"

"She has her things and I have mine." Kamal brushed off his seat before sitting down.

Perin looked askance at Nabil.

"I thought it would be nicer just the three of us," Kamal said, snapping his fingers and smacking his lips together to get the attention of the waitress at the next table.

Perin turned away; she should have called Shereen herself.

After Kamal instructed the waitress to bring him a scotch and water, he turned to Perin. "You miss New York? One of my favorite cities."

"Yes. Now I understand what people mean when they say that once you've lived there, you become a New Yorker for life. I loved—"

"I don't go there as much as I used to. Berlin's better now," Kamal said.

Perin wondered if he really meant the woman he was seeing there.

"Is this the new suit you got from that Indian tailor?" Nabil asked.

"Yes. The guy's reasonable. You should get some." Kamal straightened the handkerchief in his lapel. "He's got *L'Uomo Vogue* and other European magazines you can select from."

Perin felt awkward, shut out like old times when Nabil's friends would tell him they didn't want his younger sister around and he'd shoo her away.

"Hope you're still coming out tomorrow to work the horses," Kamal said to Nabil, who nodded. "Did I tell you we bought the land next to ours so we can plant more vines?"

"I didn't know he was selling," Nabil said

"My father convinced him." Kamal smoothed back his curly dark hair. "He had too little land for it to be profitable, and since it adjoins our property, it made sense."

"Convinced him?" Perin asked, rejoining the conversation. "Sounds like you didn't give him a choice, and from what Nabil was just telling me, he could report you."

Kamal twitched his nose. "For what? Not giving him a fair price?"

"He could say you coerced him or that you're dealing in black money."

Kamal let out a laugh. "My father would see that he has nothing left." The vertical wrinkles between Kamal's brows deepened. "They should shoot people who file bogus claims— like they did to those villagers."

"But the military shot the fundamentalists to drive them out," she said

"Is that what you read in the States?" Kamal jerked his head. "They did it to frighten the provincials into joining their cause."

"They've helped the people in the countryside. You have to admit the standard of living for most people hasn't risen in the last fifty years," Perin countered, enjoying the role of devil's advocate, especially with Kamal. "And what about the high unemployment—you read about the young men standing around."

"They should emigrate." Kamal adjusted his tie as the waitress placed their food and drinks on the table.

"Do you know what it's like for them abroad, for any refugee abroad? Do you think they want to leave their countries? No, few do." Perin turned away and shook her head, and then faced Kamal. "In Paris, they lived four to a room in seedy rooming houses, a standup toilet on every other floor." She swallowed hard. "Compatriots who lived in France for decades and were French citizens changed their last names to French ones, so their kids wouldn't face the same discrimination they did."

"Yes, yes, I've heard the hardship stories," Kamal said, nodding his head, a phony pained expression on his face. "Not my problem."

"We need to attract more foreign capital to bring jobs here," Nabil said. "Open markets, high-tech businesses."

Kamal's expression hardened. "Attract capital with these drunk-on-God idiots? Not one country run by religion has been successful, no matter what the religion."

"True," Nabil said. "Secular societies are better off— economically, live longer, better educated."

"Gender equality," Perin added.

Kamal curled his lip and continued, "Those illiterates want to destroy everything we've accomplished since independence." He raised his glass to Perin. "Welcome to the new reality," he said before taking a sip. He smiled, his grin deepening the dimples in his cheeks. "No fiancé? You didn't come back engaged?"

The gall of the man, Perin thought, as she fought back the urge to tell him off. What he was really asking was none of his business. But if she ignored his question, both men would imagine the worse—that she was no longer a virgin.

"I was busy with school. I went out mostly with classmates— in groups." As she stared down Kamal, she thought she heard Nabil exhale.

"Let's go downstairs to the discotheque," Kamal said, keeping his gaze on Perin.

"Yes, I'd like to dance," Perin said.

"I meant to listen to the music," Kamal said. "I don't like strangers touching me."

Arrogant twit, Perin thought. She wished she'd stayed home.

In the discotheque, she felt as if she was back in New York or Paris. Women, dressed in spaghetti strap dresses or tight pants with midriffs and bra straps exposed, danced with men in suits or slacks with polo shirts and jackets. Only the driving rhythms of the Rai music set the scene apart. Perin swayed to the sounds of flutes, strings, and drums as she followed Nabil and Kamal to an empty table in the back of the room.

A waiter brought them their drinks, and Perin danced vicariously with the people on the floor, while the two men sat back and watched the crowd. Kamal, a lit cigar clenched in his teeth, chipped away at the label on his bottle of ale. Perin stared at the platinum signet ring on his little finger, wondering how much longer he'd be able to wear such items. Her gaze was broken when Kamal, without saying a word, went to the bar and turned his icy magnetism on a young woman with pouty lips. Occasionally, he'd glance at Perin as if checking to see if she was watching him.

"Glad you came tonight? Kamal's great company," Nabil said.

She looked at the mirrored ceiling that reflected back the candles on the table and said, "It's rude of him to go off like that. Seems he prefers to talk to strangers. None of my friends would do that."

'Why are you taking it personally?"

Perin tightened the grip on her glass. It could seem as if she was taking it personally, and perhaps she was, but she didn't want to give any indication that he'd had an effect on her. She reconsidered what she'd thought earlier; it wasn't smoothness, it was swagger, verging on smarmy. She watched as Kamal whispered into the woman's ear; she leaned her head back and laughed. "What about his German girlfriend?"

"He doesn't go there often and he doesn't want her to come here because his parents don't approve of him seeing a Westerner."

The native music of the desert filled the room.

"I'm tired. I have to work tomorrow. Let's go."

Nabil waved over Kamal. "We're leaving."

"Get the tab," Kamal said. He gave Perin a sly smile before heading back to the bar.

"How can you can be friends with him?" Perin cradled one upturned palm inside the other, the local gesture used when a person doesn't understand.

"What's wrong now?" Nabil motioned for the waitress.

"He ignores you half the night and then he tells you to pay. He acts like a *Mawla* and you play right along."

"You're impossible. One of us always gets the check—it's easier. So what if he went to talk to someone. He tried to make conversation with you, he asked you about New York, he—"

"No, he told me how much he loved New York."

"You spoiled it by bringing up politics."

"Don't put this on me," she snapped, rubbing the scar in her palm. "Tell me. Why did you want me to come tonight? Was it really to make it up to me, or did you think I might be interested in him?"

"You could do a lot worse." Nabil looked at the bill and took out his wallet. "His family's one of the most prominent around."

"Means nothing to me." So, it was a fix-up, she thought, and she started to fume.

"I wanted you to come out with us—but the truth is ... he told me he'd like to see you."

She jolted as if poked with an electric rod. She turned to look at Nabil and shook her head. "I don't feel like running a finishing school for grown-up men. He's a master at pissing off people."

Nabil stopped and let out a laugh. "I've never heard you talk like that."

It pleased her that he'd found her remark amusing.

On the way to the car, she wondered if she'd tried hard enough to be friendly to Kamal. *No, she told herself, I'm not falling into that trap of thinking that I was the one to blame. He's an insecure, self-absorbed, know-it-all. Like many men here who are accustomed to having their way and who get angry when contradicted.*

Unable to fall asleep that evening, she emailed her friend in New York.

> *Eva, how are you? I'm thinking of you so much lately and I wish you were closer so we could talk. Remember all our discussions? I'm fine but a lot of things are going on. I knew there would be adjustments, but things are more challenging at times than I imagined. Sorry but I'm just feeling a little down tonight. Miss you.*
> *XoXo, Perin*

A few minutes later, a text from Eva came through on Perin's mobile. *Hold on. Give me a few days to get clearance from work to take time off. We'll talk everything out. Let me know, if that's okay.*

Perin replied with a quick yes. The thought that her friend might soon be with her was enough to dissipate the dark cloud, hovering above her head.

She'd be able to tell Eva about Zahara and Ali and her work, complain about Kamal and Nabil, and discuss how the life she'd known was slowly slipping away.

The euphoria dampened a little when she wondered if she would have to admit Eva might have been right all along when she told Perin it was folly to return home now. And how might her mother might react to having a foreigner in the house? She was so skittish about even the most innocuous things these days. Well, she'd have to get her father on her side.

The Bridal Purification

The satiated man and the hungry one do not see the same thing when they look upon a loaf of bread. —Rumi

Clouds flitted across the skylight of the *hammam* and a soft fragile light filtered down into the sunken pool where Perin dangled her feet and waited for her friends to arrive for Leila's wedding purification. Fearing she might run into Zahara, she kept watch for her. She was not ready to see the doctor until she was totally convinced she could write the articles she wanted.

Shereen, along with their former classmates from lycée, broke into her thoughts. Batool, Rafa, and Majida had all married after graduation, and in the ensuing years, Perin saw them mostly at social events such as weddings and birthday parties, and at the baths.

Batool sat next to Perin and in a bubbly tone, said, "Guess what Rafa had her brother get Leila—The Harem Love Potion."

"You know what they say," Shereen said. "If the husband takes it, the wife can't sleep. If the wife takes it, the man can't sleep. If they both take it, the neighbors don't sleep."

Rafa spread her legs apart and waddled around. "You walk like this the next day."

Majida shrieked with a laughter so contagious that it infected all of them, and Perin realized how much she had missed the camaraderie of these women when she was away. Here in their hidden world, they could tease, bicker, discuss risqué things, and just have fun.

"Did you know Leila's family brought in three matchmakers?" Batool asked Perin. "It was worth it. She got the second son of the family that owns the department stores."

"I heard you set the date for October," Majida said to Shereen.

"When's *your* wedding?" Rafa teased Perin.

"Have to find the groom first. One of these real men you always talk about, if they exist." Perin winked at Shereen.

"There's this website for Muslim men looking for wives," Rafa whispered as she leaned in front of Majida. "You wouldn't believe what some of them said."

"Tell us," Shereen said, her eyes opening wide.

"Well," Rafa said, "they ask normal things like if it's okay to marry a third cousin. Some ask about masturbation. *Haraam*, the imam said, forbidden. One wanted to know if he could take a shower with his wife. It's okay, but he has to be modest and avert his eyes."

"You shouldn't look at that," Majida said. "What if your husband finds out?"

"I'll tell him I was checking it out for your brother." Rafa nudged Majida. "Many said they're addicted to porn and they asked the imam what they could do to stop. And you know what he says? Go on a fast, never watch TV, walk with eyes down at all times, get married as soon as possible, and don't talk to infidel women."

"Fantasy's better than the real thing," Majida said. "Maybe the imams are right—women should cover up completely."

"Oh, please," Shereen said, amid a chorus of oh-nos.

"Just think about it," Majida continued. "No strange men ogling you, you don't have to spend time putting on eyeliner and blowing out your hair. It could be liberating."

"I like to have men turn and look at me," Batool said. "Makes me feel attractive."

"Once veils were considered sexy, those white transparent ones that let everyone see what was underneath," Perin said. "They inflamed the imagination."

"You could wear whatever you wanted in the States," Rafa said.

"Comfort was import—"

"Don't tell me you wore those ugly jogging suits, or baggy pants?" Shereen said.

"No, but I also didn't spend a lot of time trying to decide what to put on."

"They say covering up makes us feel closer to Allah," Majida said.

Perin shrugged her shoulders. "I find it hard to believe a woman who covers up is more religious or spiritual than those who don't. It really comes down to choice—whether she wants to, or not. It's her choice and either is fine."

"My God is with me all the time," Batool said, "no matter what I wear. Yours, too."

"What about your friends in America? Are they religious?" Rafa asked.

"You'll soon meet a good friend of mine from university who's coming for a visit and you can ask her."

"Is that your friend Eva?" Shereen asked in a pinched voice, her brows furrowed.

Perin nodded.

"How will we talk to her?" Batool said.

"She speaks French quite well. Her mother was from the French part of Canada. I want her to meet all of you and understand why I love it so much here."

"I don't know that she can really understand us here," Shereen said, a slight peeve inching itself into her tone. "She is a stranger."

Perin stared at Shereen, searching for words that would not offend. When none came, she was relieved when Batool said, "Aiyee, we already have many strangers here—Morocco, Iran, Egypt."

"My colleague Andrea is from Lebanon," Perin said.

"Oh, she has to come," Rafa said. "One does not know life until one spends a day with us here."

"My thoughts, exactly," Perin said, with a laugh. "Just behave yourselves and no more talk of internet porn."

"Don't you want her to see the real us?" Batool said.

A procession of women entered with flickering candles that created an undulating glow in the mist. "She's here," Batool said, standing up.

Leila sat down on a bench, surrounded by family and friends, her hands and feet covered in intricate geometric and floral henna patterns and her raven hair cascading down her ample bosom. One of her sisters began to beat a small drum, and another hit a tambourine against her leg. Perin swiveled her hips, clapped to the ancient rhythms, and called out a wish: "May Allah guide you in this new journey of a life shared."

"May you be as fertile as a pomegranate," Batool said.

"Allah looks down on you this day and always," Leila's aunt cried out.

Leila's grandmother sat next to her and ran her fingers over the seven faint scars on her granddaughter's right thigh. She took a small knife from an attendant and said, "Allah, we beseech you to take care of Leila." The grandmother reopened the first of the cuts she had given Leila when she was ten years old—cuts to protect her from harm, especially rape. "Don't let her have any problems in her marriage."

Perin unconsciously ran her fingers over her own raised bits of smooth flesh and remembered her grandmother's words when she'd opened her skin: "*You cannot trust anyone.*" Strange words, she had thought at the time, only later realizing that as a woman, she had to protect her honor for the sake of the family.

Leila winced as droplets of blood oozed out of the fresh cuts, and she turned away as her mother soaked up the seeping fluid with dates, dried figs, and a sugar cube.

With the last incision, the grandmother said, "Let her have many sons. Make her husband proud." She gave the knife back to the attendant and signaled for everyone to greet Leila.

Perin envisioned herself in Leila's place. With her mother, Aunt Safina, Shereen, and maybe even Eva beside her. She tried to imagine what it would feel like to have someone she loved, a man who adored her, believed in her, encouraged her to reach for her dreams. A man who'd let her be more than a wife and a mother. Perhaps this was where she and her friends differed. She also wanted a marriage of the minds.

At Leila's *Al Nikah*, Perin joined the families of the wedding couple in a small reception room at the Intercontinental Hotel. Radiant in her long white dress and lace veil that cascaded down her back and formed a puddle of gossamer on the floor, Leila locked eyes with her groom as her uncle started the marriage sermon. "We praise Allah, and ask for his help and guidance. There is none worthy of worship except Allah, and Mohammed is His servant and messenger."

The uncle quoted three verses from the Qur'an and a *hadith*, concluding with a prayer for the newlyweds, their respective families, and the local Muslim community. He held out a cup of honey, signifying the sweetness of life, and Leila and her husband each dipped their fingers into the cup and fed one another the nectar.

The ceremony over, the doors opened and a group of musicians entered playing bagpipes, tambourines, and drums. Their shiny silver-and-white-striped robes, bound at the waist with powder blue sashes, shimmered in the overhead lights. The wedding party followed them to the banquet hall, clapping, waving their hands in the air, and singing in piercing trills. Rafa caught up with Perin and Shereen and said, "Her family can strut like peacocks tonight," referring to the belief that the more money spent on the wedding, the prouder the family.

Perin adjusted her blue and gold shawl over her sapphire cocktail dress and said to Shereen, "You're next."

Shereen glanced sideways at Perin and smiled. "Maybe you'll be right after me."

Perin shrugged her shoulders. "Have to find my Hakim first."

"He could be right under your nose," Shereen said, with eyebrows raised.

Perin ignored the remark, not wanting to give her a smidgen of hope. "I wish Eva could have come earlier to see this."

"I'm glad it's just us." Shereen linked her arm with Perin's as they walked up the elegant staircase in step to the skirl of the bagpipes.

Ranch Aldabra

Relying upon the promise of "tomorrow," many people have wandered around that door, but that tomorrow never comes. —Rumi

Perin flaked off a layer from her croissant as Huda took the copper kettle off the stove. "I wish Nabil hadn't taken the morning paper. I need to know if they say anything more about the bans."

"Aiyee, need to know." Huda filled the silver teapot with boiling water. "It's not good to know too much." She added black tea and a sprig of mint, and swished it around before pouring off the liquid. "If you live like Allah tells you, you don't have to worry."

What did "living like Allah tells you" mean anymore? Perin knew what it meant to her, and she wasn't happy how some people interpreted it.

Huda put sugar in the pot and filled it again with boiling water, letting it sit on the table to infuse. "What are you worried about?"

"Too many things." Perin smeared plum jam on her roll.

"It's hard to come home," Huda said. "When I go to my village, I tell my mother she doesn't chop the tomatoes right and she feels bad. I tell my sister not to let her children play with the goats because they can get sick, and she thinks I'm saying she doesn't take good care of them. I tell my father he's crazy to believe the politicians and he says he'll die without hope."

"Can one ever trust politicians?" Perin mused aloud.

"Oh, those scoundrels, they came out again before the election and put up electric poles. Everyone was so happy they finally had lights. Then after everyone voted, they took them down again." Huda went ptooey toward the floor as if spitting.

Perin smiled. "How's your family?"

"My sons are playing soccer. My daughter's studying. My husband's probably drinking."

"I thought he stopped."

"Humph. He says drinking brings him closer to God and we get wine in paradise when we die, so why should it matter if he starts a little early. What can I do?"

Perin covered her mouth so Huda wouldn't see her smiling.

She poured tea for Perin and then pulled out a leather cord strung with tiny silver fish and a Tuareg talisman. "These protect me from my husband's nonsense and the bad *djinns*."

"Still eating breakfast?" Nadira said, entering the kitchen with a broom and dustbin.

"Finished cleaning upstairs?" Huda knotted her brows at Nadira. The housekeeper shook her head and scurried away. "Always looking for an excuse to hear what we're saying."

Huda placed Perin's empty plate in the sink. "Do you want me to read the tea leaves for you?"

"Not today," Perin said, undoing her beaded Navajo belt and tucking her chambray shirt into her jeans. "But I would like you to read a face for me." She took a printout of an internet photo from her bag and pointed to a man receiving an award for community service.

Huda pursed her lips and frowned. "Who's he? A suitor?"

"No, my boss."

"Okay, then." Huda studied the picture and said, "Thirty-three or thirty-five years old. Still changing to an adult. Could face big decisions about his choices in life. Long face—a quick thinker, takes other people's ideas and uses them. His eyes are deep set and almond shaped—like yours—shows intelligence. Arched eyebrows, like you, too—good communicator. His chin is round so he's generous. And he has a feminine side."

"What about his mouth?"

"Tight and flat—holds things in. Ears straight and narrow— good control. Broad forehead, he sees the big picture. He seems good." She handed the picture back to Perin and adjusted Perin's collar, placing her turquoise necklace on top of her shirt. "Stop worrying. Go have fun with Shereen."

Shereen's driver passed the port in the well-protected harbor, where the translucent silhouettes of the fishing boats glowed in the morning light. A bus came up alongside them and blocked Perin's view of the water. "Look at that," she said, pointing at the graffiti spray-painted on the bus. "'Army of the Prophet.'"

Shereen leaned across Perin to get a better look. "I thought you were for freedom of expression."

Perin kept quiet. Shereen was right and she wondered if she'd be more like her if she hadn't lived abroad, immune to incremental changes, not noticing that the life she knew was inching away. She still ached to tell Shereen about her visit to Zahara's, but something told her it had to remain a secret for now.

The city thinned out and rows of roadside stalls offering car repairs, plumbing supplies, and welding services appeared. Further along, the road became the coastal highway and the buildings grew sparser. Sandy beaches came into view on one side, and on the other, green farmlands, scattered with cattle for dairy production, while sheep and goats grazed on uncultivated land.

After they passed the citrus orchards, the driver headed inland, among the cork orchard and olive groves that belonged to Shereen's family. Surrounded by the land, Perin's concerns about Zahara, Eva's coming, and the new decrees faded.

As the driver followed the curve in the driveway through the craggy olive trees, Perin caught a glimpse of the ranch's slanted red-tiled roof. A minute later, the one-story white stucco house with wraparound verandah came into view. "It looks larger."

"We added a wing with extra bedrooms for guests."

"Like Hakim and his family?" Shereen smiled and shooed Perin out of the car.

A large shield with the image of a horse hung above the main entrance of the house. Beneath it was a plaque, scripted with an Arab legend: *"God regarded the south wind with pleasure, and decided to make of it a creature. 'Condense,' He said to the wind and the first horse sped over the earth."*

The cook turned from the pot she was stirring when they entered the kitchen. "Miss Perin, nice to see you. Mr. Kamal's coming with a guest today, too. Will you be eating with them?"

"I thought he wouldn't be here," Perin said to Shereen, trying to not sound irritated.

Turning to the cook, Shereen said, "Did he say who he's bringing?" The woman shook her head. "No matter. If it's a client, we can have lunch in another part of the house."

The news of Kamal being at the ranch dashed Perin's dream of a relaxing day. She had no doubts she'd feel provoked to argue with whatever he had to say.

Lazing in one of the patio lounge chairs, Perin gazed up at the grapevines that rambled over the wooden trellises, and breathed in the air tinged with fresh grass and the earthy scent of horses. The sun snuck through the latticework of drooping vines, its warmth coaxing away the last of her worrisome thoughts. She fancied drifting off into a luxurious snooze when she heard a car racing up the driveway.

A black BMW swirled up clouds of dust as it parked near the house. Nabil and Kamal got out. From a distance it was easy to see that Nabil was a good head taller, and five kilos lighter, than Kamal.

Approaching, Kamal flashed his eyebrow and said to Perin, "Want to come horseback riding with us?"

She shook her head. She had no intention of spending time with her brother's friend.

"We're riding on the beach," Nabil said.

That changed the equation. "If you're going there, then yes, I'd like to come."

Shereen went indoors to get hats and Perin accompanied Kamal and Nabil to the stables, stopping first at a large pasture where some two dozen horses roamed free. "It must cost a fortune to maintain this farm," Perin commented to no one in particular as she watched a filly struggle to her feet.

"Finest pedigrees. Let me show you something." Kamal moved closer to Perin, leaned over the fence, and pointed to several Arabian stallions grazing in a corner. "Look. Great leg alignment, muscular hindquarters. They're tough and yet when they run, they look like they're floating on air."

Perin nodded gently as she watched Kamal's face relax, a smile lighting up his face and eyes.

In the stable, she recognized Nabil's thoroughbred by the blaze stripe running down its face. As Nabil approached, it nickered and pressed its head against Nabil's shoulder.

Kamal tightened the girth on his horse while a stablehand held the reins of the thoroughbred saddled for Perin. She bowed her head and approached the animal from the side, holding out her hand. The horse stretched out its muzzle and sniffed.

Perin followed the others down the driveway and broke into a trot near the fruit orchards. Stopping at the highway, Perin and Shereen put on their scarves and hats.

"Put your necklace inside so it doesn't get caught on anything," Nabil said to Perin. She tucked it under her shirt as they continued down the road. A quarter of a kilometer later, they turned onto a trail that cut through the grass and led to the sea.

The palm-fringed beach was empty except for a few fishermen mending their nets near their multicolor boats propped up on small blocks of wood, their blues, reds, greens, and whites lending a festive air to the beach. A short distance away, set back from the water, was the village, a cluster of one- and two-story whitewashed houses, all with blue doors and shutters.

A black-winged kite swooped low overhead as Kamal led them toward an isolated stretch of pristine sand and pointed to a thumb-like protrusion of land that stuck out into the sea. "We'll race you to those trees before the curve."

Shereen tapped her heels into the sides of her horse, and Perin gripped the reins tighter, squeezing her thighs and calves against the horse's broad side. The animal's ears lanced forward and Perin sailed down the beach. She sprinted through the sand with a powerful rhythm. But her horse was no match for the stallions weaned to race.

"Forget it," Perin said, her hair floating behind her as she alternated between a gallop and a canter. The undulating rise and fall was hypnotic, and the rush of wind on her face and body invigorated her. Flying down the beach, nothing else mattered. Not the yesterdays, or the tomorrows. Only the golden sand, the turquoise water, and the lush palms. She fell in love with her country again.

Back at the ranch, the cook had set the long table under the pergola with colorful woven placemats. In the middle, she'd placed a dish of scallops, pomegranate seeds, herbs, coconuts, and lemon dressing. Bottles of Gulden Draak ale and a pitcher of lemonade were on a rolling cart.

"My favorite dish," Shereen said. "She always makes it for me."

"What makes you think she made it for you? She loves me best," Kamal said. Shereen squinted her eyes and tapped her foot.

Kamal unbuttoned his shirt. He had well-defined muscles and his olive-toned skin glistened from sweat; there were a few black hairs around his breastbone. *Very proud of his physique*, Perin thought to herself, wondering if being observed secretly aroused him. She felt a quiver in her stomach—excitement and repulsion churning together. There was some allure to the man, but he'd never understand mutuality in a relationship. He was definitely one to watch out for.

"I'm thinking of starting a winery here," Kamal said. "Plenty of land next to the vineyards."

"What?" Nabil said. "You heard. If more of their people are in key government posts, they'll target you if you produce alcohol."

"They're also talking about a Ministry for the Propagation of Virtue and the Prevention of Vice," Perin said.

"Oh, great," Shereen said. "They'll probably want us to go back to *purdah*."

"A woman is like a rose," Kamal taunted. "You water it and keep it at home for yourself and not let it out of the house for others to smell."

"Stop it. That's what the Taliban said," Shereen cried out.

"Our bodies exploited for political ideology," Perin added. "But it's not only here, I have to say," she added, thinking of how some States in the U.S. were trying to take away women's rights.

The maid cleared away the appetizer dishes and the cook set down a platter of roast mutton and grilled vegetables. On the way back to the kitchen, the young woman tripped and fell, dishes shattering against the stones. Kamal jumped up to help and Perin watched him clean up the shards. The cook told him she'd take care of it—she didn't want him to cut himself. With gentleness, he said, "It's fine. I'll do it." Perin unconsciously nodded her head.

"Now, where were we?" Kamal asked as he sat back down. "Ah, the Ministry of Vice."

"Prevention of," Perin corrected.

"I hope we don't end up like Iran," Nabil said.

"What do you mean?" Shereen asked.

"Once people there were for the imams ruling the county. But now many are fed up with them, old and young alike, although you mostly see young people demonstrating—they're not shackled with the memory of the shah."

"I read a woman there said something to the effect that peasants in other countries were getting more freedoms and they had to keep wearing the veil," Perin said.

"But Iran's revolution empowered woman. *Hijab* makes public places safe for women," Kamal said.

"Appeasement is the operative work," Nabil said. "It's easier to go along than fight."

The conversation stopped as the cook brought out bite-size pieces of honey-soaked pastry filled with date paste, coffee scented with cardamom, fig brandy, and two cigars.

Before she'd placed everything on the table, the maid ran out of the house, wailing, "Oh, Merciful one." Kamal stood up. "They killed the singer, Walid. They said it on the radio."

"It begins. Execution or exile for their enemies," Nabil said.

As Perin tried to register what she'd just heard about the singer's death, Rabi'a the Mystic's words echoed in her head: *Shed tears when you are aggrieved. Your grief will heal those in grief.*

"The lyrics he wrote," Shereen said sotto voce with a glazed look in her eyes. "Now songs can get you killed."

Perin's heart stumbled

Are they going to censor everything? She couldn't talk about these things any longer. "It's getting late. I have to finish some work for tomorrow."

"Stay longer," Kamal said. "We can play some poker, only small bets."

"I don't like to gamble," she replied.

"Isn't that what we're always doing?" Kamal asked.

A Turning Point

*Children tell stories, but in their tales are enfolded many a mystery
and moral lesson. Though they may relate ridiculous things,
keep looking in those ruined places for a treasure. —Rumi*

B ack at work after the weekend, Perin took every opportunity
to find out if there were other bans she'd not heard about,
particularly any that related to restrictions on women working,
or ones that could affect her job. She was still getting to know
the rest of the staff and as a relative newcomer, and a woman, she
cautioned herself against voicing any strong opinions until others knew her better—and she knew them better. In the recesses
of her mind, she heard her father's words: *These days one doesn't
know what side of the fence someone else is really on.* For now, she
was pleased they continued their conversations, apparently without censorship, when she was present.

She'd prepared her list of potential articles on desert life, and
after going over them with Andrea, she presented them at the
staff meeting: the ecosystem, animals and fauna, how to prevent
sunburn, and a recipe for the dessert she had at Shereen's—since
most of their dates come from the plantations in the region.

Ali approved the topics and told the head of photography
to assign a photographer and a driver to accompany Perin after
she'd completed preliminary research and was ready to go. She
pumped her fist under the table. *Thank you, djinns.*

Back at her desk, she began compiling notes for the desert articles when a ping from her mobile distracted her. It was a text from Zahara; she wanted to know when Perin planned to interview the women. Perin let out a sigh. She knew she could ask only Rashid to drive her there, and after bracing herself, she called him.

"I know you think it's risky, but I need to see the women again. I think I can get some good interviews."

"It's not happening. You know what father said."

"I'm not going to be out in public protesting. Really, who will see me?"

Rashid was quiet.

"You're the only one I can turn to. I'll make it up to you somehow."

"Don't sweet talk me. I don't want to be part of your crazy schemes."

"Oh, you're as pure and straight as you can be, abiding by all the rules, right?"

She waited a few seconds and finally he said, "This will be the last time."

"Definitely."

The drapes were open and the shutters closed in Dr. Massi's room; the small desk lamp gave out faint illumination and the room smelled musty. As Perin's eyes adjusted to the darkness, she noticed books and papers stacked on the floor. Zahara had prepared the women for her visit, and one by one, Karima, Ummee, and Camilia came in and told Perin their stories. Pleased she didn't have to prod much for them to answer her questions, she believed the quotes the women gave her would lend credibility to the article she planned to write.

After she spoke to the three, she told Zahara that Imene's story was also important, especially since other women had been kidnapped. Like Daesh did with the Yazidis, her story would resonate with the public and hopefully create a response.

Zahara closed her eyes and rubbed the middle of her forehead. "I see the link, but I don't think she's ready to speak to others about her ordeal. I told you she's fragile."

"I'll be gentle. But it would help if I knew what happened to her."

Dr. Massi rubbed the back of her neck and pressed her lips together. She cleared her throat and nodded her head.

Imene lived in a village in the mountains with her family: parents, a grandmother, two brothers, and three sisters. She worked in a nearby glass factory, traveling back and forth by bus every morning and late afternoon. On the way to her job one morning, guerrillas stopped her bus and pulled her off. They took her to their camp in the mountains where they hid from government troops, tied her up, and drugged her. She was a virgin and they raped her daily.

A keeper came every day to administer narcotics to her, a young man missing his left arm. Imene tried to strike up a friendship and asked what had happened to him. He told her he was preparing a bomb and it exploded. Imene pleaded with the young man to set off a bomb near her. She'd decided she would rather die than continue her existence as one of their abducted "wives." He refused and she set about rubbing her hands against the ropes that held her captive, thinking she could amputate her hands and bleed to death. Her wrists became burned and raw, but she was only able to cut her skin superficially. However, she managed to loosen the ropes.

One day, when the men were saying midday prayers, and before the keeper had arrived to drug her, she slipped out of the ropes and escaped. After walking for a day, she came across women tending goats in a valley. They took her in and cared for her until she was strong enough to make it to her village, but her family refused to take her back. They said she'd disgraced their honor and was not marriageable.

She hid for several weeks at the home of a distant cousin in another village and eventually heard about the safe house and made her way there. Since arriving, she'd barely communicated with anyone and was frightened to leave the apartment.

Perin twisted her garnet ring around her finger, slowly taking in all she'd heard. *How could Imene forget the horror she experienced?* Perin realized she'd been able to push her beating out of her conscious mind by intentionally forgetting, but if she'd had such an experience, would she have been able to blank it out? Would she have withdrawn like Imene?

"She's trapped by her trauma, can't sleep, and thinks of suicide. It's difficult to engage her and I often wonder if she will ever recover," the doctor said. "The worst of the violence is that she lost hope. Do you still think you can talk to her?"

"I'd like to try. I can't begin to imagine what she went through, but maybe if she knows someone else cares, she may reach out. Her story is important."

Perin found Imene in her room, sitting at a desk, drawing. She asked to see what she was doing. Imene put her hands over the paper and turned her head away, toward the window.

Unable to think of anything reassuring, Perin decided to face Imene's demons head on.

"Imene, Dr. Zahara told me what happened. It was terrible. I don't know if I could have survived what you went through. I admire how brave you were and still are. It took a lot of courage for you to do what you did."

Imene held her elbows tightly against her sides and clutched her hands to her chest.

"Imene, you're not alone. What happened to you is happening now to other women in other countries and some of them have told their stories, saying it helped to talk about it." Perin started to move toward Imene and then thought better of it. "Something happened even to me—but it was minor compared to what you endured. I hope you'll tell me about it. Did you know I'm a reporter?" Imene nodded. "I'd write your story so others would know about the injustice you faced. You did nothing wrong and yet you were punished. It's not right and people have to know that awful things like that happen. Otherwise, how can they be stopped? That's why the doctor wanted me to come here and meet all of you."

"My family said I dishonored them."

Perin caught her breath and hesitated, wondering what to say next to keep her talking; a wrong remark might make her close up again. "You didn't. You were not acting of your own free will. You were the one dishonored by the men in the mountains." Perin wanted to say that Imene was also dishonored by her family, but she couldn't for fear that Imene's inborn fidelity to her family might make her resent anything said against them. It was better that she came to that realization on her own.

Imene remained quiet.

"Sometimes, when things happen that tear people from their family, maybe for no good reason, people find new families. The doctor thinks of all of you here as her family."

Perin wanted to reach out and stroke Imene's hair, but again she resisted. She was still a stranger and one who was prying. She also came from a privileged background, sheltered by opportunity and resources compared to Imene's humble origins, and fates often have to do with privilege. Perin looked off into a far corner of the room. Her privilege hadn't spared her from getting attacked, it didn't make her invulnerable.

Perin turned back to Imene. "I think I hear them setting the table for dinner and I know the ladies would love for you to be with them. They're your new family, aren't they? Try eating with them tonight. I'll come with you."

Imene looked at Perin's outstretched hand and shook her head.

"Perhaps another day?" Perin said.

Imene nodded.

Back in the office, Perin told Zahara of her conversation with Imene, pleased that the young woman had opened up.

"Sometimes, a layperson can unlock the code to a patient better than any psychologist or psychiatrist. That's why I let you try."

"I think I gained some trust and I was thinking it would be good for her to take the waters at the baths—they're so healing. She could come with me one Thursday."

"Just because you got her to think about leaving her room doesn't mean she's ready for more."

"I just think it would be good for her to start to leave this reality."

"It's this reality that's kept her safe." Zahara slammed the desk drawer shut. "You made a small connection. Fine. But I decide when she's ready to do more."

Perin nodded. She knew she dare not ask for more.

She also knew that learning what these women had been through, made her want to help. And she needed to protect Imene.

The Visitor

God made the illusion look real and the real an illusion. He concealed
the sea and made the foam visible, the wind invisible, and the dust manifest.
You see the dust whirling, but how can the dust rise by itself? You see the foam,
but not the ocean. Invoke Him with deeds, not words, for deeds
are real and will save you in the afterlife. —Rumi

The aroma of cardamom-scented coffee from a nearby café drifted above Perin's head as she and Rashid waited for Eva outside international arrivals, along with taxi drivers and the throng jostling to get to the front of the railing. "There she is," Perin said, pointing to a tall, slender woman pulling a Tumi bag.

"Nice," Rashid said.

"Don't get any ideas," Perin said with a smile, glad Rashid's first impression of her friend was a good one. She watched as Eva stopped to read a bold-lettered sign scripted in Arabic, French, and English that was tacked to the wall of the arrivals area: *Local laws now require women to dress modestly and cover their heads in public.* It was odd for Perin to see her friend with a headscarf. She called out Eva's name and waved her hand overhead like an eager student who knows the answer to a question.

After introductions, Rashid motioned for them to follow as he squeezed to the end of the barrier toward the exit. He glided through the crowd with the ease of a ballroom dancer, while fending off lottery ticket sellers and men from local hotels, inquiring if they needed a room. A swarm of children in ragged clothes and matted hair surrounded Perin and Eva with extended hands. Perin led Eva away. "My father discourages us from giving. It's best they don't think begging pays."

In the distance, Mohammed's tall, slender frame was propped up against Assia's car. Curlicues of smoke rose from his cupped hand. He looked around, sneaked a puff, and then hid his hand behind his back. A smile crept up his gaunt, tanned face when he saw them approach. He stubbed out his cigarette and opened the back door of the car for Perin and Eva, while Rashid got in front; a pungent odor from his cheap black tobacco lingered.

Traffic on the congested highway stalled; Mohammed tapped his fingers on the steering wheel and other drivers honked their horns. The faulty exhaust pipe of the rattletrap car in the next lane clacked, while a donkey pulling a wooden cart brayed as the driver swiped it with a stick.

"Wow, quite some noise," Eva said with a laugh as she glanced at the nearby bus with teenage boys spilling from its open doors, hanging on with only their fingertips.

"You live in New York," Rashid said with a mock frown. "It was noisy there from what I remember."

"It's different here—there it's … I don't know."

Mohammed hit a pothole as the cars moved on, thrusting Perin into Eva and pushing her toward the car door.

"Organized? Refined?" suggested Perin. "It's definitely worse here."

"Organized, refined noise," Rashid said, brushing his thick hair out of his eyes. "Interesting concept."

"Close your window. Dust's flying in," Perin said to her brother. "It's not good to breathe it in."

Rashid turned to Mohammed. "Ever since she's returned, she thinks everything's bad."

Perin put her hand over her mouth so Rashid wouldn't see her smile. She'd never complained about the dust and noise before. She sounded like one of those returning natives she despised—the ones who are overly critical and tend to compare everything at home to where they've been, with the home country coming up short. But she wanted everything to be perfect for Eva. She wanted Eva to love her country, her city, her people as much as she did.

Unadorned cinderblock high-rises demarcated the city limits, towering like raptorial gargoyles over nearby cardboard and corrugated metal shacks. Traffic halted again. Bicyclists, and a child with a younger sibling straddled across her back, wove in and out among the vehicles. Car fumes and rancid odors from a nearby fish canning factory stung Perin's eyes, and she noticed Eva had covered her mouth with the end of her headscarf.

Eva scooted to Perin's side of the car and looked out at the high-rises with rugs and clothing strung from window to window, flapping in the breeze like flags of distinct lands.

In front of one of the buildings, two bearded men in black turbans and gray robes were talking with a woman dressed in slacks and wearing a scarf. One of the men raised his baton and slashed at the front of the woman's legs. A thwack rang out as the wood hit bone. Perin cringed and balled up her fists. The man struck the back of the woman's legs; the force of the blow buckled her knees. She put a hand on the ground to keep from falling. He hit her on the shoulder until she stumbled and fell.

Eva grabbed Perin's arm. "Why are they hitting her?"

"The religious police," Rashid answered, biting off a hangnail.

The policeman struck the woman above the eye and blood gushed down her face.

"We have to help her," Eva said.

"No way," Rashid said, his voice pinched.

Perin remembered the women who had come to her rescue in the Casbah and she wanted to do the same now. She also didn't want Eva to think she wasn't the person she imagined her to be. She jumped out of the car and yelled at the policeman, "I want your name."

The man stopped beating the woman and looked at Perin, his eyes narrowing. "No, I want yours," he said. The man's companion started toward Perin.

Rashid whipped out of the car and yanked on Perin's arm. "Get in," he said with a harshness she'd never heard before.

She struggled to shake her arm loose. The policeman thwacked his baton in the palm of his hand and continued toward her. Rashid forced her into the car, slammed the door shut, and propped his body against it. "Everything's under control," he said to the man before getting back in and telling Mohammed, "Get us out of here."

Mohammed clicked the doors locked and veered onto the roadway's dirt shoulder, swerving to avoid a boy and his goats. "Too dangerous, Miss," he said to Perin, his voice quivering as he motioned for the drivers in the next lane to let him through.

Perin heard the blood rushing around in her head as she stared at the back of Mohammed's graying and balding head.

"Those were the religious police?" Eva said. Perin nodded. "You said they were thugs, but to see them beat a woman—it's completely different—horrifying."

Perin re-envisioned her last image of the woman, scrambling in the dust, blinded by gushing blood, and wiping her eyes while trying to escape her attackers.

"I know you say it's dangerous, but if we'd all gotten out, couldn't we have helped?" Eva asked.

"You're a foreigner here," Rashid said, pulling on his earlobe. "They could have made an example of you. You could have been—we could have been—jailed. It would kill our parents if anything like that happened."

"You're right," Eva said. "Sorry, it was just a normal reaction. I won't give you cause for worry."

Perin screwed her body around and peered out the back window, struggling to catch a glimpse of the woman, but a river of cars blocked her view. She felt Eva's eyes on her and remembered the only argument they'd ever had, the night Perin said she wanted to return home and work. Eva told her she was an idiot for wanting to subject herself to "patriarchal tribal traditions." It had angered Perin to hear a Westerner say those words and she refused to admit there might be some truth in what Eva said. She only replied that this was all the more reason why she should return home. People of their generation had to stand up to the clerics because her parents and their friends wouldn't—they had too much to lose.

She had also told Eva that she ached to be with her family again, not knowing how else to explain homeland and roots, things you feel in your bones but don't fully understand yourself. Molded by memories, home was where she believed she belonged, comfortable in her own culture, protected by her family, able to peel off all pretenses. She came from a lineage buried deep in the North African earth; it sought her out and beckoned, and she was determined to follow.

"What did she do? What will they do with her?" Eva asked.

"Who knows? Maybe they saw a lock of loose hair," Rashid said, cracking his knuckles. "They do that to scare people. They'll probably let her go so she'll tell people. Not a very nice introduction for you."

"Don't worry. You'll be with one of us all the time," Perin said, gazing beyond Eva, past the women walking along the road, erect of carriage, like models on a runway, balancing bundles of firewood on their heads as if they were bags of feathers.

Mohammed turned onto the large boulevard that ran parallel to the sea. In the distance, fishing boats bobbed between ships moored at anchor in the docks. Perin tapped Eva's arm and pointed to Aunt Safina's villa perched on a cliff overlooking the water, before pointing in the opposite direction to the sprawling city built on the hillside, where the minarets and gold dome of the central mosque jutted into the sky, and whitewashed houses tumbled down to the sea.

It was late morning when they entered "colonial town," the part of the city built during the French occupation, and the lull before lunchtime had not yet set in. Near the central commercial area with its theaters, museums, churches, and cafés, people queued up for taxis outside one of the luxury hotels. Women, now all with coverings on their heads, bustled in and out of shops. Patrons sat in the worn leather chairs of the open-air barbershop and delivery boys, with packages tucked under arms, dodged between pairs of men hunched over backgammon boards set up on the sidewalk. The familiar scenes comforted Perin. Not everything had changed.

Mohammed guided the car up the hill past the thick sixteenth century walls that embraced the interior labyrinth of byways. Perin nudged Eva. "That's where we'll take the baths on Thursday with my friends. They're eager to meet you."

"As I am to meet them." Eva squeezed Perin's arm.

Farther on up, Mohammed arrived at the family's beige stucco, Moorish-style house, and parked in the driveway. Rashid bounded across the lawn in front of Perin and Eva and swung open the front door. Nadira was coming down the staircase, a plate of pomegranates in one hand and bolts of red and yellow silk tucked under her other arm. Excited to see their first American guest, the sinewy woman's mouth flew open and the pomegranates rolled off the plate, thudding down the stairs. As Nadira reached out to catch them, the fabric grazed the ornamental iron railing and unfurled, cascading down the steps. The fruit landed on the floor and one cracked open, scattering red seeds on the black and white tiles.

Assia stood at the top of the stairs, shaking her head, her eyes laughing. She maneuvered around Nadira, saying, "I tell you not to do two things at once." As Assia kissed Eva, Rashid stepped on the pomegranate seeds, squirting juice on Perin's shoe, red drops, the color of blood. "It was terrible," Perin said, placing her hand on her cheek.

Assia looked to Rashid for an answer and he told her what happened. She glanced down and shook her head. Then as if someone had pulled a string attached to her head, she straightened her spine, smoothed her toffee-colored straight skirt over her hips, and told Nadira to clean the floor. She adjusted the knot on the silk scarf around her neck and led Perin and Eva into the living room.

"I wanted to help. But there was nothing we could do," Perin said, taking off her tunic and placing it on the sofa along the wall.

"You know your father doesn't want us to get involved."

"We live here, Mother, we are involved," she said as she thrust her hands into the front pockets of her stovepipe jeans.

Assia fidgeted with her earrings of interlaced gold bands. "I prefer you discuss it with him later."

"I want to know what you think," Perin said as she sat down next to her, motioning Eva to join them.

Assia pinched her lips together and her eyes took on the glazed look that appeared whenever she wanted to evade something unpleasant. "The last few months, Eva … it's been more difficult," she said as she stared at the garden through the window, "with the ones … the ones who back the clerics. We have to be patient and wait until things get back to normal."

"What if they don't get back to 'normal'? Mother, they want to make us an Islamic state."

"*Tawakilt Ala Allah.*"

"Trust in God? To do what? Give people a spine to fight back and not passively agree to do whatever they say?"

"You think it's possible to reason with these people? Have a dialogue with them?" Assia said as she stroked her dark hair, bound behind her head in a bun.

Tension hung in the air and separated them like an invisible drape. Perin picked at a tattered edge of the sofa.

"Please don't pull those threads," Assia said.

Perin put her hand in her lap and debated whether she should press for answers. She looked at her mother, dressed as if ready for a tea party. She hadn't always been like this.

In the late 1960s, when most women her age stayed home and married, she defied convention and studied abroad at the Sorbonne, working part time in a fashion showroom. Now she was indistinguishable from other women bound to the traditional roles of wife and mother—and to the local customs.

Perin decided it was best to keep quiet; she did not want to argue with her mother when Eva had just arrived.

"See if Huda has the tea ready," Assia said to Perin. "And tell her to listen for the vegetable truck."

As Perin led Eva to the back of the house, she said, "I'm sorry. I didn't mean to get so upset … it's just … I'll tell you about it later."

The scent of spiced eggplants grilling on the stove filled the kitchen and Huda, a long black veil on her head, was chopping walnuts, her stout form silhouetted against the green, blue, and white floral tiles of the backsplash. She dropped her knife and wiped her hands on her apron. "Blessed be Allah, in the name of God, the most gracious, the most merciful. You're here safe." She cradled Eva's hands in hers and looked into her eyes before kissing her on both cheeks. Perin translated for Eva what Huda said.

"Very nice. Is this new?" Perin asked, pointing to Huda's navy dress decorated on the bottom with bands of red, gold, and purple ribbon.

"It's a special day," Huda said, a blush appearing on her checks.

"And veil at home?" Perin said, with lightness in her voice. Huda nodded and adjusted the flowing fabric. "Does your husband want you wear it all the time now?"

"No, I like it," Huda said with an edge of defiance before making another comment.

Perin turned to Eva. "She said we're both pretty and should wear a *chador* when we go out because men will be attracted to us and it's a sin."

"It's enough we have to wear *hijab*," Perin said to Huda. "We'd suffocate in a tent."

Huda picked up a dish covered with cheesecloth. "Some fresh goat cheese with an orange and melon?"

After Eva learned what Huda said, she told Perin, "Thank her for me, but they fed us well on the plane and I won't be able to eat for a while."

"Just tea," Perin said, eyeing the pomegranate juice out of the corner of her eye; the bright red color made her stomach queasy as she remembered the woman in the street.

As Huda prepared the tea, Perin watched Eva take in the room with the copper pots hanging over the stove, ceramic plates with

Moorish designs dotting the walls, and the tops of the cupboards lined with antique Bedouin stacking boxes and *ibriks*, the brass coffeepots with large drooping beaks.

"I'm glad the *djinns* are still taking good care of you," Perin said to Huda, the person who had taught her to communicate with them. Perin explained to Eva that *djinns* were spirits who protected people, and there were others one had to appease—the ones that caused blinding sandstorms and mirages in the desert, and tempted people to do evil deeds.

Perin realized how difficult this was going to be having to translate everything for Eva with the staff. At least all the family and most of her friends spoke French and quite a bit of English.

Huda shooed them her toward the living room. "Go be with your mother. She's been waiting to meet your friend. I'll bring the tea."

"Huda's wearing a veil," Perin said to Assia as she came back into the living room. "She's not getting crazy about this, is she?"

"No, it's fine." Assia looked down at her hands and ran her finger over her gold wedding band. "I don't know what I'd do without her."

Perin took her mother's hand and caressed it. Afternoon sunlight filtered in from the verandah that ran alongside the living room. It accented a swath of the red carpet, imbued with blue, green, and brown medallions and arabesques.

"I must remind Nadira to water the plants. Some are getting yellow edges," Assia said as Perin continued to stroke her hand. "How was your flight, Eva?"

"Lovely. We flew over the Sahara and the mountains as dawn was breaking. The peaks were bathed in a pinkish-orange glow and the green fields near the coast looked so fresh and vibrant, it was magical."

"Now you know how I feel when I come home," Perin said, taking in a deep breath.

Huda brought in the tea with a dish of almond biscuits. Assia moved a turquoise ceramic vase and onyx bowl to the edge of the coffee table to make room for the tray.

Eva took a framed photo from her bag and handed it to Perin. "I don't want you to forget." As Assia looked at the picture, Eva continued, "We took it Perin's last week in New York. There's the Statue of Liberty in the background."

"Is this how you went around New York?" Assia asked Perin, pointing to the black Lycra shorts and tube top she had on in the picture.

"Only when we skated—it's no big deal. Everyone dresses like that."

"I hope I haven't offended you," Eva said to Assia before touching her lips with her fingertips and seeking guidance from Perin.

"It's fine, Eva, mother is more enlightened than she puts on at times."

Assia frowned at Perin and then turned to Eva. "How is your work?"

Eva explained she was working with a local daily paper in New York and was able to take a week off as they'd put in a lot of overtime lately and things were slower in August. Eva yawned. "Excuse me. I didn't sleep much on the plane."

"Of course, you must rest. We can talk later," Assia said. "Perin, run a bath with lavender salts for her."

"Sounds delectable," Eva said, with another yawn.

Altered Reality

Love alone cuts argument short, for it alone comes to the rescue when you cry for help against disputes. Eloquence is dumbfounded by Love: it dares not wrangle; for the love fears that, if he answers back, the pearl of inner experience might fall out of his mouth. —Rumi

Perin helped Eva unpack and was about to run a bath when Eva said, "Wait. I want to know what's going on." She motioned for Perin to sit down on the bed next to her.

"You saw what happened to that woman, and as mother said, it hasn't always been easy."

"No, I want to know about you. What's been going on?"

"I … well, well, it's not easy for me to tell you this, and my family knows nothing about it, and they can't know, but I was also beat in the street the other week. Like that woman."

Eva stiffened. With her voice catching, she said, "No. What happened? Were you injured?"

Perin described the incident. "I was wearing a tunic and pants so they didn't splice deep into my skin. The marks lasted only a day or two." Perin stroked her arm. "I forced the whole thing out of my mind. I won't let fear hold me hostage. Don't worry, it won't happen again."

"You're so certain? And you mean to tell me you have no lingering psychological effects? No flashbacks?" Eva creased her brow. "I think I would."

"I told you, I've blocked it out."

"Like you always think you can. It could pop up at any time." Eva took Perin's hand and squeezed it. "I had bad feelings about your returning, but you know that. I wonder now if you plan to stay."

"Yes, this is my home."

"Okay. But if you change your mind, you know our advisor will help you get a job in the States. But wait." Eva put up both her hands. "Let's back up and start at the beginning. I want to know everything. You said it was difficult to find a job."

"It was. No one responded to my job queries and I wondered how I ever thought I could get hired immediately. After a week, I was a bit depressed, which upset father, so he spoke to his friend who's the managing editor of *The Gazette*, the country's most prestigious paper. I was thrilled to meet with him, but wished I could have done it on my own."

"You need connections everywhere," Eva said. "Go on."

"I was afraid he might consider me too green for a reporting position, especially after he mentioned I didn't have a list of contacts, so I told him I'd learned a lot about news gathering models and I'm good at fact-checking and research. Then he went on a rant about how in America they make stories out of the smallest crumb of news and then rile up people, and not only that—he talked about the tendency to make idols of celebrities, even minor ones. He said he didn't understand this desire to worship, to bow down to others."

"There's truth in that," Eva said. "Anyway, we know there's a trend everywhere toward soft news—entertainment mixed with news. And then what?"

"He told me the government planned to institute regulations for the workplace and some stated it was a woman's duty to stay home, marry, and have children, and not comingle with men. Women on his staff had been harassed, and families were afraid for their daughters and wives and wanted them to leave their jobs."

"You told me women here have always contributed, even fighting during liberation."

"Yes, and I told him the country would come to a halt if all women stopped working, and I asked him if he wasn't concerned that if they take away a few rights and freedoms and no one stands up, nothing will keep them from taking away more and more. Well, I was rude, speaking to someone of his position that way, and if my father found out, he'd be angry. So, I softened my tone and asked if a paper as respected and influential as his was planned to write critical analyses of proposed regulations. Then he goes off and mutters something about the voice of the people and the paper is a 'servant of society', and doesn't make policy."

"Many votes were probably in protest."

"Exactly. The politicians failed to resolve problems with unemployment, education, healthcare. I was stunned. I had a completely different idea of this man who'd reported from every hot spot in the Middle East. I don't know if I mistook his acquiescence, his willingness to go along, for cowardice, or if he's just trapped like many others. But the part that angered me the most was that he thought teaching French in a lycée for girls would be a better place for me, and without asking, he set up an interview with the principal."

Perin ran her hands through her hair. "Principal Meriem was her name. Dour woman. Oh, but that's not all. He said I was a lovely young lady and that many women who think they want careers find that true contentment comes when they have their own families, just like his wife did. Can you believe it?" Perin fingered the stones of her necklace and gently rocked back and forth.

"Men of his generation tend to say patronizing things like that," Eva said. "Listen, I know how much you want a career here, and now, don't get angry with me, but I think you have an altered sense of reality—you knew what was going on and you somehow thought it would be different for you."

At that moment, Perin's professor's words sounded in her head: *You really think you can get a good job there? Come on, you've got fundamentalists in parliament now, and you can bet they have their own agenda. Or maybe you're planning to throw a hand grenade into the system—save your homeland, or something like that?*

It hurt to acknowledge what she knew on a deeper level—that Eva was right and doing important journalism was a dream that might not work out, and only because she was a woman, subject to clerics who wanted to institute archaic rules that would thrust women back centuries.

She went on to tell Eva about Zahara and the women and how she wanted to help them. Eva encouraged her to write about their plights, and offered to do all she could to get Perin's articles published in the States, if she couldn't publish them locally.

"Did I ever apologize for calling you an idiot?" Eva said. "You know I don't think that. I just didn't want to see you leave—for selfish reasons and also because I was worried."

Perin found her comment ironic, as she was about to agree with what Eva had said.

"I'm going to say this just once more, Perin," Eva said, rubbing her eyes. "You shouldn't rule out returning to the States, especially while you're still a recent graduate."

In spite of all the opportunities, openness, and freedom the States offered, Perin knew she didn't want to go back. There was comfort being in her homeland and in her own culture. No problem could erode the bonds that resonated deep within, nourishing, comforting, and breathing life into her. It overrode any desire to live a life abroad. She didn't want to become a foreigner.

"You'd better rest. I'll run your bath. We'll talk more later."

Eva hugged her. "I'm so happy to be here. I'll always be here for you."

Seaside Restaurant

When Eva woke up a few hours later, Perin told her, "Father and Nabil have a business dinner tonight, so Rashid thought it would be nice to go to a seafood restaurant on the coast and you can see some of the local life."

"I'd love that," Eva said.

Before leaving, Perin asked Rashid, "You're certain it's all right to go there, no?"

"Better there than in town." He turned to Eva and continued, "People on the coast have more freedom—they're not constantly watched like we are in the city."

Rashid asked Perin to sit in front so he didn't look like a chauffeur. He drove first to old town, heading up a narrow street, lit only by weak lights emanating from the small shops and open-air restaurants that lined the sidewalks.

"It's about fifteen kilometers from here on the coastal highway—but nothing to worry about," Rashid said to Eva. "Nothing forbidden in the car." Rashid winked at Perin.

His wink made Perin wonder if he was teasing her, or if he really had something "illegal" in the car.

Eva propped her arms over the front seat. "Like tobacco? I've heard it's considered a drug. But from what I've seen, a lot of people smoke."

Rashid scoffed. "True. The clerics say Muslims don't need stimulants. Most people figure they won't get caught, and if they do, the first time they get a suspended sentence and a fine. After that it gets more serious. Suppose you've also heard what the Qur'an says about wine: *There's a devil in every berry of the grape.*"

Eva laughed.

Rashid glanced over his shoulder. "We have another saying: 'If a man and a woman are alone in one place, the third person present is the devil.'"

"That saying's probably in use in a lot of countries," Eva said.

Rashid turned right onto the main artery that ran parallel to the sea. Traffic was light and the car's headlights gave glimpses of the roadside stands where men congregated, chatting. A few walked along the dark road, visible only when the lights struck them.

"Talking about restrictions," Eva said, "was it only incompetence and corruption that got the fundamentalists voted into office?"

Gazing out at the darkening countryside, Perin carefully composed her words. "It's complicated." She tugged on her ear. "Yes, there *was* a lot of corruption—money that should have gone to social services, especially in the countryside, was funneled into the pockets of officials. There's high unemployment, especially for young men, and they provided jobs for many. They also played on people's feelings that the West marginalizes us, and then there was influence from countries like Turkey and Iran."

"I see parallels with the States," Eva said, "and the reactionary stance by those who think they're being left behind. And they've done a good job of making them believe immigrants are responsible for all their problems. Rashid, let me ask you, do you ever think of leaving, studying abroad like Perin did?"

Rashid looked at Eva through the rearview mirror. "Not really. Did you know that in Europe we're discriminated against and considered blacks—*les noirs*? Here we're white." Perin turned and frowned at Rashid. "We have a different mentality," he continued, "maybe because we were dominated by others for centuries. We're good at adapting until things change, and they always change."

"We don't like being migrants," Perin added. "This is our country, no matter how many faults it has. Would you get up and leave the States if some government came in that you didn't agree with? I doubt it. You'd stay and try to fight it."

"Right. There's a lot of resistance in the States and in other countries now against corruption. And talk about fundamentalists, we have our own who want to strip women of their rights and allow religion to dictate policy." Eva shook her head and chuckled. "I even worry about my father's family. They're so far right I often wonder how they make a left turn."

Perin liked that Eva found similarities and gazing at a sheaf of moonlight on the ruffled surface of the sea, she reflected on what Eva said. They could leave, if they really wanted to, but she wanted to believe that the little she might be able to do, if only writing about Zahara and the women, could made a difference that might prevent the ideologues from flourishing and completely taking over.

Rashid turned onto a road that traversed a dark stretch of sand that led to a ramshackle wooden shack near a clump of palm trees. Its walls came halfway up to the frond roof, and a torch-lit walkway extended from it to the beach. Two men squatted against the wall that faced the parking lot and smoked, the tips of their cigarettes glowing in the dark.

Gusts of wind cooled the night air and waves lapped onto the shore. The breeze shifted and the fragrance of seafood roasting on charcoal floated toward them, melding with the sounds of sizzling hot cooking oil. Perin breathed in the sea air and exhaled slowly, like a valve releasing coiled-up tension.

At the entrance, a beggar held out his hand in supplication. Rashid gave the man some coins. "*Sadaqua*. Charity. One of the pillars of Islam," he said to Eva. "We consider it a loan to Allah. Father doesn't like us to give, but a few coins is fine."

"Flamenco from Cuba tonight," Perin read from the chalkboard near the entrance. "I wonder if it's any good?"

The patrons paid scant attention to them as they entered. There were only middle-aged men and a few young people in the restaurant, obviously locals from the cut of their hair and their casual clothes.

"The girls don't have their heads covered," Eva said.

"More freedom here," Perin said. "We don't have to wear them now, either."

"A group of Saudis tonight," Rashid said.

After Perin's eyes adjusted to the darkness, she saw, on the far side of the room, a table of men in long white robes and red checkered *kaffiyehs*.

The owner, a stocky man with a fringe of hair around his head and a bushy black mustache, greeted them. "*Salaam.*" He took a drag on the cigarette wedged between his chubby fingers. Rashid returned the greeting and asked for a table facing the sea. The manager motioned to a waiter and the man ambled over with a board listing the specials of the day. He escorted them across the room and placed the menu in the center of the table. Perin took off her scarf and placed her tunic on an empty chair and Eva did the same. A wind arose and the table candle flickered, sending up a plume of smoke dispersed by the breeze.

Rashid suggested they have the combination seafood platter, fresh fish and vegetables, and a beer. Perin was glad Eva declined the latter and asked for bottled water. One never knew if a sympathizer would appear.

Rashid tried to get the waiter's attention, but the man was busy collecting flatbreads from one of the cooks seated on a low stool in front of a clay oven, her colorful print dress spread around her like an open parachute as she flipped the dough from one hand to the other, patting it flat. On the wall above her was a calendar, its edges sooty from the ash from the fire. It was turned to August and had a photo of an exotic foreign car Perin couldn't identify.

"What are those Saudis doing here?" Eva asked.

"Things they can't do at home," Rashid said. "Once I was out in the desert in Jordan, near Iraq, and there was a highway that seemed to go nowhere. I asked my friends why they would build it in the middle of nowhere, miles from Amman, and they said it was for the Saudis who sneak over the border to go to clubs and bars."

"Many hoped the new crown prince would be a beacon for reform," Eva said, "and do more than curtail some of the power of the religious police. But now I'm not so sure. No dissent allowed."

"They treat foreign workers badly. Some have to live in shipping containers," Rashid said.

"I've read about the maids who were tortured," Eva said.

Perin leaned forward. "Modern-day slavery. Did you know slavery is legal in Muslim law?" Eva shook her head. "It only exists in Sudan nowadays and most Muslims deny it, but it's in legal manuals." She sat back and crossed her arms. "Here's another truth—we're a shame culture. A Muslim feels he has to kill someone who he *thinks*—and I emphasize *thinks* because many allegations turn out to be false—has disrespected him or his family. Even though the Qur'an says not to kill."

"If you're a shame culture, what are we in the States?"

"A guilt culture."

"Interesting. I need to think about that," Eva said, pinching the skin at her throat. "Other religions have had reformations. Do you think it could happen with Islam?"

Perin tilted her head to the side. "Hard to say. There's no central authority, only opinions. Laws but no formal theology. Changes come from imams and it's all about how they interpret the law."

"Many fractions to satisfy—Shiites, Sunnis, reformers, traditionalists," Rashid said. "But as Father says, things always change, and it's possible nationalism could take its place. Do you practice a religion?"

"I was raised Catholic but I haven't practiced it for a long time. I recently received Tao."

"What's that?" Rashid asked.

"I have to start at the beginning—I have a dear friend in Thailand who discussed it with me for a while, believing I was supposed to receive it and obtain its protections. My friend said it was not religion per se, but the root of all religions, including Christianity and Islam, and it has wide meaning. Before, only the elites could receive it, but now Tao Masters decided that with all the disasters in the world, anyone who is meritorious, as they say, and has a sponsor can receive it. I'm just studying it now so I don't know a lot. Maybe the best way to explain it is by telling you the answer a person in the temple gave me when I asked him to define Tao. His answer was one word, 'Love.'"

The waiter put three large platters in the middle of the table: grilled octopus, mussels, scallops, and squid; a fish, complete with head and tail; and a steaming mountain of couscous with vegetables. An oily piece of eggplant landed on the table in front of Perin. She picked it up with a thin shiny paper napkin and pushed it to the side.

"Like the blackened catfish we have in the South," Eva said as Rashid handed her the serving utensils. Perin looked at Eva's immaculate hands with elegant oval nails, and then glanced down at her nub-like fingertips, the nails chewed off.

From the stage, the manager announced the flamenco troupe from Santiago de Cuba. A spotlight shined on a guitarist playing a haunting song. A few minutes later, two male singers came out on stage, singing and clapping their hands to the polyrhythmic beat, and calling out, *Vamos! Venga!* Four elfin dancers with weary smiles appeared, followed by a striking brunette with a sultry smile and pale skin who towered over the other women. Her eyes roamed the room, targeting individual men, each for a moment.

The dancers gyrated their hips, stomped their feet, and clicked castañets. *"Ale, Ale! Toque de palmas!"* They swung their skirts up and around their bodies with one hand, while their other hands twirled and flicked above their heads as if they were picking fruit from a tree, bringing it down to place in an imaginary basket at their side. *"Dale más, guapetona. Tome."*

Perin loved their strong defiant stances, the passionate, explosive, masculine character of the dance. The intense pulse of the music and the rhythmical clapping of hands reminded Perin of some of their native music. Eva rapped her fingers on the table, keeping beat to the music.

"Vaya, cosita! Venga, muchacha!"

Perin found it hard to keep her eyes off the tall dancer. Rashid's eyes were also riveted on her. At the end of the set, the Saudis puckered up their mouths and made sucking noises. One stood up and went to the foot of the stage, pulled out a shiny gold bracelet, and handed it to the statuesque woman. With a coquettish downward glance, she wordlessly took the bracelet and placed it on her wrist. Then she gave the man an alluring look before disappearing behind the curtain. He returned to his seat with a sly grin.

"They seem so ... so comfortable in their skins," Perin mused.

"Sure you're not thinking something else?" Eva said with a smile.

Perin felt her face get red. "Isn't the fish delicious?" she asked, ignoring Eva's remark.

Mystical Dunes

God has given you the polishing instrument, Reason, so that by means of it the surface of the heart may be made resplendent. —Rumi

Two days later, as dawn's soft light was breaking through the leaves, Fuad drove his gray Mercedes along the tree-lined street and headed up the hill that skirted the villas and luxury condominiums.

Perin turned to Eva. "Up so early reminds me of the quote from the Prophet Huda always said when she woke me before dawn: *When you wake before the light comes through the slats of your shutters, an angel cries out, 'Glory to the Lord, the Most Merciful.'*"

"What a lovely way to be awakened," Eva said

The first signs of life were beginning to percolate. A gardener, caged behind an iron-rail fence, trimmed a rose bush. A maid opened a window and hung a coverlet over the sill to air. Down the road, a peddler, overloaded with brooms and cleaning supplies, readied himself for his daily round.

The two-lane paved roadway that led to the desert was crammed with brightly painted flatbed trucks carrying goods to the oasis cities, and buses brimming with commuters en route to the factories outside of town.

"One of Huda's cousins prepares meals for the workers out here," Fuad said. "Cooks in the middle of the night, and in the morning sets up her stand outside the plants. All her family's hardworking."

"Except her husband," Perin said. "You'd think she'd realize she might be better off without him."

"Women of her generation don't think like that. They stick with the givens," Fuad said as he drove past the natural gas plant. "I'm getting hungry."

Perin reached into the basket on the backseat and handed out the flatbread and goat cheese sandwiches Huda had prepared. The container of sliced nectarines she placed on the armrest in the middle of the front seat, after offering some to Eva.

"I'm so happy Ali approved you taking us today, Father. Much better than a driver from the paper."

"Maybe Eva's accompanying you to work yesterday helped."

"I'm sure it did and she helped me so much with research."

"Her boss was very accommodating and said Perin could take photos instead of assigning a photographer to come along," Eva said.

"He also said that if mine didn't turn out, they'd get stock photos or send a photographer later," Perin said. "He covered his bases."

"And it was quite serendipitous that I mentioned the trip to Omer, who knows this scientist working there," Fuad said.

"Do you know much about this man uncle arranged to meet us?" Perin asked.

"Not much. His name's Yousef and he's from Lebanon. A biologist, I believe."

"A good source of information for one or two articles, Perin," Eva said.

"Hopefully. And please take notes, Eva. And lots of photos in case yours turn out better. Oh, and Huda warned us not to do anything to disturb the bad *djinns* that live in the desert,"

"I love how she takes care of you," Eva said.

Fuad changed gears as they climbed the foothills of the "Tell" region of rugged high plateaus. Forests of cedar, pine, and eucalyptus came into view. Perin rolled down the window and breathed in the crisp air, lightly scented with arbors. At the higher reaches of the mountains, there were still traces of snow, even though the ski slopes, and the Alpine-style chalets built in the 1930s, had been closed since late March. A few forlorn roadside food and drink stands remained open. Next to a mountain stream, a woman sat chilling sodas in the running water and behind her loomed a battered metal Pepsi-Cola sign with "Drinks For Sale" scribbled over it.

Traversing the mountains, Perin's eyelids grew heavy and she saw Eva was already dozing, no doubt still on jet lag. Placing her head on the headrest, she asked her father, "Would you mind if I take a nap?"

"Not at all. I'll let you know if I need you to keep me awake."

She closed her eyes with delicious anticipation, the same feeling she had when she awoke early and found she had another hour to sleep. But it was not easy to rest, as Zahara and the women crept into her thoughts, and she kept rehashing the conversations she'd had with Eva.

When she opened her eyes again, the fringe of the desert was coming into sight, followed by purple-, rust-, and ochre-hued crescent dunes—undulating waves of sand like a lightly rippled sea, what the locals had in mind when they called the desert *erg*, their word for ocean. She reached behind and gently shook Eva. "Sorry to wake you, but you must see this."

Eva's eyelids fluttered and she stretched her arms. "Thanks. I don't want to miss a thing."

Fuad pointed to a stone building. "Eva, see that desert palace?"

"Yes, and it looks like there are tents and camels, too."

"Bedouins live in the tents and tether their camels to them. The building is from the seventh century and was a former hunting lodge built by the caliphs of Damascus."

"It's in amazing condition," Eva said.

"Tuaregs also live in the desert," Perin said. "But they stay farther to the south."

Before long, the oasis appeared with its mud-brick villages and little plots of land for growing vegetables and grains. After the second village, there was a roadside sign that said "Government Research Center. 5 Kilometers. All Visitors Must Register."

The country's green and white flag atop the center's concrete structure rippled and snapped in the wind as Fuad maneuvered the car into one of the empty slots for visitors, marked off in the sand with rows of white pebbles.

Perin motioned for Eva to put on her tunic and scarf, and she did the same.

Inside, a burly mustached soldier in fatigues, with a beret jauntily pushed down over one eye, commandeered a reception desk that obstructed the rest of the room. On a bench next to him was a stocky middle-aged man in rumpled khakis and a tan shirt. In his hand was a book, titled *The War for Lebanon, 1970-1985.* "You must be Fuad," the man said, approaching. "Yousef. Nice to meet you. Right on time. You must've missed the road repair crews. Let's get you all signed in."

The guard transcribed information from Perin's and Fuad's national identity cards and Eva's passport into a worn oversized leather ledger with cracked edges. They signed next to where he printed their names.

"Our escort's waiting," Yousef said. He put on wraparound sunglasses and a floppy canvas hat covered with pins from nature reserves around the world.

"Do you always have an escort?" Fuad asked, squinting up at the sun.

Yousef nodded. "They say it's for our safety. But they really want to be sure we're doing what we say we're doing, and we don't take any artifacts we run across. It's not a problem, but they can get in the way. Once we were looking for beetles; a big shiny black one came out of his hiding spot and a soldier stepped on it before we could catch it. Squashed." Yousef's sturdy, bear-like frame shook as he let out a hearty laugh. "The French set up this center in the 1950s for the archeologists they sent to hunt for Roman and Phoenician artifacts. They chose the site because it's near the oasis, and there are reserves of underground water."

As they neared the jeep, a soldier in desert camouflage slung his rifle over his shoulder and pushed the driver's seat forward for the three of them to get in the back.

"We'll start at the basin where we set traps," Yousef said as the escort drove out of the lot. "We're a mixed lot here—a bug man, a lizard guy, and others who study rodents, ants, and grasshoppers. Also, a botanist who observes the plants and shrubs adapted to this region."

Bumping up and down over small dunes, Perin's head kept hitting the top of the jeep, and dust flew up from its wheels. She placed a tissue over her mouth and nose and gave another one to Eva. Fuad took out his handkerchief.

"Hold on," Yousef said, "we have to go fast over the ruts or we'll get stuck in the sand."

Perin's stomach bobbed around and she was glad she hadn't eaten much for breakfast. Her hand on her diaphragm, she kept one eye on the escort's rifle perched against the dashboard. Its constant rattling unsettled her. "Is it safe to keep that gun there?"

"The safety's on," Yousef said after checking.

Reassured, she looked around to capture to memory the shifting palette of colors and how the sun cast shadows, like figures guarding the landscape and dunes.

At the basin, four soldier-escorts in camouflage milled around a van and two jeeps that had a tarp stretched between them for shade. A soldier smoking a cigarette squatted on the ground under it. Yousef took three goatskin bags hanging from the grill on the front of the jeep, handing one to each of them and reminding them to drink plenty of water. Perin swung the bag's palm-frond strap over her shoulder as they followed Yousef up a small embankment. "Let's see if they caught any rodents last night," Yousef said over his shoulder.

At the top, Perin paused to look around and take photos, enveloped by a mystical feeling of being surrounded by sand and sky.

"It's mesmerizing," Eva said. "Just beautiful."

On the other side of the mound, near a rocky area with scrub, were three men, a woman, and two escorts. Perin kept her attention on the scientists as they traipsed down and didn't notice a scrawny soldier break away from the group and come toward them.

"Stop! Show your passes." He pointed his rifle at the three of them. Perin instinctively stepped back behind her father and pulled Eva with her.

Yousef smiled and explained they were his guests and didn't need passes.

"They're not authorized to be here," the soldier replied, his rifle still pointing at them.

"My good man, they're not going to disturb anything. I take full responsibility for them." Yousef's voice emphasized *full*. "No one ever asked for passes before."

"Orders. They have to leave," he said, jutting out his rifle, his eyes tiny black slits.

Perin glanced at the other scientists who watched, immobile, as if any movement on their part could escalate the situation.

"I apologize," Yousef said to Fuad, his ruddy complexion turning redder. "I'll have to speak to the captain back at the center. The guard's new; I've never seen him before."

"Can't you do something?" Perin whispered to her father as they walked back to the jeep. "I bet we don't need papers."

Without looking at her, Fuad shook his head and followed Yousef.

Back at the convoy of vehicles, Perin propped herself against one of the jeeps while Yousef pulled up his baggy jeans, got into a jeep, and drove off with the escort.

"Shouldn't he be able to bring whoever he wants?" Perin said after they left. "He's heading up this expedition, isn't he?"

"That's not how it works and you know it," Fuad said. "They're guests and the military has authority and control over this area. And in case you didn't notice, he had a gun."

Perin pinched her lips. It was hard for her to look at these soldiers, and especially the one back there, and think they represented the government. She kicked a pebble and watched it bounce across the sand. "You're good at reasoning with people."

"But apparently not you. It's for Yousef to handle, not me." Fuad softened his tone. "I know you're tired, but we're here because you wanted to come, so let's enjoy the day." He slung his jacket on top of a jeep and fanned himself with the map of the desert he'd brought from home.

Eva nudged Perin. "It's fine. We can wait. I'm happy to just soak in the ambience and take more photos."

Perin nodded. She had so wanted this day to be perfect. She wondered how much of her mood was because she hadn't slept much, and how much was due to her irritation at the soldier stopping them for no good reason. And then there was the deep-seated anger she felt regarding what was happening to her country.

Perin scraped away the top layer of sand with her foot. The sun was intensifying. She adjusted her sunglasses and pulled the brim of her hat further down on her face. "We should have brought umbrellas," she said as the sound of an approaching jeep was heard.

Enveloped in a cloud of dust, it pulled up alongside them. Yousef and a broad-shouldered man wearing a billed cap got out. "The unit's head." Yousef put his arm around the man, whose stomach protruded over his belt. "He says it's fine you're here as long as you've registered. He'll speak to the young man."

Yousef led the group back to the embankment where the soldier who'd stopped them was anchored in the same spot; the scientists and the other escort had moved to another area about fifty meters away. As Yousef and the Captain spoke to the young man, he kept his body rigid; only his eyes darted back and forth from his superior to Perin and the others, hardening with each glance.

Yousef motioned for the three to join him, saying all was worked out. He led them over the crest of a dune to an area with sparse vegetation, pointing to *jujuba* shrubs, where ants harvested seeds. Fuad bent over and Eva and Perin got down on their haunches with Yousef, their heads nearly touching. "They move en masse in search of food. Not afraid of being seen." Excitement imbued Yousef's voice as he pointed to dots scurrying out from the shrub. "There's some ten thousand types and they've been everywhere for millions of years."

Yousef pulled a bandana from his back pocket and wiped the beads of moisture from his forehead. He wrapped the red-and-white patterned cloth around his head with its thinning hair, and placed his hat on top of it. "Did you know that each ant can lift fifty times his own weight?"

Yousef retied the shoelace on one of his scuffed white sneakers, stood up, and brushed sand from his knees. "Next stop, the traps. Watch out for scorpions."

"Really?" Perin said, scanning the ground.

Yousef chuckled. "Nothing's going to get you. They're almost always nocturnal and hide under rocks and groundcover during the day."

"It's the 'almost always' that bothers me," Eva said as they approached several spring-loaded traps spaced several feet apart among bushes and rocks, their locations flagged with bright red streamers tied to adjacent bushes. A slender woman with a clipboard tucked under one arm was checking them. She had a long skirt over her jeans and wore a headscarf.

Yousef introduced Yasmina, his colleague from Beirut, and asked her to talk about her work. "To the right are traps for rodents that I baited with sunflower seed and barley yesterday, just before dark. They're nocturnal and I didn't want the birds to eat the seeds before night. I found two in the traps this morning."

"From what we've seen and heard so far," Perin said, flipping to a new page in her notepad, "you're researching things I would consider ordinary, common—ants, spiders, rodents, lizards. Why are they so important?"

"To unravel the mysteries of the different species," Yousef said with a verbal flourish and a smile. He resumed his professor-like tone and said, "We take tissue samples from the animals we collect and compare them to see if the DNA is the same from place to place. Or we see what differences there are. Then we trace the relationship between the species, and if we're really lucky, we stumble across their origins, which tell how animals get from one place to another."

Perin felt the sun beating on her head, and sweat dripped down her back. Her shirt was sticking to her skin. She bellowed it in and out in a fruitless attempt to let in air.

She saw her father fanning himself with his map, sweat beads dropping from his forehead. He sat down on the sand and took a drink from the goatskin bag.

"Did you take your medicine today?" Perin asked. He nodded.

Yousef came over, took one of Fuad's arms, and motioned for their escort to take the other. "We'd better get you back to the jeep." As he started to walk away, he turned and said, "You stay and talk to Yasmina."

Perin watched her father go down the embankment and debated whether to accompany them.

"It's too much for him to be out at midday," Eva said. "He was up before dawn and the drive had to tire him out. I can keep him company."

"Yousef's with him," Perin said. "He'll feel better in the shade. Let's speak to Yasmina and then we can leave."

Approaching the scientist, Perin said, "What's the biggest obstacles you face in your work?"

"We have to document as much as possible while we have the chance. With all the minerals and gas underneath the desert, it's only a matter of time before the government grants exploration rights and destroys habitats." Yasmina wiped her flushed face and brow with the tail of her scarf.

"Can't you take it off here?" Perin said, pointing to her headscarf. "No one's around."

"I feel more comfortable with it on. It sends a message and the guards look at me less."

Yasmina looked over Perin's shoulder and bit down on her lip. Out of the corner of her eye, Perin saw the form of a man, his feet spread apart. The soldier who had stopped them earlier stood a few feet behind her, his eyes piercing through her like lasers as if undressing her, and stroking the butt of his rifle with his sweaty hand. Perin's stomach somersaulted; she wanted to tell him to go away, but she had to play along.

Eva grabbed Perin's hand and led her down the embankment. "We'd better not rile up the *djinn*."

Perin laughed. "Now even you believe in them." She managed to not even glance at the soldier as she passed him.

They arrived at the jeep just as the escort finished letting air out of the tires to give it traction on the sand that was softening with the heat of the sun. She was relieved that color had returned to her father's face, and he was not perspiring as heavily.

The escort maneuvered around the bones of a camel splayed in the sand and Perin swayed right and left as the jeep bounced along, stirring up dust that lodged in her eyes and throat.

"Why don't we stop at the oasis for a coffee?" Yousef said.

"Good idea," Fuad said. "I want to get something for us to eat on the drive home."

Perin gave one last lingering look at the hypnotic sands and dunes, carved and molded into sensuous forms by the wind, and wondered what enigmas and secrets they held.

The Oasis Café

His words were filled with such eloquence and wisdom, as though an ocean abided inside him, and the ocean filled with eloquent pearls. The light that shone from every pearl became a criterion of right and wrong. —Rumi

At the edge of the sand-strewn village, Fuad slowed down to maneuver past a donkey cart heaped with dates. Near a stone well, three women beat wet clothes with palm fronds, and behind them, a camel with a beam attached to its back walked in circles, turning the stone wheel of a press. Perin watched it plod around and around, head hung low, bobbing like the head of a toy doll on a dashboard. Her heart went out to the animal, trapped and resigned like so many others.

Fuad turned into the main square ringed with one-story mud buildings and parked next to Yousef's dust-clad jeep. They joined him in the center of the square, where meager stalls sold homegrown root vegetables, packages of figs, and hats and baskets made from palm fronds.

"Can we see the sand paintings?" Eva asked, pointing to a young boy, sitting at a table covered with about twenty bowls of colored sand, ranging from earth tones to pastels of pink, aqua, powder blue, and canary yellow. With a metal funnel, he poured a tiny amount of persimmon-colored sand into a miniature bottle, like the ones used for serving liquor on planes. He added the colors of pistachio, nutmeg, and champagne. An intricate, clearly delineated design of a date palm and a nomad on a camel slowly took shape.

"Pick out one. A memento of our day," Fuad said to Perin and Eva.

While Perin perused the designs, a goat wandering among the stalls brushed against her legs. She shooed him away and selected a scene of a camel train traversing the desert at sunset, the sky ablaze in reds and golds. Eva chose a scene of dawn breaking over the Mediterranean that reminded her of the view she saw from the plane.

Yousef led them to a rustic building with a crude hand-painted sign over the door that said Oasis Café. Along its façade and the adjoining row of buildings, robed and turbaned men with weathered faces puffed on water pipes and watched the goings-on in the square. A youngster sweeping sand from the entrance stepped aside as the group entered.

A long bar with stools abutted one wall, and behind it, shelves were stacked with dented aluminum pots and cups in various shapes and sizes, glasses for tea, and tiny porcelain demitasse cups. A photo of the country's president beamed down, alongside an Egyptian movie poster with scenes of men with rifles and women in combat uniforms; one woman, her blouse open to mid- chest, sat on the back of a motorcycle.

"*Salam*," Yousef greeted the café owner. "I brought my friends to my *home away from home* for some of your Turkish coffee. Told them it's the best they'll find in the whole country." The man folded his hands in prayer pose and bowed his head before rushing to wipe off a table in the middle of the room. He flicked his cloth across each chair, scattering dried breadcrumbs and used toothpicks. A waiter shuffled over and asked if they wanted anything to eat.

Fuad ordered to go, falafel, bottles of water, and two packages of dates.

"What a wonderful collection of copperware," Eva said as her eyes roamed the small long-handled pots on an overhead shelf.

"*Ibriks*," Perin said, "used in the desert for making coffee and tea."

The owner returned with three demitasse cups of steaming coffee, glasses of water, and dates dipped in butter.

"*Bismallah*," Yousef said, raising his cup first to his guests, and then to the other men in the café. The men nodded, returning his greeting.

"'Sweet as love, hot as hell, with a foam so thick you could stride across it in boots.' An old saying we have," Yousef said. "Did you know that when Ottoman men married, they had to promise to keep their future wives supplied with coffee, or the women could legally divorce them?"

Eva smiled at Yousef and touched his arm, saying, "You know so much. I love hearing all your stories." Perin gave her a kick under the table. Eva glanced at her and removed her hand.

"They call me the trivia king at home. I know a little about a lot of things." Yousef sipped his coffee and let out a sigh. "Did you ever visit the date plantations here?"

"Years ago, when Perin was young," Fuad said.

"We stopped at a stand and had date milkshakes made from camel's milk," Perin said, pulling up her drooping socks. "It was good and I still remember its tang." Turning to Yousef, she said, "I'd like to ask you more questions about your work. Yasmina said when you're at a site, you rush to fit in as much as you can because you never know when some species could disappear. Can't you find the same insects and animals in neighboring countries?"

"The Sahara's over nine million square kilometers and nothing's exactly the same even within a small geographic radius."

"There are similarities, aren't there?" she said.

"We learn more from the differences."

"Of course," she said. "What's your favorite thing about your work?"

"Nighttime. You'd be surprised what goes on when it's dark. Jerboas search for plants and seeds and the foxes hunt the jerboas. Both burrow beneath the sands during the day because it's too hot. We set up motion-sensor lights and cameras, and sleep nearby. The sunsets are glorious and then there's darkness and silence." Yousef looked off into space.

Perin imagined what it would be like to be engulfed in the absence of sound, under the inky blackness of a moonless night when all the stars flickered like small explosives on the end of firecrackers. "But it's near freezing at night," she said.

Yousef agreed and remarked that the cold was more dangerous than the heat. "You wear the right clothes and we light bonfires."

"I hope you don't mind me asking," Eva said, "but since you're from Beirut, I hear it was great before the war."

"The Paris of the Middle East it was called before *the events*— that's what we call it."

"Did you see a lot of fighting?" Perin asked.

"Perhaps he prefers to not talk about it," Fuad said.

Yousef stirred his coffee. "It's the only way to get rid of the hatred." He stopped twirling and put his fork down. "My wife was killed. She was twenty-four. We'd been married two years."

"I'm so sorry," Eva said, placing her fingertips to her mouth.

The same age as me, Perin thought. She saw her father looking at her and knew he was thinking the same thing.

"I didn't have time to grieve. I'm the only son and I had to take care of my parents and three sisters." Yousef scratched the back of his head and was quiet.

"That's what happens," Fuad said, "in times of difficulty, families have to close ranks."

"Was anyone else in your family injured ... or killed?" Eva asked.

"No. The only scars left are those on our hearts and souls."

"Such a tragedy," Eva said with a shake of her head.

Yousef nodded. "I hope others learn a lesson from us and don't become intolerant and so entrenched in their positions that they think violence is the only way to justify their cause. We paid the price for too many years."

Perin watched Yousef. He had more layers than she previously thought.

The waiter placed a paper bag on the table in front of Fuad. As he paid for the food and coffee, he said, "Yousef, I hope you'll visit us the next time you're in the city. I'd like to return your hospitality."

Perin was pleased her father invited Yousef. They'd have the chance to learn more about this man. She sensed a gentle heart beat under his burly exterior.

On the outskirts of the village, a ragtag group of boys played soccer in a field near drying piles of dung the village used as fuel.

"Yousef's an interesting man," Eva said. "Passionate about his work. I like that."

"It's hard to imagine someone getting so excited about bugs," Fuad said with a yawn.

"You're tired," Perin said. "If I knew how to drive, we could switch from time to time."

"Have Mohammed teach you."

A thrill tingled down Perin's spine. "I'd like that. Thank you. I will."

"Both of you must be tired. Go ahead and take a nap. I'll wake you if I start to feel drowsy."

Perin awoke when Fuad put on the brakes to slow down.

Ahead, two policemen manned a roadblock. Perin quickly put her scarf back on and motioned for Eva to do the same. As her father pulled up to the barricade and turned off the motor, a policeman motioned for him to lower his window. He scrutinized the three of them and asked for their documents.

The officer took Fuad's driver's license and identity card and held the pictures up to Fuad's face, alternately looking at them and at Fuad. He conducted the same ritual with Perin's and Eva's documents.

"I need you to open your trunk." Fuad followed the officer to the rear of the car while the other officer stopped a car in the oncoming lane.

Perin twisted around to see what was happening.

"What's he looking for?" Eva asked.

"I'm not sure. Maybe goods smuggled through the desert or drug traffickers. I can't see with the trunk raised." She tore a loose thread from the sleeve of her blouse and twisted the filament around her finger.

Don't get paranoid, Perin told herself, picking at her cuticles. But why was it taking so long? All the officer had to do was see there was nothing in the trunk. What if he was accusing her father of some trumped up charge?

"I need to check what's going on," Perin said as she opened the door a crack.

"Maybe you should wait," Eva said.

Straining to hear the muffled voices, Perin started to slide out of the car when the trunk slammed shut. She scooted back inside and closed the door. Fuad got in and handed them their identity documents. Perin asked why they were stopped.

"They're checking all main roads. He said a mob killed the imam who preaches at the mosque near the club. They think some of them may come this way."

Perin's lower lip quivered.

"The legislature voted today," Fuad said, "and I suspect the clerics got their Family Code passed. It's probably emboldened some of their followers. The imam they killed was a moderate who supported a secular state. It'll be tense the next few days— or longer."

Perin felt queasy, as if her body was signaling a foreboding before her mind could register all the implications of what was occurring. *Please angels and djinns*, she prayed, *keep the country and all of us safe.*

"I hope you won't be alarmed, Eva," Fuad said.

"Thanks for your concern, but I'll be fine. It's good to experience this to better understand what's happening here."

Eva appeared so calm and Perin wondered if Tao helped her. She wanted to know more about it.

At the city limit, a crowd of men, most of them young, strutted through the streets with fists raised, chanting and waving banners. Some put posters of a radical cleric on buildings and light posts. Others spray-painted walls and the sides of idling buses: *"Islam is the only way to live,"* and *"Peace for our Brothers in Palestine."* Her professor's words haunted Perin as she watched: *I've seen how things can get out of hand. And how easy it is for people to get riled up and swept along with a movement.*

Assia was waiting in the hallway when they returned home. "Of all days for you to go away. I've been so upset. They killed the imam, and the decrees. They said on television no singing in public, no alcohol, no gambling, no smoking." Assia shook her head. "What are we going to do about Rashid? Nabil, too. But I'm more afraid for Rashid. He thinks I don't know he smokes, but Nadira shows me the butts she finds in his room. And I smell it on his clothes."

It hurt Perin to see her mother so distraught and she wished she could think of something to say, or do, to mitigate her anxiety. But she couldn't even think of something to reassure herself.

Fuad rubbed his forehead. "I'll have a talk with him."

"And foreign music. You have to tell him he can't go around with those things in his ears. And that music of that singer they killed. They could put him in prison."

"We didn't raise idiots. He knows what the consequences are. I'll talk with him."

"And I don't want you going around alone," Assia said to Perin. "They could pick you up for some infraction—accuse you of something and there'll be no one to protect you."

"I hope my being here doesn't create more problems for you," Eva said.

"You're fine here with us," Fuad said. "You're our welcome guest."

"Did they say anything about restrictions on businesses?" Perin asked, her job utmost in her mind.

Assia shook her head.

"They want people to see visual representations of the bans. That's all they can control at this point," Fuad said. "They have to ensure things keep running smoothly and panic doesn't set in. I don't think they'll interfere with companies. At least not yet."

"I'd feel better if you didn't work in an office," Assia said to Perin.

Perin remained silent; there was no sense in adding to the tension. And she couldn't tell her mother that the real danger was in reporting from out in the field, not from an office.

"We're going on with our lives," Fuad said to Assia before turning to Perin, "but with extra caution. Especially in public."

On her way out of the room, Perin overheard her mother say to her father, "Safina's worried about Tariq and is thinking of sending him to Paris."

"I doubt that's necessary," Fuad said. "He'll be fine here, as we all will."

Perin hoped one day she could emulate her father's calm under pressure, and gain some of his wisdom.

Upstairs, Perin and Eva discussed how Perin could approach each article she planned to write on the desert for her column, after which she again brought up how she wanted to write about Zahara and the women, saying she hoped Eva could meet them while she was here.

"Your father just cautioned you. Will writing about the women put you in danger?"

"Like we discussed—I don't have to put my name on it. You could put your name."

"I'll do what I can. Just think about what your father said." Eva opened one of the shutters and looked down on the courtyard. "You don't know how fortunate you are to have a father who's present in your life and cares about everything you do."

"But your parents are supportive," Perin said.

"Maybe more now that I'm grown, but it wasn't always this way. My father couldn't relate to a small child and he was rarely home. Work took priority over family. He provided well and we lived a good life, but I never had the closeness with my parents that you have with yours."

"And your mother?"

"I don't think she ever wanted to have a child. She also was an only child and very pampered. You know what one of my earliest memories of her is? She would lie in her chaise lounge in a long dressing gown and call out for me: *Eva, come here and entertain me.*"

"I always thought your family was like mine."

"You have such warmth surrounding you and you're able to go out in the world because you know they'll always be here for you. I envy you." Eva gazed down and rubbed her cheek. "I've had to realize I can't capture now what I didn't get as a child."

"Oh, Eva," Perin said, embracing her. "Friends are family and think of us as your family."

"That's nice of you to say, and I'd love to consider you family, but you're not and you'll never be."

"Don't say that. We are, if you want us to be." Perin stroked her arm. "My family is one reason I returned, but here family's extended and it can get suffocating."

"Perhaps it seems that way now. Being on your own and making your own decisions can change you."

Perin tilted her head and stared at the ceiling. "I don't know. Maybe." She shook her head. "I can't think about that now. I better get to bed so I can function tomorrow. You're welcome to come with me again, or I could see if Rashid and mother could take you to a museum."

"I'd like to visit a museum. And Perin, I want you to know that I had a fabulous day. Saw and learned so much, enjoyed every moment, even dealing with that dreadful soldier—it gave me material for an article. Thank you."

Perin woke sometime after 2 a.m., her stomach grumbling. Warm milk and a banana would help her sleep. She tiptoed downstairs and saw light coming from her father's study.

Fuad was asleep in his chair, chin resting against his chest, an open book in his lap: *The Origin of Species* was written across the headers of the pages. His head drooped and made him seem older, barren of the vitality he'd always had. Perin's heart felt like it was expanding to contain all the love and affection she had for him at that moment.

She gingerly lifted the book from his lap. He blinked several times and struggled to get up from the chair. She extended her hand. He waved it away, grasped the armrests, and pushed himself up. He stretched, adjusted his glasses, and turned off the desk lamp. "Go back to bed. I'll get the other lights."

She kissed him on the cheek. "Thank you for taking us to the desert." He hugged her and gently nudged her toward the door. She forgot she was hungry and went back upstairs to bed.

Interludes

*When the ocean of Mercy begins to foam, even stones drink the water of life.
The face of the earth becomes lush green, the dead wood springs to life, the lamb
and the wolf together play, the despairing becomes valiant and strong. —Rumi*

"I wish I could have brought my friend with me tonight," Perin said as Zahara drove them to the apartment. "I wanted her to meet you and the women before she leaves."

"They're just getting used to you. They're not ready to meet a new person, and especially a foreigner who doesn't speak their language."

Perin let out a heavy sign. "I understand." She also realized how tiresome it would have been to translate everything for Eva. She appreciated that Eva didn't mind and insisted she keep the appointment, assuring Perin she'd be fine at home with the family, and she'd support Perin's excuse of having to work late.

At the apartment, Perin spent a half hour with Imene, slowly gaining her trust. She was finally able to persuade the young woman to venture out of her room and join the other women.

Imene slithered into the living room, shoulders hunched and face averted, her eyelids fluttering. Gradually she relaxed as the women included her in their conversations and encouraged her to help them with dinner preparation. Perin allowed herself to think that Imene had always wanted to participate, but needed assurance that the women wouldn't shun her like her family had done, or hold her responsible for what had happened to her. Now she hoped that by engaging with the others, Imene would eventually be able to open up and purge some of the shame she felt.

Perin could not explain the strong connection she felt toward Imene. As she watched the young woman, a verse from the Qur'an came to mind: *Every good deed will be repaid tenfold; if you have faith and do good works, God will never impose a duty on you greater than you can bear; those who show compassion to the weak and pardon the enslaved shall be granted an easy death and the delights of paradise.* But she wasn't doing it because she wanted repayment, even of the heavenly kind—she was doing it because she wanted to.

As Perin watched the nearness of Imene and the women, she thought of Eva's departure. Soon she'd no longer have her friend next to her to say whatever she thought, without thinking of how to say it, someone who really listened, empathized and encouraged her. They'd keep in touch, certainly, but it wasn't the same. Nor was it quite the same with her friends here.

The following day, as Perin and Eva prepared to go to the *hammam*, Assia instructed Mohammed to drop them off at the back entrance because she did not want them walking unescorted through the Casbah. But Perin had other ideas and on the drive there, she said, "Mohammed, Eva must experience the ways of our hidden city. It's fine to leave us at the main entrance."

"Can't, Miss. Your mother told me not to." Perin saw him looking at her through the rearview mirror with a pasted-on smile. "I'll be in trouble if she finds out."

"Eva and I lived in New York and you know how dangerous it is there," Perin said, with a wink at Eva. "She won't ever know."

At a stoplight, he ran his hand back and forth across the top of the steering wheel, brows crunched together. He shook his head.

"I can't let her go without seeing the Casbah," Perin said.

He closed his eyes and nodded. "You must never tell your mother."

Perin took Eva up a crooked alley lined with wooden-latticed Ottoman balconies that jutted out from the whitewashed buildings. Underneath one of them were two teenage boys hawking batteries, cigarettes, and chewing gum, all contained in little boxes that hung from ropes around their necks. Feeling their eyes on her, Perin's chest tightened, and her mind reactivated memories of the beating. She took Eva's arm, quickening her pace and nearly bumping into a woman carrying an overloaded striped plastic bag on her head. Perin hastened toward the souk, where they could mingle among shoppers ambling through its twisty lanes, and the open stalls of the food vendors with their neatly arranged mounds of vegetables and bowls of cinnamon, henna, saffron, cumin, and sage, formed into pyramids.

Farther on, a whiff of perfume floated by. "Father says a blind man could find his way around the Casbah by following his nose—sweet cinnamon in the spice market, the fruity smell of olive oil in food section, the rusty smell of raw meat hanging from hooks, the smell of leather."

"So true. A marvelous adventure for the senses here. Is that hashish?"

Perin nodded. "You often smell it here."

Eva grabbed Perin's arm. "Come. I'm eager to see what's around the next corner."

The perfume vendor, a grandmotherly woman with a gap between her front teeth, sat beside her trays of bottles topped with colorful glass stoppers. "Come, come, try my *1001 Nights*."

"Even though I can't understand what they're saying, I love the way the vendors call out to you in such a sensuous tone and with such familiarity," Eva said, extending her wrist.

The woman dabbed the scent on her and Perin. "Scheherazade used this to entice King Shahriyar. It'll bring you untold blessings."

Perin scrunched up her nose. "Too sweet."

The woman tipped back her head and laughed; her black scarf slipped down, revealing a mass of bright henna-red hair. "If it smells too sweet, then you are not accustomed to sweetness in your life and you need it."

Perin was tempted to tell the woman she had plenty of sweetness in her life and more than what she imagined the vendor had, but she only said, "Another day. Peace be to you," as she led Eva away. The woman's smile vanished and she muttered something under her breath.

"What did she say?" Eva asked.

"Cursing me because we didn't buy something."

"Ha. And I thought she was so nice."

As they rounded a corner, avoiding the ubiquitous piles of garbage that resembled ancient burial mounds, someone half-hidden in a doorway called out, "Let me tell your futures, my dears." A fortune teller with a fake mole above her brightly painted lips picked up a deck of cards and shuffled them. "Don't walk away. You'll regret it."

Perin motioned for Eva to hurry. "Huda says these women frighten you by saying they see evil things, and then insist you buy their charms as a protection, expecting you to pay astronomical fees."

"Same in the States."

Perin followed a web of lanes until they reached the jewelry section, stopping at a wedding shop with its ostentatious eighteen-carat gold belts set with semi-precious stones, where a boy in a sweat-stained undershirt stood, eating a mandarin orange and dropping the peels on the ground. "Husbands buy the belts as gifts for their brides on their wedding day. Most of the women are from the lower classes and the belts will be the one thing that is truly theirs—not their homes, not their children—and it's their alimony should they divorce."

"It hardly seems sufficient to support a woman," Eva said as *"Balek! Balek!"* rang out from a porter lashing the rump of a braying donkey laden with bags of carded cotton wool.

"Our taxi of the Casbah," Perin said.

"I'll remember his smell for some time," Eva said, referring to the heavy musty odor.

"The baths will wash it away." Perin led her friend toward the main square and down the alleyway to the *hammam*. "I wish you'd stay longer. Can't you call your boss and tell him you've got some good stories here?"

Eva shook her head. "Not this time, but I'll be back."

Sitting in a corner of the baths, Perin and her friends—except Shereen, who stood aloof—explained some of the bathing ritual to Eva, including how women must come fourteen days after giving birth, and that no boys over the age of three were allowed to enter. It bothered Perin that Shereen was distant, but she thought it best to ignore it for now.

Gradually the women grew more comfortable with Eva and asked about her life. Batool wanted to know what she thought of their country and Eva said, "Apart from the fascinating history and culture, I love the everyday rituals and unhurried rhythm of daily life, and the closeness of family and friends. And the colors and sounds are mesmerizing."

Majida wanted to know if Eva spent much time with her family and Eva tried to explain that they were not a constant in her life, as they were here; her world revolved around career and lifestyle.

"You'll conjure up bad *djinns* if you don't see your family," Batool said.

"*Haram, haram, haram.* You'll pay in the hereafter," Rafa joked.

"Maybe her parents don't need her," Shereen said in English. "Parents there want their children to leave home."

Shereen's snippy tone annoyed Perin and she looked at Eva to see if she'd taken the comment to heart. But Eva showed no sign of irritation.

"We heard the stores there have too many things and it's impossible to decide—one hundred types of cheese, twenty types of olives, and the shopkeepers are not helpful," Majida said.

"You have lots of hair on your arms," Batool said. "We have sugar wax here that can help you."

"I don't mind the hair," Eva said. Batool frowned and shook her head.

Rafa nudged Batool and said, "How do the men there compare to men here?"

"I really can't say, but I guess there are more varied backgrounds and religions than there are here. Perin could answer better."

Perin thought for a few moments. "They don't look at women in the same way as men do here. There's not that male-female playfulness with sexual undertones. Well, maybe with some. But I think American men, especially in our age group, are more considerate and treat women as equals. Like say if a group of us met for dinner at someone's apartment, the men would help cook and clean up."

"Who wants a man who does women's work?" Majida said.

"They have to," Eva said. "Most women there work and they don't have household help, so it's difficult to manage a job, a family, and a house."

"Some men here cover their heads piously and yet can't stop looking in every direction," Batool said.

"Here you'll both find a real man," Rafa said to Eva and Perin

"Did you date much before you married? Were you intimate?" Eva asked the women.

"Oh, no," Majida said. "We were virgins when we married."

"But we knew a lot," Rafa said with raised eyebrows. "We played around."

"We did not," Majida said.

As the women bantered, sadness engulfed Perin. She still had things she wanted to talk to Eva about, if only to clarify things for herself.

"Perin," Shereen said, "it's time to get ready to leave for the hairdressers."

"Yes, we'd better go now so we can get home. Father is taking us to Coruma this afternoon." She thought of asking Shereen to accompany them and decided against it—she wanted Eva all to herself.

Perin parted the plastic-beaded curtain for Eva to enter the hair salon. In a corner, a black television with a white doily and a vase of plastic flowers on top of it stood out against the newly painted chartreuse walls. An emotionally charged Egyptian soap opera blared away.

"Take a seat. It won't be long," a stylist said as she blow-dried a client's hair.

Perin and Eva sat down on the green, rust, and yellow floral print sofa. Shereen sat on an orange plastic chair across from them, took one of the curl-edged Egyptian and Lebanese gossip rags resting on a side table, and flipped through its pages.

"Anything of interest?" Eva asked.

"Sort of. Stories of Iranian movie stars, regional television celebrities and singers, royal Saudi princesses, the Queen of Jordan."

Perin remembered what Mr. Garib had said about Americans idolizing celebrities—it wasn't only in the States and she wished she had pointed it out to him.

"I only read them here. My mother won't let them into the house," Shereen said.

Perin was glad Shereen seemed more friendly now toward Eva, possibly because she knew she'd be leaving soon.

A woman told Perin she was ready to give Eva a manicure and Eva followed the woman to the back of the salon.

"You have such beautiful hair," one of the stylists said to a client as she sprayed lacquer on it. "It's a shame you have to cover it up."

"I want to be a singer," the woman answered, "but if I have to wear a scarf, it won't be a good image. None of the popular singers wear one."

"The clerics banned music," another stylist said. "What will you do now?"

"I know. I can never go on the stage."

"You could sing at private parties at homes," the owner said. "Or go to Egypt or Lebanon. It might be better there for singers."

The woman shook her head. "I love my country. I don't want to leave it."

Perin gazed at herself in the mirror that ran the length of the opposite wall. I love my country too, she thought. I wouldn't let anyone force me out.

"They're almost ready for you," the owner said, motioning for Perin and Shereen to follow her to the washbasins. She wiped down each chair with a damp cloth, and asked, "What kind of rinse do you want today."

Perin and Shereen answered in tandem, "Rosewater."

At the edge of a red-brown, mud-brick village along the coastal highway, Fuad turned inland onto the dirt road that led to the ruins of Coruma, where small makeshift stands selling soft drinks, candies, and handmade crafts greeted visitors. A rattletrap taxi, two private cars, and a donkey cart sat in the parking lot; he bypassed them and wedged the car in the shade between two trees.

"Do you know what Huda said to me when she heard we were coming here?" Perin said. Fuad shook his head. "She thought we were crazy coming to visit a bunch of old stones."

Fuad laughed. "I had lunch yesterday with Yousef and I asked him to come with us today, but he had too much work."

"Too bad," Perin said. "Please invite him another time."

"I gave him a standing invitation any time he's in the city," Fuad said. "We'd better visit before it gets too late." He escorted Perin and Eva to the entrance booth, a wooden shack stuck in an opening in the wire fence.

"*Salaam.* Excuse me, sir. Would you like a guide to show you around?" said a casually dressed young man, with deep-set eyes, greased back hair, and tobacco-stained teeth. A sharp odor of sweat assailed Perin's nostrils and she began breathing through her mouth. Fuad agreed and the guide said, "Sir, you will not regret your decision. We'll start on the *decumanus*, the main street of the Roman town built here in the fourth century before the Prophet." He took out a book displaying an artist's rendering of what experts thought the site looked like at the height of the Roman occupation.

As the guide explained the importance of olive groves in the area for the oil used for lamps and cooking, Perin stared at the worn stones and heard the tinkling of bells in the distance. A herd of goats grazed on a nearby hill. Captivated by the past, she liked to think they were being tended by direct descendants of the long-vanished peoples who populated this site centuries ago—the threads of life that traversed the centuries.

As they were nearing the end of the tour, Eva nudged Perin and pointed to a young couple kissing behind several slabs of stone, only their heads visible above the broken boulders. Perin smiled and said, "They have to sneak away from the watchful eyes of guardians. Ruins and cemeteries for young lovers."

"Quite ingenious. Who would think to look for them here?" Eva said.

After Fuad paid the guide, two boys scurried over. One had a large basket of homemade breads balanced on his head, and the other a wooden shoeshine box.

Fuad selected a loaf of bread and handed the child some coins, telling him to keep the change. The boy's eyes widened and then he ran off with his friend toward the candy seller.

Outside the gate, an older woman twirling wool into yarn on a long wooden spindle was selling goat milk and silver filigree bracelets and earrings that were spread out in front of her on a faded vegetal-dyed blanket. Fuad offered to buy Perin and Eva something. Perin touched her turquoise necklace and said, "This is all I want."

On the way back to town, Perin gazed at her reflection in the car window. Framed by the green farmland, it was like she was fused with the earth.

"Thank you for a wonderful excursion," Eva said. "I felt stranded in time, seeing such true sublimity, like in art."

Yes, sublimity—an apt description for her homeland, this place of her roots where her ancestors had lived for centuries that had seeped deep into her being, demanding complete loyalty. But yet, she wondered if she could remain faithful to it now that it was changing in ways she didn't want to acknowledge.

"Don't let your dreams and hopes for a career wither away," Eva said to Perin the next morning as she was packing. "I know you, like all of us reporters, have visions of writing about major events, but often it's articles about everyday occurrences that enhance and change lives."

"Are you saying this to make me feel better?" Perin asked.

"No, I believe it. And I believe you can be a conduit to cultural understanding and bring attention to important issues. After your years in the West, you better than anyone can attest that there are more similarities than differences between us and your heritage."

Perin hugged Eva.

"You have much beauty here. I'm glad I came. Now I understand better why you wanted to return."

Seventh Heaven

*Melancholy may enter your soul, and ambush your happiness;
but it will prepare you for true joy. Melancholy drives out all other emotions
and feelings, so the source of all goodness may occupy the whole house. It shakes
the yellow leaves from the tree, allowing fresh leaves to grow. It pulls up old bodily
pleasures by the roots, allowing divine spiritual pleasures to be planted. Melancholy
takes many things from the soul, in order to bring better things in return. —Rumi*

A few days after Eva left, Perin broached the subject of Zahara with her mother to see how she would react, not by telling the truth, but by saying she was collecting things for the less fortunate. Assia said she always believed her work with the needy women at the mosque was important, and she was pleased it had influenced Perin. "What group are you collecting for?"

"One at University Hospital. They have some indigent patients who need things."

"You don't have to spend time with these people, do you?"

"No, I just drop the things off," Perin said, chewing the inside of her cheek.

"The doctor, how did you meet him?"

"It's a *her*, Mother, and I met her through work." Perin's skin prickled. She was not a good liar and it was as if *LIAR* flashed on her forehead whenever she spoke an untruth.

"Safina and I can find things for you, and ask Huda to check with the maids in the neighborhood to see if their families have things."

Perin found Huda washing the dinner dishes. Umm Kulthum's *El Alb Yeshak Kol Gamil* filled the room. "I'm collecting things for poor families. Mother thought you might be able to help."

"I'll see what I have at home."

"No, I didn't mean for you...." Perin sprinkled salt in her palm and licked it. She was surprised to hear herself say, "The truth is, there's a group of women who've been thrown out by their families or had to escape their husbands and I'm thinking of helping them."

Huda let the dish she was holding float into the soapy water. "What? They'll come after you. Better mind your own business."

"I thought you'd be supportive. The same thing happened to friends of yours."

"It's bad to get mixed up with other people's troubles. Next thing, you're in trouble."

"Women should stick together and help other women."

"Not if it kills you," Huda said with a frown.

As she left the kitchen, Perin heard paper rustling in her father's study, where she found him hunched over a large sheet of paper that he covered up with folders when she entered. She kissed him on the forehead and put her arm around his shoulder. Blue lines extended from the section of the paper that was not covered. It looked like a blueprint.

"Are you enlarging the mill?"

"Since you caught me, I might as well tell you. I have some property on the coast, not far from Kamal and Shereen's ranch. I'm thinking of building a villa to live in part of the year, when I retire. Your mother loves the sea."

Fuad moved the folders away and Perin bent over the scale drawing, commenting that it seemed large for the two of them. Fuad said it was for all of them. He pointed to three extensions off a central patio, a wing for each of them for when they had their own families and came for visits. "It'll be a great place for grandchildren."

"You've thought of everything—except the spouses," Perin said. Fuad laughed. "What's there now?"

"Only a shack the previous owners left. I'm keeping it for the caretaker I'll hire once construction starts. Another villa's going up next door and it should be finished in a couple of months."

"Can I visit the lot with you one day?"

"Yes, but you must promise not to say a word. I want to keep it a secret until everything's set with the architect."

"I promise."

"So, tell me, what things are you writing about this week?"

"Following up on the Middle Eastern cuisine trend in the States and Europe—chefs there are sprucing them up with things like lemongrass. And since it's almost time for kids to go back to school, we have another article about after-school activities. And I'm hoping to do one on Persian fairy tales."

"You learn a lot writing about so many topics."

"True. I met an interesting artist last week. She makes hand-painted scarves with ethereal designs, like photos taken by the space telescope." Perin fiddled with the pens and pencils in his marble box, debating whether she dare tell him about Zahara. Surely, he would understand her need to write about something more important.

And before she realized it, Perin blurted out the story of Zahara. "She thinks if people in other countries know what's happening, they'll help, and governments will protect these women if the international community is watching. Like the women in India where families kill their sons' wives so they can get new dowries. With awareness there have been demonstrations." Perin held her breath and waited for her father's reaction.

Fuad stroked the corners of his mouth and asked if she had considered the risks. Then he echoed something she had said to Zahara, "These stories are not exactly news."

"She says it has to be mentioned constantly. The squeaky wheel theory. This woman has so much courage—"

"Courage without wisdom is foolish." Fuad rolled up the blueprints. "It seems you've made up your mind."

"Well, not really. I'd like your opinion."

"What do your dreams tell you?" His eyes narrowed and his lips pressed together as he put a rubber band around the blueprints and stuck them in a corner of his study.

"I know, the hieroglyphics of the mind. But my mind has been in a muddle lately." Her father often spoke of how her dreams would tell her the truth and give her answers to guide her daily life, if she learned to understand and read their images. It was wisdom passed down by his maternal grandfather, the religious scholar and professor.

Fuad looked directly at Perin. "I want to protect you. I know it's not always possible, but I like to think I'm here to intercede should something happen."

"I want to … I feel I have to do something. There's this young—"

"What do you mean have to? There's no such thing. I've always supported you, but this time I prefer you don't get involved. It's not a good idea."

Fuad blinked a few times. His hand shot up to his jaw, his body tensed, and his face contorted in pain.

"*Baba*, are you all right?" She jumped up from the chair. "What is it?"

"I'm … lightheaded." Fuad leaned his head against the back of the chair.

Perin ran to the living room, where her mother and Rashid were watching Hitchcock's "Notorious." "Father's not feeling well. Hurry. Come now."

"It's not his stomach, is it?" Assia asked. Rashid stood up.

Huda's wails bounced off the hallway walls. "Oh, no. Allah, merciful One, no. No!"

Assia and Rashid rushed out of the room. Perin stood inert, like a mayfly trapped in amber. A moment later, her mother's shrill cry crashed through her entombment and she bolted out of the room. In the hallway outside the study, Huda was on her knees rocking back and forth. Her hands in prayer position, she looked at the ceiling and cried out, "Aiyee, Aiyee."

Perin looked inside the room and saw her father's prostrate body. Assia knelt beside him, stroking his cheek. Rashid shook him and felt for a pulse. He dropped his father's hand and pounded on his chest.

Assia kissed Fuad's hand. "My love, please wake up. Fuad, my life."

Rashid looked up at Perin. "Call Dr. Kareem, and find Nabil."

Dread filled Perin's heart. Dazed, she waited for her father to tell her it was just a little spell; he was resting and would be fine. But he didn't move.

"Perin. Call Dr. Kareem and Nabil." Still she couldn't move. Rashid came over and shook her. She broke away from his grip, slumped to the tile floor and wept into her hands. Wrenching sobs shook loose from the depths of her soul. "No! No! Father, no!"

Dr. Kareem arrived shortly after Rashid's call and confirmed Fuad had died of a heart attack. Nabil rushed home from the club. Unusually pale and unable to speak, he only nodded when Dr. Kareem asked him and Rashid to help wash and prepare the body. Rashid put his arm around Nabil and their bodies heaved as they held back their cries.

The doctor gave Huda two vials of tablets. She was to give Perin and Assia one of each straightaway and another dose in the morning.

Assia flung herself on Fuad's body again, refusing to leave her husband. Nabil and Rashid pried her away to take her to her room.

Dr. Kareem clasped Perin's elbow and walked her to the bottom of the stairs. She remained there like a mannequin until the doctor shepherded her upstairs.

Perin was curled in a fetal position, fully clothed, when Huda entered to give her the two pills. She refused them. She didn't want her senses dulled and her anguish numbed; she needed to experience the heartache and feel her loss to make it real, to connect with her father's spirit. Her diaphragm quivered and she gasped for air as the pain erupted from deep within her belly. Huda cradled her, rocking back and forth, humming a tune, the lullaby she sang to her when she was a child. She longed to be that little girl again, safe and protected.

"Life never ends," Huda told her. "He's in the seventh heaven." Perin visualized the seven concentric spheres of Islam's heavens—the seventh, the highest, the place of pure bliss, the empyreal. After Huda covered her with a coverlet and turned out the light, Perin lay watching the whirling blades of the overhead fan. She buried her head in the pillow to muffle her cries while Huda sat beside her, stroking her head. Before her tears ran out, Huda made her take the pills and soon they took effect and she dozed off.

She woke later to find the room dark except for the eerie green glow emanating from the bedside digital clock. It was 4:44. Dawn had not yet begun to creep around the edges of the shuttered windows. A soft chant was coming from outside her room. She pushed herself out of bed and went into the hallway. A fluttering light spilled from the doorway of a guest bedroom. As she walked toward the beckoning room, she heard Nabil's and Rashid's voices from downstairs.

Large white candles were placed around the body. Smoke from burning incense snaked around the flames. On the bed her father lay, facing Mecca, his body wrapped in a simple white gauze shroud that appeared as light as a butterfly's wing. But in Perin's mind, the cloth created an impenetrable barrier, as if he were encased in white marble, separating him from her. The quietus, the cessation of life, screamed at her. Tomorrow she wouldn't even have this; the body would be buried.

At the foot of the bed, Huda knelt, rotating her upper body in a trance-like circular movement, as she said the *salat*. Dear devoted Huda had stayed the night so her father wouldn't be alone, while Nabil and Rashid arranged the funeral, and she and her mother slept to exorcise the twin demons of pain and sorrow. Perin knelt down beside Huda and joined her in the prayer for the dead. The sweet smell from the incense turned her stomach. She started to gag and rushed from the room.

A light drizzle fell on the mourners gathered around the grave. Perin felt its taps on her head and hands. She recalled that the Prophet said an angel accompanies every raindrop because each one is an expression of being. She looked over the rim of her sunglasses. The sky was delft blue. Wisps of gossamer clouds floated across it, strewn out like the faux cobwebs she saw adorning shops and apartment windows for Halloween in New York.

Nabil and Rashid were to her right, shoring up Assia. Out of the corner of her eye, she saw her mother shake and heard her sobs. Fearing they would tripwire her own tears, she leaned closer to Aunt Safina and silently recited a few lines from the Qur'an: *Mankind is ordained to show kindness toward their parents. Lord, inspire us that we may be thankful for the blessings You bestowed upon us and our parents.*

"Seek Allah's forgiveness for your deceased brother," the turban-clad imam intoned. "Pray for his steadfastness because he is now being questioned about his faith. His soul departed the moment he died, and now he is with Allah."

The moment he died. The words thrust Perin back to the previous night. She blamed herself for his death. She shouldn't have brought up Zahara.

"No harm will come to those who believe in God and who gave generously to others from what they had," the imam said. "God knows all and will not be unjust to anyone. All good deeds will be rewarded."

Perin looked down at her father's coffin and squinted. The clouds had passed and the sun hurt her red-rimmed eyes. She adjusted her sunglasses and glanced around at the bent heads of family and friends, Fuad's business associates, and workers from the factory. Ali stood with several associates from the sports club; she was pleased he'd come. Off to one side she saw Yousef, also pleased he'd come; Omer must have told him.

She watched Huda and Nadira as they rocked forward and backward, their lips moving in silent prayer, their upturned palms cupped before them. From time to time, they converted their pleas to heartrending wails. Perin blinked to clear away the film on her eyes.

The imam raised his book toward Perin and the family and intoned, "The Qur'an says, 'After the death of a person his actions stop, except for three things he leaves behind—continuous charity, knowledge from which some benefit may be obtained, and a virtuous child who prays for him.'"

Father, I'll pray for you every day, she promised, stroking her turquoise necklace.

The imam motioned Nabil forward. He took three handfuls of soil and poured them into the grave. Assia and Rashid went after him. Then it was Perin's turn.

Trembling, she picked up the dirt and held it over the grave, her heart shriveling up. Hand suspended in midair, she held the earth between her fingers—dry and devoid of life. Brown nothingness that signified her emptiness. She couldn't release it. She couldn't accept that her father was gone from her life forever. Never again would she be able to speak with him, hold his hand, feel his lips on her forehead, see his face light up when she entered a room.

The imam stepped forward and nodded at her. "He is with Allah now."

Perin dropped the soil on the grave and stepped back. Other mourners came up and tossed earth on the grave. She stroked her necklace again and reaffirmed what she'd said to him that evening—she'd never take it off. A tear reached the corner of her mouth and she caught it with her tongue.

"Weeping is simply mercy, the softness of the heart," the imam said.

Willing herself to think of something else, Perin followed the wanderings of a solitary goat grazing on tufts of grass among the simply carved whitewashed tombstones covered with bird droppings. She heard the sound of wood on stone reverberating through the cemetery. She turned to see where the noise was coming from.

Two religious policemen were walking toward them. One struck his baton against the headstones as he passed. *What are they doing here?* Perin wondered. The women are dressed modestly, with covered heads, the service is in accordance with Islamic laws, the presiding imam, while not one of their firebrands, had studied at the main mosque in town.

Omer left Safina's side and approached the men. One of the policemen stuck out his lower lip and smugly raised his chin as Omer handed the men something; Perin surmised it was his official government identity card. They said something to Omer and then pushed him away. They waved their batons in the air and one screamed out, "Women have to leave. Only men can stay. Out. Now."

Perin remembered reading something about the clerics wanting to institute a decree that only men may attend burials. For as long as she could remember, tradition held that women and children attended funeral services. There was no way she would let them deny her this right.

A dozen or so of the male mourners held the policemen back while Omer called someone on his mobile, and the imam kept on with the service, refusing to be rushed.

At that moment, the image of the religious police at her father's funeral burned onto the lamina of Perin's mind, and fertilized the abhorrence that was brewing beneath her deceptively calm exterior.

The first of the three days of the traditional mourning period, friends and relatives came to extend their sympathy and brought prepared food. Perin tried to be gracious, but the callers forced her to think about her loss. Only at night, when she retreated to her room, did she feel a release, and where once again her tears became a salve for her soul.

On the last day of the grieving period, Perin sat outside in the courtyard with Uncle Omer and Aunt Safina. "A wonderful testimony to your father that so many people are still coming," Omer said. "Nabil will have a big job filling his shoes."

Perin nodded and looked over at Nabil. Eyes rooted on the ground, he raked his fingers through his hair as he talked with a family friend. Grief had etched new lines in his face. He was now head of household and had total responsibility for the family and for the businesses. How he had struggled against their father, wanting to modernize and update the factory systems, and now he could put his convictions into action. It had to be overwhelming for him. It was easier to have boundaries.

"Let your memories comfort you," Aunt Safina said to Perin. "Think of all he gave you. And don't be afraid to grieve. Let it run its course; don't hurry it."

Yousef came over, greeted Omer and Safina, and then said to Perin, "I am very sorry for your loss," his eyes full of concern. "I know you loved him very much, and someone so loved never truly dies. He'll always live within you."

"Thank you. It's comforting to think that." Perin cast down her eyes. When she looked up again, Ali was standing next to Yousef.

"A fine man, your father, a man of integrity, which is rare these days. I wish I would have known him better."

Perin's eyes misted over. Afraid of unleashing a flood of tears, she excused herself and went inside.

The dining room was empty when she entered. The table, with all its leaves, stretched nearly to the window and was laden with foods Perin loved. But she had no appetite. She sank into a chair in the corner, relishing a moment alone, with only thoughts of her father.

A few minutes later, she sensed someone's presence. Through pitchers of iced tea, and sorrel and pomegranate juice, she saw Ali. She stood up and words tumbled out, "I was just resting. I didn't know you were coming ... I saw you at the funeral. Thank you for coming. I'm sorry I didn't call you myself. I wasn't...."

"Perin, it's fine. I understand. How are you?" Ali came around and stood next to her.

"It's painful to accept the finality that he's really gone." Perin looked down at the border of the carpet and rubbed her shoe across the ripe pomegranates intertwined with garlands.

"My father died two years ago," Ali said, "and it took at least six months for things to feel like they were halfway back to normal. Whatever normal is."

Everything about Ali comforted her—his presence, his words, his smile. Perin's eyes grew watery and she longed to put her head on his shoulder. But he was not a member of the family. She reined in her emotions and asked how everything was at the paper. He told her all was fine; they'd manage until she was ready to return.

"Work might help me forget. My father was proud of my working. He liked to read the articles." A tear rolled down her cheek.

Everything stopped for a moment as Ali brushed away her tear.

He took her hand. His touch was sensual as he rubbed his thumb over it. She didn't know what to do or say, but she didn't want to let the moment pass without giving him an indication of how she felt. "I'm glad you came," was all she managed.

The clink of china took her out of her reverie. Kamal was on the other side of the table, placing a serving of scallops with pomegranate seeds and herbs on a dish. He was staring at the entwined hands, his eyes narrowed.

Perin slipped her hand from Ali's and put it behind her back. Ali moved away from Perin and greeted Kamal. Kamal nodded and the room became quiet except for the sounds of Kamal crunching on an almond. Kamal kept his gaze on Perin, scrutinizing her like an insect under a microscope. It occurred to Perin he could distort what he saw, insinuating to Nabil that much more had gone on between her and Ali, which would cause Nabil to feel he had to protect her good name, and possibly put more constraints on her.

"Ali was a good friend of my father's." Perin twisted a corner of the tablecloth and watched Kamal's unchanged expression. "He spoke to Ali ... about my working for the paper."

"I heard," Kamal said, a sharpness clinging to his words.

"Were you looking for Nabil?" she asked. Before Kamal could answer, she said, "I'll go find him."

Nabil was sitting at the desk in their father's darkened study, his forehead in his hand. Perin asked him if he was all right, and if she could get him something, but Nabil only shook his head. She embraced him; he didn't resist and nestled his head against her abdomen.

"We still have each other," she said as she hugged him closer. She decided not to tell him Kamal was in the dining room. He also needed time alone.

Vestiges of a Life

*What did you accomplish in your life? How did you consume your
sustenance and strength? Where did you lose the luster of your eyes?
Where did you lose all the five senses? I gave you bounty. Where is your gratitude?
I gave you the capital. Come show me the interest. —Rumi*

To remember Fuad and close the official mourning period,
Huda prepared a special meal for the immediate family.
After the dinner, Assia went upstairs and Nabil told Perin and
Rashid he wanted to speak with them. As Nabil paced across the
living room, Perin noticed how hollowed out his eyes looked.

Nabil leaned over their father's overstuffed chair and rested
his hands on its back. "I'm going to need your help."

"Of course," Rashid said. "What do you want us to do?"

"You'll have to drop out of school next semester. This will be
a full-time job." Rashid's jaw jutted out ever so slightly. "You can
oversee order fulfillment and maybe exports. I don't want to lose
orders because the factory hasn't been operating at full capacity."
He turned to Perin. "You'll have to supervise the house."

"Mother and Huda manage the house. They'll consider it an
insult if all of a sudden I'm looking over their shoulders."

"I don't want the staff taking advantage."

"Huda's been with us over twenty years, Mohammed nearly
as long. Tell me one thing they've done to take advantage," she
said with an edge. "On the contrary—we take advantage of
them. Huda comes here on her days off, she works late—"

"The house is your responsibility now." Nabil's eyes reinforced
the firmness in his voice.

Perin looked at the potted plant in the hallway. "Did it occur to you that Mother may think we're pushing her aside? She's not incapacitated, she's grieving."

"Right," Rashid said. "You can't act like she doesn't matter just because Father's gone."

"Don't exaggerate," Nabil said with a shake of his head. "All I'm saying is that she can't concentrate on what needs to be done right now."

"This is no time for dictates," Perin said. "Ask Mother first. And I hope you'll listen to what she thinks—and what we think."

"I'll consider your opinions. But in the end, I'm the one who makes the decisions."

"Okay," Rashid said, standing up. "We'll talk after you speak to Mother."

"Think it's easy for me? Worrying about the family, the businesses, the employees, the finances." Nabil sank into their father's chair and splayed his arms over the sides.

Perin wanted to sympathize with him, but she was too annoyed with what he'd said. She also didn't like that he wanted to change things so soon after their father's death.

"Mother shouldn't be alone," Nabil said. "People won't be stopping by as much now." After a pause he said to Perin, "You have to stay home and take care of her."

"She's not really alone ... okay, fine. I'll stay one or two weeks, but then I have to get back to work"

"We'll discuss your working later."

"I'm going back. Father approved of my working."

"I said we'd discuss it later."

Nabil got up and grabbed a roll of papers standing in a corner and sprawled them out on the coffee table. "Do either of you know what these are?"

"They're father's plans for a new home by the sea," Perin said. She pointed to a section of the prints. "Those are the three wings, one for each of us, that father planned. He had dreams of playing in the sea with his grandchildren."

"You knew about this?" Nabil asked. "Why didn't he tell me?"

"I just happened to see them the night he died—he was looking at them when I came into the study. I'm certain he would have shown them to you later."

"What are you going to do with them?" Rashid asked.

"Nothing," Nabil, said rolling up the prints. "I've got enough without starting something new."

"It would be nice to finish something father wanted," Perin said. "Mother loves the sea."

"You never listen to what I say." Nabil snapped the rubber band around the roll.

"Yes, I do. We *all* realize you took on a lot after father died." Perin reached out and touched Nabil's arm. "You're making it harder on yourself than it needs to be."

Nabil shook her hand from his arm. "How asinine is that. All you think of is yourself and what you want; you don't really know what it's like for me to have all this responsibility, how I worry about everything, can't sleep at night … and have to put up with you and your demands."

"Don't go into that again," Rashid said.

"And you," Nabil said, pointing to Rashid. "You come to work, do what you're assigned. No playing computer games there while—"

"You have to micromanage everything, don't you?" said Rashid. "Even your managers say it. Sure, I'll do all you say but I'm tired of your constant criticism and you watching over my shoulder. Either you trust me or you don't."

"Hush, you'll wake up Mother," Perin said. "Let's not discuss this more right now."

"Don't tell me what to do," Nabil said. "You're the one who jeopardizes this family with that silly job."

Perin was about to rebut him, but she knew Nabil would not back down. She'd have to rise above the argument instead of digging in her heels and having the last word.

Nabil threw the blueprints in the corner and left the room.

Rashid gave Nabil a salute behind his back.

Three weeks had passed since the close of the official mourning period and Perin thought she'd have been back at work by now. But Assia remained in her room, retreating further into her anguish. Perin looked in on her several times a day, encouraging her to take her meals downstairs or sit in the courtyard. But she refused. It was heartbreaking to see her mother so grieved. Perin pretended she was coping well to not add to her mother's sorrow.

One afternoon, Perin went outdoors to get some fresh air. She saw the red rose petals Huda placed in the fountain; she said they brought comfort to a heart broken by grief, and their aroma would make everyone feel better. Perin stirred them, willing them to work their magic.

As she sat under one of the palm trees to shelter herself from the sun's harsh rays, Arabia nuzzled up to her and begged to be petted. She stroked him a few times and he put his chin on her knee, looking up with mournful eyes, intuiting her sorrow.

The sun's warmth soaked into her skin while random thoughts bombarded her with the *what ifs*, the *whys*, and the *if onlys*. Why did her father have to leave them now? Why did she have to bring up the subject of Zahara with him? She could not banish the thought, the burden, that she may have contributed to his death. If only he could have stayed to see what she would eventually accomplish with her career. If only he could have known her husband and her children. And what if he'd built the villa along the coast? She pictured him frolicking in the sea with his grandchildren. He would have been a wonderful grandfather.

Her thoughts shifted to Ali and she wondered what he might have said to her if Kamal hadn't entered the room when he did. She'd been awkward with him. She really didn't say what she wanted. Her stomach fluttered as she remembered the feel of his hand on hers. She refused to believe that such a touch was sinful.

She tried to think of topics she could use for her column once she returned to work, but memories of Zahara and the women fractured her thoughts. The last time she spoke with the doctor was shortly after her father's death when she rang up Perin to offer her condolences. She picked up her mobile.

Zahara answered on the second ring. "Again, I'm very sorry about your father's death. I haven't called because I wanted to give you time to mourn but you really must get to writing about the women. It may be hard to hear this, but your father's dead and there's little you can do. The women are still alive."

Resentment rose from the pit of Perin's stomach. "You're really too— I lost my father; you don't care that my heart is breaking."

"Perin, listen, you know—"

"You pretend to be one of the good ones, sacrificing for others. What you really care about is what you want. Everyone should give up everything for you."

"What I am trying to say, and I admit that I'm a bit abrupt and for that I apologize, but I just think it would help you to focus on others now. You must have heard that they lowered the marriageable age of girls to twelve. Write about it, let the world hear your outrage—and okay, mine, too."

Perin hadn't heard that this decree had passed. She knew it was on the agenda, but she had hoped reason would have prevailed, with the moderates influencing the final version. It would be more rewarding to write about girls' childhoods destroyed than doing a story on how to set a table for a dinner party, but she couldn't extract herself from her shroud of inertia.

A strong gust of wind flapped the top of the canopy over the table and beat the palm fronds against her bedroom window. A red haze encircled the sun and Perin felt gritty crystals on her lips. The siroccos had arrived, bringing the Saharan sands.

"Just let me be for a while," she said to Zahara before hanging up.

She led Arabia to the room off the pantry, where he licked crumbs off the floor. She settled into her father's chair in the study.

The silver-framed photographs of the family Fuad had always kept on his desk were now on the side credenza, alongside his wooden in-box and the leather folders he used for his papers. *Humph, Nabil. Why did you have to move his things?* She needed the outward manifestations of her father's life to remain intact longer.

She opened the middle drawer of the desk. Everything seemed the same—his lapis lazuli letter opener, business cards in the silver case monogrammed with FH, address books, sets of pens and pencils they'd given him for his birthdays, and a second pair of glasses. Vestiges of a life.

In a side drawer was his agenda. A verse from the Qur'an with an artist's sketch of a palm tree and pomegranates adorned the first page: *God sends rain. The palm trees yield clusters of dates, and the olive trees bear olives; it brings forth all manner of pomegranates. This is a sign for true believers.*

Perin scanned the entries—lunch appointments, meetings with clients, a cousin's birthday party, the wedding of an employee's son, and a circle around the day she returned from New York. She closed it. It was too painful to think that nothing more would be added.

Returning the agenda, she saw a small silver box at the very back of the drawer. Inside was a lock of blond hair with a frayed blue silk ribbon around it. Whose hair was it and why did he keep it? Although intrigued, she didn't want to ask her mother about it. There were too many other things for her to think about now than to concern herself with something that had no relevance to her life. She resigned herself to the possibility that she'd never know the story behind the lock of hair.

In another drawer was a bundle of papers. She pulled it out and recognized her stationery and her handwriting. French and American stamps flashed by as she flipped through the letters she'd written her father while studying abroad. Her eyes welled up. She shoved them back in the drawer and turned on her father's CD player. "I've Grown Accustomed to Her Face" drifted across the room. Tears rolled down her face. The past was present in everything she touched.

"Perin? Perin, is that you down there?"

Her mother's voice startled her. She wiped her eyes with the corner of her blouse and went to the bottom of the stairs. "Is the music disturbing you? I can turn it off."

Assia stood at the top of the stairs in her dressing gown, looking off into space. "It reminds me of when your father and I met in Paris."

Perin went up, took her mother's hand, and led her back into her room. Assia, her hair flowing loosely down her back, sat at her dressing table and stared at herself in the mirror. "Do you think a lot about those days in Paris?" Perin asked.

Assia nodded. "I can still see your father sipping his coffee at Les Deux Magots—he got upset if he drank it when it was still too hot and burnt his tongue. And the way he'd flip open his Dunhill lighter, bend his head to the left and bring it close to his cigarette. I remember every gesture." Assia smiled in the mirror. "Did I ever tell you about the time after we were married and we were skiing in Gstaad? A snowstorm blanketed the town and none of the small planes were leaving. Your father had an important final exam and had to get back to Paris. When we got to the airport, we found people who had been sleeping there for two days, hoping to get out. Your father talked to the gate agent and we were the first ones on the plane. He could convince people of anything."

"What did he say that you departed before the others?"

"I wish I could remember" Assia stared off to the left. "I don't think he ever told me. Oh, there was another time he told a man he liked his tie, in his charming way. The man took it off and gave it to your father." Assia stared at her image in the mirror. "Everyone loved him. We were happy in Paris."

Seeing her mother savor her memories, Perin hoped that someday she'd also know an enduring love. And she wished she'd heard these stories before; she'd have loved to have asked her father what he said at the airport.

"It helps to talk, doesn't it?" Perin said.

"Silence has its own beauty." Assia continued to stare at herself in the mirror. "We can't improve on it."

Perin was worried. Her mother seemed to be resigned to hopelessness. Then she remembered what her father said the night he died: "Your mother loves to be by the sea." She told her mother that Aunt Safina had invited them to stay with her for a few days. Assia, the veins in her temples beating, said she didn't want to go anywhere.

Later, Perin called her aunt from the courtyard on her mobile. On the other end of the line, Safina sighed. "It's not good for either of you to stay cooped up. She has to get on with things or it'll be harder and harder for her to break out of her gloom."

"But what can we do?"

"Let me speak to her."

Perin took the phone to her mother and waited outside the bedroom. She tried to divine what Aunt Safina could possibly say to entice her mother to go out. A short time later, Assia called to her. "Tell Mohammed we're going to Aunt Safina's tomorrow at six. And tell Huda we won't be back for dinner."

Perin cocked her head, unsure she'd heard correctly. She started to ask what made her change her mind, but thought better of it. It was enough to know her mother was going to leave her room. She didn't want to break the spell Aunt Safina had cast.

The Trance of the Stimbali

Day and night he danced in ecstasy, revolving on the earth like the heavens. His ecstatic cries reached the zenith of the skies and were heard by all and sundry. —Rumi

The sun's fiery rays etched out a pathway from the horizon to Safina's villa as it slowly dipped below the water like a swimmer inching into a liquid basin. Choppy waves jounced around the fishing boats still at sea, and breezes rippled the moonlit water. The sirocco winds from southern Africa made the air heavy, but the soothing rhythms of the waves created a lullaby as they lapped against the rocks below.

A warm breeze grazed Perin's neck and for the first time in weeks, she thought of nothing in particular—a relief after so many days of remembering. Even her mother seemed more relaxed. Dina, still in her gray-dress-white-apron day uniform, wobbled out onto the terrace with dishes of nuts and dates.

"Your shoes—isn't it difficult to work with them on?" Perin said.

"Madame gave them to me." Dina lifted up her foot and waved around a black stiletto with ankle straps. "Like the ones the models wear."

"Dina does just fine," Aunt Safina said, waltzing into the room. "She looks so sexy."

"You want her to look sexy?" Assia asked with a frown.

Safina shot Assia a "don't-say-more" look. After Dina left, she whispered loud enough for Perin to hear, "It makes her feel special. What's wrong with that?"

Dina walked back in with a tray with glasses and a pitcher of dark liquid. Condensed water streamed down its sides, leaving abstract designs in its wake.

"Look what Dina made for you—blackberry lemonade." Safina extended her left arm. "Oh, I haven't shown you the new watch Omer bought me."

Assia, with a vexed air, glanced at the shiny gold watch with black hands and said, "You have enough watches already."

Safina tossed off the remark with a shrug. "There are sales all over since they banned insignias and logos. You must get some things before they're gone, and later we might not be able to bring foreign goods into the country."

Assia twirled a strand of hair. "You're not supposed to wear them and you go and buy them. Really, Safina."

"If we pay attention to everything they say…." Safina twisted her emerald ring around her finger and looked around the terrace as if lost.

Dina handed Assia and Perin each a glass of the amethyst-colored liquid, topped with a pineapple slice.

"Now that you're both here," Safina said, "I want your opinion on the dress I'm wearing to the dinner at the Italian Embassy. It may be the last one, so I want to look special. And you know how those women critique every inch of you. They say the Germans look like potatoes, and the Americans are so loud and—"

Assia shook her head. "I've heard all your stories. I don't know why you care. It's none of your business what others say about you."

"You always look delicious, Aunt, so I wouldn't worry, if I were you," Perin said.

"Delicious is for here, darling. For there I need sumptuous. Dina, please get my dress." Dina nodded and went out. "No one will be able to compete with it."

"Why do you always think you're in a competition? Honestly, I don't know what gets into you sometimes," Assia said. "You could be more generous toward others."

Perin was surprised how edgy and aggressive her mother was. She and Safina always had their little tiffs, but this seemed different.

Dina came back with a long red chiffon dress, pleated and shirred like a toga. Safina handed the dress to Perin and said she could borrow it any time she wanted. Perin held the dress under her chin and twirled around.

"Now what's your surprise?" Assia said.

Perin stopped whirling. She'd figured it out. Assia was not upset because Aunt Safina was carrying on about her new clothes and her engagements. It was because she knew she'd no longer attend gala functions—she had no husband. From now on, she'd only be invited to weddings, birthdays, and other intimate gatherings of family and friends. Nabil would decide what she did and where she went. She'd even have to go to him for money. At fifty-one, she was still young and attractive. It was too soon to cloister herself in widowhood.

"I've invited over a *Stimbali* group," Aunt Safina said, beaming. "We'll begin at dusk."

Perin felt a surge of excitement rush through her. She'd heard much about these trance dancers, but she'd never seen them. They usually performed in villages, where they were revered and hired for all occasions, from birth celebrations to mourning rituals. Rural people thought the *Stimbali* had magical powers and could cast spells, dispel bad *djinns*, and bring good fortune.

Assia stood up and placed her hands on her hips. "You're crazy. I'm not staying for that. Does Omer know you're doing this?"

"Yes, and he doesn't mind." Safina put her hands on Assia's arms. "Listen, we've had a terrible shock and this'll do us good."

Assia gestured for Perin to get her things.

"No, you're not leaving," Safina said. "I've read that we only start to live when someone important dies. Maybe this will help you realize how much you have to live for."

The family had always respected traditions and ancient rites, and Perin loved all of them—the purification ceremonies, face reading, tarot cards, reading of coffee grounds. But for some reason they never entertained the idea of dancing with the *Stimbali*.

"In the States they have dance therapy," Perin said. "I want to stay. It might do us good."

Assia sighed. "I need to sprinkle water on my face."

After she went inside, Perin asked Safina. "What did you say to make her come today?"

"If I told you, I'd lose my trump card. I'll go see if she needs anything."

Perin didn't press her aunt; she figured she'd find out eventually.

Safina called out that the *Stimbali* had arrived. In the hallway, Perin found her mother hugging the wall. "Come on, Assia," Safina coaxed her. "It's no different than dancing at weddings and parties. They say the *alima* has the gift of second sight. She can see the *djinns*. She'll be the messenger between you and the spirits."

Assia rooted herself to the spot. "I don't want any messages."

Safina tugged on her sleeve and pulled her into the room. Perin entered behind them, her every sense heightened.

A dozen candles lit the room and large fluffy pillows had been placed on the floor. The heavy scent from sandalwood incense and jasmine flowers stung Perin's eyes. She started to cough.

"It's bothering Perin's allergies," Assia said. "We can't stay."

Perin, holding back a cough, said, "I'll get used to it."

On the far side of the room, engulfed in smoky haze, stood five women clad in colorful floor-length print dresses. In the middle was an older woman. The way the others deferred to her, Perin surmised she was the *alima*—the "one who knows," the experienced one who would lead them in the trance dance. Clustered in front of them on the floor were native instruments: cymbals, a tambourine, a *laúd*, and two *daffs*. There were also swatches of organza fabric in red, the color of the fire spirits; black, the color of the earth spirits; and blue for the water spirits.

"*Alima*, this is my sister, the one who lost her husband, and this is her daughter. It's for them we're doing this."

The *alima* extended her palm and directed Assia and Perin to pillows adjacent to the dancers. Perin tucked her chin in as the *alima's* piercing eyes penetrated her façade, as if exposing her deepest thoughts.

"The dance will heal your spirits and make you whole again, sisters," the *alima* said softly, but with a dictating power. "Take off your slippers. Spread out your legs. Move them up and down. Let energy enter your stagnant parts."

Something in the *alima's* voice reassured Perin and made her feel safe.

"Get up on your feet."

Perin and Safina stood up; Assia hesitated. The *alima* approached Assia and held out her hand. Assia met her gaze and then, like a lost child, she took the woman's hand and rose.

"Use the earth to ground yourself."

Perin stomped on the rug and felt its soft bristles under her bare feet.

Aunt Safina leaned over to Perin and whispered, "This also helps problems that come from suppressed wishes."

Perin stopped moving. *Does Aunt think I'm repressed?*

She didn't dwell on the answer. The *alima* started beating a *daff* that was nearly the size of a satellite dish; a painting of a woman with a diaphanous veil and coquettish smile adorned its head. With closed eyes, she held it vertically in her left hand and swayed her head. She shook it against her body and snapped her fingers against its head, building up an ancient visceral rhythm that resonated deep within Perin. These rhythms of her culture were part of her marrow and they transported her far away. And yet she was closer than ever to home.

The other musicians joined in with various other rhythms, moving to the beats of their instruments.

As Perin undulated and swayed her hips, Aunt Safina said, "She knows the rhythms the *djinns* like. They'll tell her their wishes. She's falling into a trance now."

As the crescendo increased, Aunt Safina called out, "Lead with your wrists, it's more graceful." Perin smiled to herself.

One of the *Stimbali* draped a red swatch of sheer fabric over Perin's head and face. Another woman put the black one on her mother, and the blue on Aunt Safina. The cloth on Perin's head cast the room in a rosy glow. She felt strangely protected, as if in a cocoon. The blinking candles framed and muted the women's forms. She saw her mother twirl without inhibition as if in another world, a smile on her lips.

The ancient rhythms pounded into Perin's soul, reaching deep to massage the sorrow. She began to move in counterclockwise circles with the stamping tempo, swaying with abandon.

"Let your emotions out. Let yourself be free," the *alima* called out. One of the *Stimbali* danced next to Perin and picked up a corner of her clothing—connecting, supporting, one woman to another. The music grew louder and the gyrations more intense.

"Seduce the air," the *alima* said.

Rumi's words came to Perin: *Day and night he danced in ecstasy, revolving on the earth like the heavens.*

Perin closed her eyes and entered into the darkness of vacant thoughts. She twirled to the vibrating percussion in a tight circle and then spun around, her arms up in the air, left hip out to the side, shooting up and down. With each spin, she threw off another layer of the West she had accumulated the past three years: the need for empirical evidence, the shunning of superstitions like the evil eye and various talismans, the implication that their culture was superior.

As the beat of the music grew less intense, a rush of heat rose from Perin's feet and up through her body, like a long stagnant worm extricating itself. She crumbled to the floor, exuberantly exhausted. Blood flowed anew through her veins, purging the old that carried the imprint of the pain. A *Stimbali* took off the cloth and cradled Perin in her bosom. Another woman sprinkled rosewater on her head. She surrendered completely.

The *alima* placed her hand on Assia's forehead. "Remember the past. Heed its teachings." She smiled at Assia, her eyes tender. "The *djinns* said your husband is watching over you and your family. And my dear, a woman doesn't need to be loved. She is to teach love."

Next, she cupped Perin's chin in her hand. "My child, the *djinns* said you must come to understand the sacred mystery of Astarte." She took a small blue bottle of pomegranate flower essence from her skirt pocket and handed it to Perin, telling Perin to take a dropperful each day. Perin was baffled and wondered what she had to understand about Astarte, the ancient goddess of the Phoenicians, a symbol of fertility, like the pomegranate.

After Safina escorted the *Stimbali* out, she said, "Aren't you glad you came?"

Assia shrugged. "Like you said. Dancing at a party." She straightened her spine and told Safina not to plan on inviting her for another one.

"You always do this, Assia. Ever since we were children, you have to judge me. You never like anything I suggest." Assia started to protest, but Safina cut her off. "But I know you really liked it. I saw you. You just don't want to admit it."

Perin smiled to herself as she watched the familiar scene play out. And she thought about what she'd just experienced. It was doubtful the *Stimbali* could banish her heartache quicker. She'd have to accept grief as a companion for as long as it took. Maybe her mother wouldn't dance again, but she knew she wanted to, and she wanted to do it with Imene and the other women. It was another way she might possibly help them.

Astarte Missing

*When the mirror of the heart becomes pure and clear, impressions
of the other world will become manifest. The image and the image-maker
will become visible, like the carpet and the carpet-spreader. —Rumi*

The Saturday after she danced with the *Stimbali*, Perin and
Shereen wandered through the Phoenician galleries at the
National Museum. "The trance dance must have helped, because
Mother didn't object when I said I'd like to come here."

"Let's go find your Astarte so you can complete your
assignment."

"What do you think the *alima* wants me to *understand*
about her?"

"It's obvious. She's the goddess of love and war, so you're
going to fall in love and it will be tumultuous—a war."

"No, it's more like she represents the divine feminine. Aunt
Safina said something to me about repressed dreams. Do you
think she said that because I'm not married or engaged?"

"Possibly. You know how families are. They may pretend they
don't care, but at our age, they panic. Thank goodness I met
Hakim." Shereen paused. "You're reading too much into what
she said. If someone asks you why you aren't married, say you're
barren and that will shut them up. But you seem keen on Ali."

"Remember the adage—one shouldn't combine work with
pleasure."

"If it's right, it's right and it doesn't matter where you meet.
Where else are you going to meet men?" Perin raised her

eyebrows and nodded. "Has Nabil said anything else about your going back to work?"

"We've conveniently not brought it up. It's been a month and Mother's better. I don't want Ali to find out that they can do without me."

In the next room, Perin whisked Shereen to a glass-enclosed case in the far corner where terra cotta votive statuettes of the orchard goddess Nikkal were placed, but no Astarte. "They removed it," Perin said, pointing to a rectangular space that was two shades lighter than the surrounding area. In front of it, a tag read: *Ivory plaquette for the shrine of Astarte.*

"What could possibly frighten them about an old artifact?"

"She also represented the cult of sacred prostitutes." A chill ran up Perin's arms. "They probably threatened to close the museum if the curators didn't take it away."

"Well, nothing to be done. Let's go have tea in town." Shereen grabbed Perin's arm and led her into the next gallery, where across the room a couple stood examining the Roman amphorae.

Even though their backs were to her, Perin thought the man looked familiar. He stood as close as possible to the woman without touching her, and their posture indicated they had a relaxed familiarity with each other. He leaned his head toward hers when pointing to an object, and while he explained something, her eyes were riveted on him as if she wanted to etch the moment on her memory forever.

When the couple turned to face each other, Perin saw the man's profile and gasped. She rushed down the main staircase without stopping until she was outside the museum.

Shereen caught up with her across the lawn in front of the museum. "Why did you run out like that?"

"Shereen, that was Ali and he was with a woman."

"Maybe it's his sister."

"Oh, please. What man comes to a museum with his sister?"

"Plenty. The family won't let her go out alone, and she cajoles her brother into taking her." Perin crossed her arms and shook her head at Shereen. "You have to admit it's a logical assumption."

Perin had never asked if Ali was married or engaged. How could she? People might suspect she was interested. She'd always assumed he was not attached.

Shereen waved over her driver. "Did you see those scruffy shoes she had on? Flat like a man's loafers. They made her ankles look thick. And that tacky scarf with all those flowers. Wait and see—you'll find out it's his cousin or something."

Perin appreciated Shereen's attempts to make her feel better, but she could tell by the way the two looked at each other that the woman was not a blood relative. But who was she?

When Perin arrived home, she told her mother she needed to rest and went directly to her room. She didn't have to explain anything. They all had their days, when staying self-contained was the only way to get through the daylight hours.

She plopped down on her bed. The scene of Ali and the woman played continually in her head, like a bad song. Why, if there was another woman, did he hold her hand?

Let it go, she told herself.

She turned on the television and got up to hang her tunic in the armoire. A news bulletin interrupted the regular programming. "It has been confirmed. Four twelve-year-old girls died after being shot in the head. Teachers reported that members of the fundamentalist party entered the schoolyard during recess and singled out the four girls who did not have their heads covered."

Perin grabbed the remote and checked other stations; the coverage was the same, except for the state-run programming, which did not feature it. She backed up against the armoire and stood there numb. She covered her ears and slid down the grained wood, sinking to the floor. She placed her head in her hands, wanting to cry. But no tears would come. She sat there, unable to move. Through her daze she heard the announcer speak of the new regulations for girls at schools and she remembered Principal Meriem.

A moment later, Zahara and the women in Satellite Village paraded across her mind, one by one: Imene whose family wanted to kill her, Fatma and her scars, Camilia with callused feet and hands, arthritic Ummee, and Karima who had been abused by her brothers. Zahara's indignation became hers. She went to find her interview notes.

Perin struggled to shape her piece. She scratched out sections and contemplated her choice of words, knowing the power each had, if correctly placed, to make people stop and think. She also knew she had to phrase it right to get past the censors, especially if they were monitoring the internet as Rashid thought. Then, after weeks of not being able to string thoughts together, the words started to flow. Two hours later, she had a rough draft that captured the horror of what the women's lives had been reduced to. She edited it, satisfied it communicated what Zahara wanted the outside world to know. And it was the story she wanted to tell, the story of the women from her perspective as a native returning to a changed homeland. She reread the last paragraph:

To silence the wisdom that only women can impart, and to deny women their rights, rendering one half of the human race powerless and ineffective, will only hold our society back. Women and men alike must reexamine our sacred writings, emphasizing a common humanity instead of preaching violence and intolerance. Only then will our country become my country again.

Perin sent the copy to Eva.

It had felt good to write again.

She looked down on the courtyard. Assia had spread her watercolors on the table and was painting the likeness of the fountain. Her mother seemed relaxed; Perin doubted she'd heard about the murdered girls yet. She joined her outside.

"I like the colors in this one." Perin held up a painting her mother had done of the sunset from Aunt Safina's terrace; the sky was a mélange of grays, pinks, and yellow, and the diffused rays of the sun darkened the blue sea. "Mother, I want to go back to work."

Brush in midair, Assia stared straight ahead. "It's been so nice having you home."

"You know how much reporting means to me."

"Why do you make it so difficult for me?" Assia swished her brush around in the water. "You could be in trouble if the clerics—"

"It's the women's page. How controversial can it be?"

"You won't give up, will you?" Assia shook her head and rubbed the brush on a paper towel to absorb the excess water. "I won't give you my blessing."

"But, Mother, you wanted a career. You told me many times how much you loved working in Paris. And you even thought about being a painter."

"That was long ago—now things are different."

"Mother!"

Assia let out a sigh. "Go get Nabil. We'll discuss it."

"You know what he'll say."

Assia dabbed gray at the base of the fountain, creating a shadow. "*Inshallah*. If it's God's will, you'll work. Go get him. And that talk about my career...." She stared into space for a few moments. "...the *alima* said to look to the past."

A few minutes later, Perin returned with Nabil, pool cue in hand. She motioned for him to sit down. "Is this going to take long? I'd like to finish my game."

"Rashid can wait." Perin swallowed hard. "I was talking to Mother about going back to work. I want to go and they're expecting me to return."

"Don't you need her here with you?" Nabil asked Assia.

Assia shrugged her shoulders. "I can't really say I *need* her."

Having expected her mother to agree with Nabil, Perin was surprised at her answer.

"You didn't answer my question," Nabil said. Assia shrugged again. "If you're not going to answer, I'll tell you what I think— it's not a good idea. It's dangerous for women to work. Perin's place is here."

"Father would never say such a thing." Perin tightened her jaw.

"He let you get away with too much." Nabil bounced the end of the cue stick on the ground. "Perhaps you don't know, but they're checking out everyone who lived in the West."

Perin had heard that they put together a watch list of people they condemned as corrupted by the West. But she wasn't about to admit it to Nabil.

"The family comes first. You can't always have your way," Nabil continued. "Do you want to give them an excuse to take away our businesses?"

Perin's stomach cramped.

"Omer said the paper wouldn't let her work," Assia said, "if the editors thought there was a danger."

"Now you're on her side? I thought it was only Father."

"There are no sides here. You may be the head of the house, but I'm still your mother." Assia twisted her wedding ring around her finger.

"Okay, let her go back to work. But if she gets into trouble, don't say I didn't warn you." Nabil stormed out, slamming his fist against the frame of the door as he walked into the house.

I hope he hurt himself, Perin said to herself as she rubbed the scar in her left palm.

It couldn't have been easy for her mother to go against Nabil. She took one of her mother's hands and held it between hers. "Thank you. It'll be fine."

"You were right. I did like working," Assia said, smiling.

Chains, Guns, and Lashes

*If in the darkness of ignorance, you don't recognize a person's true nature,
look to see whom he has chosen for his leader. —Rumi*

Perin's pulse quickened when she entered the newsroom, just as it had that first day, several months ago. She was a part of humanity again, like a patient who, after convalescing for months, ventures out onto a busy sidewalk and delights in being alive, not minding if jostled by passersby and startled by car horns. Although she could never forget the loss of her father, work allowed her to move on.

As she reviewed the topics Andrea had listed for next week's column—making herbal bath salts, painting rooms with bright colors, how to care for silver—Andrea brought her a cup of cardamom tea. "It's good to have you back. Ali also said he was pleased you were returning."

Her heart beat an extra beat, but only one, tamed by the image of him with the woman. She didn't want Andrea to detect that she might be interested in Ali, but her having to know overrode this concern. "I was at the museum the other day and he was there with a woman." Her breath suspended while she waited for a response that she hoped would tell her something.

"Probably his fiancée," Andrea said. Perin coughed, splattering tea on her desk. "Are you all right?" Perin nodded. "Fourth cousin or something—his mother arranged it."

"*He* agreed to an arranged marriage?"

Andrea nodded her head. "After his father died, his mother was lonely with her husband gone and her three married children living elsewhere, and she thought it time Ali—he's the youngest—got married. There was a distant relative who had a marriageable daughter."

Perin stared at the front wall of her cubicle. Her instincts had been correct. The woman was not a blood relative—at least not a close one. Something inside of her made her want to tell Ali she'd seen him with the woman. As she was trying to think of a clever remark that would send him the message, Astarte popped into her mind; was there something about Astarte that had meaning for her and Ali? She wanted to research the goddess and then write about her personal experience with the missing statue, and at the same time expose how the clerics were stripping the country of its cultural heritage. Perhaps by doing so, she'd understand what the *alima*, and Aunt Safina, meant. But first she'd have to finish next week's copy.

She was so engrossed in researching websites relating to how to get a good night's sleep that she didn't notice Ali when he came up alongside her. "It's good to have you back, Perin."

He seems genuine enough, she thought. "Thank you for being so considerate." She was unable to say more, as the scene of him and the woman at the museum swirled in front of her eyes, taunting her.

"Did you know that one of the staff missed reading your work?" he said.

"Really?" A rush of adrenaline shot through her veins. "Who?"

"I did." Caught by surprise, she didn't respond. "I like the twist you give to pieces and your voice—I've noticed how it's become more distinctive in just a short time. And I guess I miss having you around to prod me to cover more diverse topics."

Ali smiled and sat on the edge of her desk and leaned toward her, reminding Perin of how he had leaned toward the woman in the museum—one of his seduction techniques, she thought, willing herself not to fall for it or interpret it as any sign of intimacy. "I wanted to call again to check on you, but a lot of things came up."

"I understand," Perin said, adding to herself, *more than you realize.*

After Ali left, she found it difficult to concentrate, her mind playing tricks on her, one moment letting her think he really was interested in her, and the next, painting him as a blackguard, used to toying with the feelings of women. Here she was again driving herself wild with notions; she pushed them away and forced herself to concentrate on her articles.

While polishing her draft on painting, she heard shouts coming from the editors' offices. She peered over her cubicle and saw Ali arguing with Ghazi, his hand cutting the air between them like a sword. Moving closer to hear, she stopped and asked one of the fact-checkers what had happened, and the woman told her a fire broke out at a girls' school downtown, and some of the students were trapped inside.

"You left us exposed with no metro reporter available." Ali curled his hands into fists.

"There's a lot going on—two are covering the king's visit, another the president's speech, the other the groundbreaking for the new mosque." Ghazi's teeth moved up and down, as if chattering. "I don't know if—"

"You'll have to go," Ali told Ghazi. It was the first time Perin had seen Ali so agitated. "What school is it again?" Ali asked one of the researchers.

When Perin heard the response, and before she realized what she was doing, she stepped forward. "I'll go. I know the school. I met with the principal once." Ali's and Ghazi's eyes locked on her like heat-seeking missiles. "It's a girls' school. I can talk to the girls and the mothers. The other reporters can't do that."

Ghazi looked at Ali. "She's inexperienced covering breaking news." He started to walk away. "I'll see who I can get over there right away."

"Wait," Ali said. "She has a point."

Ghazi turned around, his mouth agape, words lodged in his throat. Finally, he said, "Even if she goes, she can't go alone. It could be dangerous."

"We can't wait. I'll go with her," Ali said.

Perin was stunned. The editor going out to report—and with her? But she sensed he was too agitated to stay behind a desk when a story was breaking.

Ali told her to wait out front while he got his car, and while she stood outside, Perin remembered the day she interviewed with Principal Meriem, the interview Mr. Garib had set up for her.

Principal Meriem, a woman in her early forties, with a long, narrow, pinched face, and slightly crooked front teeth. From the little else she revealed in her *chador*, Perin could see she was exceptionally thin. She told Perin the school was one of the best in the city, and it stressed academics; the girls studied the classics, mathematics, geography, and writing and grammar in French and Arabic, and when they reached sixth level, they started literature and the home arts.

Perin recalled thinking what a nice euphemism *home arts* was.

The principal went on to tell Perin that the staff didn't want the girls to be distracted, emphasizing it was important to set good examples for them, and because of this, Perin would be required to wear a *chador*. Amused that Principal Meriem had assumed she would take the position, no questions asked, Perin had only nodded, and thought it odd that a woman who worked with children never smiled. Even now, as she imagined herself in a *chador*, feelings of claustrophobia rose up in her.

For the second part of her interview, she'd been whisked away to sit in on a fifth level lesson to observe their methods. The teacher was conjugating a French verb on the green blackboard, and the girls, about thirty of them, answered when called on and followed instructions without question, never raising their voices, never laughing, and rarely turning to look at a classmate—a contrast from the rambunctious fifth level classmates Perin remembered from her school days.

Midway through the lesson, a girl in the back row had turned and smiled at Perin, her dark doe-like eyes sparkling. Perin returned the smile, and continued to do so each time the girl sneaked a look. When the class was over, the girl took Perin's hand and asked if she could show her where the drinking fountain was. The simple gesture had melted Perin, and for a brief second she thought it might not be so bad to work at the school, since at that time her chances of getting a reporting job seemed slim. But later at home, she realized she could never work in such a stifling environment, no matter how much she wanted to be employed.

Ali maneuvered through the clogged streets of the lower town while Perin told him what she remembered about the school and read the printout the research assistant had given them. "It was rated number four on the list of the top ten primary and middle schools for girls. Student population around 350. Principal is Mme. Meriem." The principal's grim face popped into Perin's mind, but was instantly replaced by the image of the young girl who took her hand and led her to the water fountain.

"Search her out. We'll want her side of the story."

Police cars with flashing blue lights blocked the road leading to the school, and in front of the school's closed gates, three city policemen in their navy uniforms struggled to contain the crowd that clamored to be let in. Ali drove down a side street and found a spot that was too small to parallel park in; he drove onto the sidewalk, leaving the rear of the car sticking out in the street.

Perin followed Ali down the street; rounding a corner, she saw flames shooting out from the top floor of the building and smoke steaming from adjacent windows, filling the air with a toxic smell. The girls' high-pitched screams were mixed in with the cries and wails of parents and bystanders. Dogs leapt around, their chorus of wild barks and yelps adding to the chaos.

As she pushed through the crowd, Perin repeated a prayer offering, "*Tawakilt Ala Allah.*"

"They're letting innocent babies die," a black-shrouded woman howled while striking the chest of one of the policemen guarding the entrance. He pushed her away and aimed his gun at the crowd. The people moved back and then started hollering and advancing again.

"If you won't save them, we will," a man shouted out.

Ali waved his press pass in front of the policeman's face and Perin held up her badge. As the officer started to open the gates, the throng behind Perin surged forward, squashing her against Ali. Someone's elbow jabbed her in the ribs. As the officer opened the door a crack, his colleague pushed back the people with his baton.

"Get as close as you can and see what's going on," Ali said to Perin after they squeezed through and entered the cement-walled compound. "I'll find the fire marshal."

She quickly scanned the scene. On the upper floor, flames bellowed out in long tongues, and on the lower ones, little hands, imprisoned by grilles, frantically shook from jagged windowpanes. The girls begged for help, their shrieks piercing and stabbing at Perin.

Nozzle handlers were directing spray to the upper windows, while vent men were on the ladder, headed for the roof; two Red Crescent ambulances waited nearby.

Perin ran to the main entrance, where a group of firefighters and city police stood among the dozen or so parents who'd made it into the compound before the gates were closed. Some held up their arms in prayer, calling on Allah, the angels, and *djinns* to help. Others beat and slapped their heads and chests. The smoke stung Perin's eyes. She wiped them with the sleeve of her tunic and asked a city policeman why they weren't getting the girls out.

"The religious police won't let us in," the thickset man answered, straightening his holster. "They say they have to protect the girls."

"What do they mean protect? They're going to die in there." Perin wedged herself between two of the men in the front, where three religious policemen and their rifle-toting escorts blocked the school entrance. When one of the militias turned sideways, she saw chains on the doors.

"Can't you rush them? They can't shoot everyone," Perin screamed to the firefighters, who only shifted their stance and remained rooted to the spot.

A television cameraman bumped up against Perin and a parent behind her shouted at the religious police, "May Allah blind you and boil you in oil."

Perin felt a helplessness she'd never known before and then she knew what she could do. "I'm from *The Daily*," she yelled at the morals police. "I'll write that you're responsible for killing these girls. Break the chains."

A chant of *break the chains* rose up from the parents behind her. One of the religious policemen barked back, exposing stained teeth, "We are the keepers of the laws of Islam."

The wails of sirens broke through the confusion, silencing the crowd for a moment. Then Perin heard what sounded like large vehicles pull up outside the school. Soldiers with rifles drawn stormed through the gate toward the burning edifice, and running awkwardly behind them was a portly man Perin recognized as the head of the Department of Education.

The soldiers pointed their rifles at the robed men and their escorts, and up the rear came their captain. He faced off with them and said his men had orders to shoot, if they didn't open up.

"It's Allah's law. Men must be segregated from girls," a religious policeman said.

The officer motioned to the soldiers and they cocked their rifles and moved closer. The armed escorts lowered their rifles, but the turbaned men refused to budge. A group of firemen stepped forward and pushed them away, while another hacked at the chains with an axe until the doors flung open.

Young girls surged out, holding their scarves over their mouths and noses. Firefighters barreled into the school while the soldiers held back the parents and onlookers. Perin thanked the angels and then saw that the morals police had grabbed three girls, forcing them back into the burning building. "Cover your head, *keffir*," one said, twisting a girl's arm as he dragged her on the ground. The children flailed their arms and kicked the shins of the morals police. Perin tried to grab one of the girls, but a soldier pinned her back with his rifle. And then the captain stepped forward and ordered the morals police held at gunpoint. Released, the girls ran into the yard, struggling to put on their scarves, calling out for their mothers.

Two firefighters came out of the building, each carrying a limp body, and laid the inert forms on the ground, near the female nurses and paramedics. As Perin looked on, a man passed her and pointed to her head. With the panic and confusion, she hadn't noticed that her scarf had slipped off. She scooted it back on her head and looked for someone to interview. She spied a mother and daughter huddled together near the concrete wall; the child was engulfed in the woman's black *abaya*.

She squatted down next to them and introduced herself before taking out her notepad and asking if they were all right and if she could ask them some questions. The mother hugged her daughter closer, swaying back and forth, muttering prayers and her daughter's name, Thara. Both sets of eyes were fraught with terror.

"I know this has been a terrible shock for you, Thara—"

The mother let out a piercing wail and kissed her sobbing child. Think, Perin told herself. Think of something that will make her want to talk. "People have to know why this happened, so it can be prevented in the future," Perin said softly. "No one should suffer what you're suffering." The woman watched Perin and remained silent. "How old are you?" Perin asked the daughter.

The girl wiped her nose and looked up at Perin. She was covered with soot and her tears had left squiggles and uneven streaks down her checks. "Ten," the child muttered.

"Ten. I remember when I was your age. Can you tell me what you saw?"

The child hesitated and looked at her mother. The woman closed her eyes and nodded. "The teacher yelled 'Fire.' I smelled smoke. I was scared."

"I would have been scared, too. What did you do then?" Perin kept her eyes focused on the child, scribbling her responses without looking at the paper, hoping she'd be able to read her cryptic scrawl later.

"I ran to the door, but teacher said to go to the windows for air." The child pointed to one of the broken windows.

Another mother and father came over and sat on the other side of Perin, but she kept her focus on Thara to help the child maintain her concentration. "How did you get out?"

"Teacher told us to follow her." The child started crying. "Maya was behind me. She fell down." The girl looked around the yard. "Where is she? I don't see her." Her cries turned to sobs again and she nuzzled closer to her mother.

The woman opened her *abaya* and enveloped her child like a bird protecting its young in its wings. "Leave us alone."

"One more question, please. Why didn't someone unlock the doors as soon as the fire started?" The woman cradled her daughter and shook her head. Perin sensed that to ask more would be an offense.

The man next to Perin answered. "A fireman said the guard went to run an errand." He spat three times on the ground.

"Which fireman?" Perin asked, catching her scarf as it inched off her head. The man shook his head. "Is the guard here now?" He shook his head again.

"Allah is my witness. If I see him, I'll beat him to death." He spat again on the ground.

"Do you know what caused the fire?" she asked him, glancing back at Thara, who had her hands over her ears.

"All merciful Allah, I am not deserving." He picked up his daughter to leave.

"There will be an investigation. My paper will report the findings." She took out two business cards and handed them to the man and the woman. She told them to call her at any time if they remembered anything, or heard something they thought was important. "May Allah watch over you and your children."

Two metro reporters from *The Daily* had joined those from other papers and local TV and radio stations. They all fanned out to talk to parents, emergency personnel, and soldiers. The metro guys would write the lead story, and if Perin had any hope of writing a sidebar to accompany it, she needed more information.

On the ground near the ambulances was a row of small shrouded bodies, grieving families hovered over them. A firefighter carried out another child, arms and legs dangling like a cloth doll, and laid it next to the others. As Perin approached, she heard a nurse say to the firefighter, "Five dead."

Perin looked down at the white mounds, and asked a paramedic how they died.

"We'll know for sure after the coroner examines them, but it looks like they were trampled."

A nurse standing nearby told her about thirty girls were injured; most sustained smoke inhalation or broken legs from trying to jump from the roof. Others had first-degree burns; their polyester clothes caught fire and stuck to their skin.

A mild stench of burnt flesh wafted up. Perin ran over to the wall and vomited. She wiped her mouth and took several deep breaths. When she stood up again, she saw a woman mourning over the body of one of the children. *How do I know when to let them grieve and when to persist with questions?* she wondered as she approached the woman. "I am so sorry for your loss. I can only try to imagine the depth of your grief. Is this your daughter?"

The woman nodded, tears running down her face.

"Do you feel like talking about her? Is there anything you'd like to tell me about her?"

"Maya," she said, sorrow dripping from her words.

Maya. Thara's friend. It was a name she didn't want to hear. Tears clouded Perin's eyes. "Did she like school?" she asked gently.

The woman looked off in the distance, her eyes glazed. "She liked poetry. She wrote poems about peace, nature—birds, streams of water in the mountains, the sea."

"I'd like to read some. Maybe I can see if we could put one in our newspaper."

The woman gave Perin her number and then fell into her arms, sobbing. "She's with Allah now," Perin said, remembering the imam's words at her father's funeral.

The fire was extinguished, leaving a charred and scorched façade. Wisps of smoke rose from the top windows. In one corner, near the wall, metro reporters were interviewing the head of the Department of Education and a military official.

Perin walked among the articles littering the yard—little shoes, scarves, singed schoolbooks, and chairs the firefighters had thrown out of the windows. She hadn't seen the girl who'd accompanied her to the water fountain that day months ago.

Movement in a far corner caught her eye where a reed-thin, chador-clad woman wandered alone, dazed. "Principal Meriem? I don't know if you remember me. You interviewed me—for a position teaching French."

Eyes fixed on the ground, the principal paced, repeating, "My girls are the best. Our teachers are the best. We have the top academic students in the city."

Perin put her hand on the woman's shoulder. She raised her narrow face and stared at Perin for a few moments and then cast her eyes down again, resuming her march, lost in a sea of confusion. Then she stopped, put her hands on her head and shook it, letting out a wail. Perin knew Ali wanted the principal's story. She also knew there was little the woman could tell her now. What would happen to her? The school had seemed the most important thing in her life.

As parents left with their daughters and the ambulances pulled away, Perin sought out Ali. She saw him standing with uniformed men near the fire chief's car. Two of the men had red morals police insignias emblazoned on their gray robes. To avoid them, she hugged the wall and scuttled along it toward a scraggly tree near the entrance. An emaciated cat jumped down from the ledge of the wall and prowled around her feet, scars and patches of skin shining through the spots where its fur had not grown back. Another battle-weary survivor, she thought, her sadness growing into despair. It was too soon after her father's death to face such a tragedy. The world was going mad around her. Who would believe this had actually happened?

Ali gazed over the heads of the men and motioned for her to go outside. A morals policeman turned and saw her and he said something to Ali. She hastened out the gate.

Outside the compound, she became angrier and angrier, thinking of what these gray-robed men had done. Crude, uneducated peasants, rewarded with jobs for their loyalty to the fundamentalists, blindly obeying orders, unable to think critically, and yet they were becoming some of the most powerful people in the country. Didn't anyone else see this?

Ali exited the gate and she followed him to the car. He wiped soot from his glasses, placed them on the dashboard, and stared ahead. Perin wanted to reach out and touch his arm, to feel a connection, share the agony. But it remained only a longing. A glint of a tear appeared in his eyes, followed by a flash of anger. The moment passed and Ali put his glasses back on, becoming her boss again. "If we do this right, we might be able to turn some tide against the clerics."

"You really think so? People were paralyzed—frightened to death of the religious police. They had total control." It dawned on her that words and threats were the only weapons people had dared use to challenge and confront them. If it hadn't been for the military, many more girls would have perished.

"What did you get?" Ali asked as he backed out of the space. After she recapped what she found out, including Principal Meriem's state of shock, she asked if they knew the cause.

"One of the firemen attributed it to faulty wiring, another said it started in the kitchen. I want our reporters to investigate until they have all the facts. I want to identify those responsible. They must be accountable." Ali looked over at Perin. "There were over 300 students and teachers in that old building. And no fire escapes. The chief told me it was coded for only 200."

"They're all responsible—the guard, building inspectors, civil defense, Department of Education, religious police," she blurted out.

"The facts will condemn them." Stopped for a traffic light, Ali pushed his glasses on top of his head and rubbed his eyes.

A man, laden with tin plates and pots slung together over his shoulders, tapped on Perin's window. Ignoring him, she asked, unable to squelch her curiosity, "What did the religious police say to you?"

"That the fire was God's will."

"How could they think such a thing?" Ali stared straight ahead and didn't respond. "What else?"

Ali turned his head a few times and glanced at her. "They asked what you were doing there." Perin breathed through her nose with a humph. "I told them exactly what you said, that someone needed to get the women's and girls' stories."

The police, she figured, saw her with her head uncovered. She was doing what they considered a *man's job*. She had yelled at them to open the doors, and she was alone. Enough for 500 lashes of the whip—if they stuck by the book.

All Men Have Nightmares

*Sever the chains of the ego. Set yourself free and witness the
bright essence of your inner being. Discover within your heart the wisdom of
a prophet without books, without teachers, and without prudence. —Rumi*

Arriving home after work, the local television newscaster
greeted Perin as she walked into the living room. "The official death toll is not in yet. Firefighters say they negotiated with
officials from the Ministry to open the chained door." The anchor paused before continuing, "The head of the Department of
Education defended their actions, citing the decree that dictates
that women and girls must be protected with heads covered in
public."

Perin sat down on the sofa and took out a copy of the sidebar
she'd written, recalling how she'd struggled while doing it. She
glanced at her last sentence that quoted one of the paramedics
who tended the injured and dead: *It just seems wrong that we put
greater value on outward manifestations of our faith than on life
itself.*

Ghazi told her she'd get her first front page byline. But it was
bittersweet. Lives were lost for it to become reality and her father
was not there to see she'd handled an important story well.

Her mobile rang. She scrambled to fetch it out of her bag.

"I hope you're as outraged as I am about what happened at the
school today," Zahara said on the other end of the line. "Some
colleagues and I are organizing a protest march tomorrow. I

want you and a photographer from your paper to join us. Some must work freelance."

Leave me alone for a moment, Perin screamed inside. "I don't have home numbers."

Assia appeared at the doorway. "Who is it?" Perin held her hand over the mouthpiece and mouthed, "Work." Her mother came in and stood behind one of the chairs.

"Meet me at the hospital around 7:30 a.m.," Zahara said on the other end of the call. "We plan to walk to the university a little before eight, just before classes start."

After ending the call, Perin wondered if she could get a follow-up to her sidebar.

"What did the office want?"

"For me to interview someone tomorrow morning."

"You must have heard what happened today," Assia said with a pained look on her face. "Tragic. Those poor girls and their parents."

"I was there, Mother." Perin shivered, thinking of the little bodies on the ground.

Assia put her hand on the back of the chair to steady herself. Perin started to go to her, but stopped when Assia straightened up and tucked in her chin. "Why were you there? You could have been hurt."

"The paper sent me. I had the chance to write about something important," Perin said, second-guessing her decision to tell her mother. "Here. Read it." She held out her story.

Assia shook her head. "The only thing that's important is that nothing happens to you. Is it going to be published?" Perin nodded. "Will your name be on it?" Perin nodded again. "Perin, how could you do this to me? You disregard my feelings, put yourself in danger, and us, too—you really are hurtful." The color rose in Assia's face. "I assured Nabil you were only writing for the women's page. You'll have to tell him. I don't want him finding out about it from someone else."

"He doesn't have to know. No one really reads bylines."

"You're acting very sure of yourself."

"People have to know what happened," Perin tried to explain. "Even you said it was barbaric to lock up girls."

"I said it here—in the privacy of our home. I didn't go out in public and then write about it." Assia pounded her fist on the back of the chair.

Perin remembered how frightened the firemen and city policemen had been of the religious police, and her father's last words rang in her head: *What if I'm not around to help if something should happen to you.*

"The interview tomorrow better not have anything to do with the fire."

"No ... it's on ... it's on flowers, making potpourri. An interview with one of the gardeners at the botanical garden."

"Keep her safe," Assia repeated as Perin left the room.

She sat on her bed and ran her finger over the ink stain on the green and white floral coverlet, debating whether she should go to the protest. Zahara was depending on her to write more stories, especially since Eva got her article published on an online news site. She was pleased it was out there, and it wasn't as painful as she'd thought to not to have her name on it. She told herself it wasn't about her, it was about what really mattered—not that she get credit for it. She recalled the Qur'an said that *"the self is an advocate of vice."*

There was always the possibility of violence at a demonstration. What if she was beaten—or worse, taken to prison where anything could happen? The thought of losing her freedom made her question going, and she wondered if she was really strong enough to endure deprivation should she be taken away. And then there was her mother. Should anything happen to her, it would devastate Assia, and Perin would be caught in a lie. Trust within the family was becoming more fragile every passing week.

The next morning, Perin stopped in the kitchen doorway that led to the dining room and peered in. Nabil was eating breakfast, his face half-hidden by the sports section of the paper. He appeared relaxed, so she assumed he hadn't seen her name on the article. Itching to get her hands on the front section, she was tempted to stroll in and ask him for it, but he knew she read the paper at work and she had to play it safe and not arouse any suspicions.

She whipped across the passageway and joined Huda, who was rolling dough for flatbread. The radio was on low and she hummed along to a popular song. Seeing Perin, she stopped and wiped her flour-dusted hands on a dishtowel, telling Perin her breakfast was waiting for her in the dining room.

"No, I have to go. I have an interview this morning and Mohammed's waiting. I'll just grab something to take with me."

"Why are you whispering?"

Perin looked out the window at the irises and papyrus in full blossom and wished she really had an interview at the botanic gardens instead of going somewhere that would remind her of yesterday's horrors. As she thought this, she was, at the same time, trying to come up with an excuse to tell Mohammed about why she had to stop at the university before going to the gardens. "Nabil hasn't been in a good mood," Perin said, nodding toward the dining room. "I don't want to remind him I'm working."

"All men have nightmares and he has a lot now. You should have compassion."

All men have nightmares, Perin repeated to herself. "I'll try to be more understanding," she said to Huda, wanting to add that her nightmares were much worse than Nabil's.

A nebula of apprehension surrounded her as she looked for Zahara among the men and women mingling together near a new wing of the hospital. The majority of the men were dressed in green scrubs and the women wore the approved colors of navy, black, and brown.

On the ground lay homemade banners and signs: *Your beards are smeared with blood; You can't hide behind the Qur'an.* Several people were reading the morning paper. A photo of the charred school was prominently displayed on the front page. Perin borrowed a copy from a woman and found her article starting in the lower left-hand corner of page A-1, and continuing on A-4. Seeing her byline, she was energized.

"I saw your article," Zahara said as she greeted Perin.

"I'm glad it ran."

"Too bad you couldn't bring a photographer. Pictures get attention."

Perin pulled out a camera. "My brother's. I'll take some."

A man with a bullhorn instructed people to listen to the directions for the march.

Handing the paper back to the woman with a thank you, she asked Zahara, "How did you get this together so quickly? There's quite a crowd, at least a hundred people."

"The injured girls were brought here and the doctors and nurses were appalled when they heard what happened. Wait here. I have to get people lined up."

"Before you go, I need to talk to someone you think would be a good source. Preferably a man—it'll carry more weight."

Zahara pointed to a trim man in his early thirties, dressed in hospital togs. "He's an attending physician. He treated some of the girls and one of his patients died." Zahara nodded at the man.

Perin approached the doctor. He told her his name was Lyes; his last name would remain a secret.

"Dr. Zahara said a girl in your care died. Was there any way she could have been saved?"

The dark circles under Lyes's red-rimmed eyes cut into his face as if scooped out with a melon baller. "If she'd got here sooner, perhaps."

"Why are you marching today?"

"For all the girls lost and injured, and also for my daughter."

"What do you hope these demonstrations will accomplish?"

"Let's be realistic," Lyes said, with a trace of defeat. "We've already let them amass too much power."

"Is there anything that can be done to change things?"

"Civil strife, civil war. Sometimes you have to break something before you can put it back together. We see it in medicine. If a bone is broken and improperly set, we re-break it and set it right."

Zahara ran up and said to Lyes, "Get in line. We're leaving soon."

"Thank you, doctor." Perin said. "I hope this helps accomplish what you want." She then went on ahead to get wide shots of the marchers as they arrived.

Early morning breathed life into the streets as Perin walked the few blocks from University Hospital to the campus. Tradesmen and students scurried past sidewalk cafés that were filling up with men who worked in the surrounding offices and stores. Most of the shops were still shuttered, but curbside vendors had set up their umbrella-topped kiosks stocked with balloons, pyramid stacks of oranges, and piles of bananas. A boy arranged orderly rows of pulp magazines on the sidewalk, while lines of buses clogged rush-hour traffic and spewed plumes of black smoke. Perin put her hand over her mouth and nose as a barrier against the flecks of soot that floated in the air.

As she rounded the last corner, she passed two men putting up a billboard painted with the face of a woman wearing a black scarf, and in the background were two white-bearded, turbaned clerics and a mosque. Its caption said: *Veils are for protection, not limitation.* She scoffed and adjusted her scarf, double-knotting its ends around the back of her neck.

She strode up the steps that led to the main square of the university, stopping at the top to catch her breath. Young men in jeans or casual slacks were arriving for classes from every angle of the quadrant, while others sat studying on the grass encircling the square, or on the steps of the library that formed a backdrop for the central fountain. She was the only woman in sight.

Near the liberal arts building, two students in skullcaps handed out literature and proselytized to passersby. Behind them, plastered to the walls, were multiple posters of a hard-liner mullah with slogans scrawled beneath: *All the learning of men is not equal to one drop of God's wisdom. A return to Islam means social justice and fulfillment. World domination by Islam is the only way to salvation.*

She distanced herself as much as possible from the bearded students to prevent them from targeting her. It was best to not be noticed. She headed toward a cement pillar at the edge of the stairway that overlooked the street, from where she'd have a clear view of the marchers when they appeared. Soon the man with the bullhorn came into view, leading the way, while protesters who followed waved banners or held up newspapers with the photo of the charred school. Their rhythmical chants grew louder and louder, and amid the navy-, brown- and black-clad women, the green hospital scrubs stood out like islands of hope, screaming their own protest.

Perin shot frame after frame as they came down the street, and by the time they reached the bottom step, students had surrounded her. "Don't block me. I'm taking pictures." She elbowed one away, but they ignored her and jostled for a front-row position. She raised the camera over their heads, peeved that they'd interfered with her sightline.

Someone behind Perin yelled and she turned to see a professor with a halo of frizzy white hair, slapping students on the shoulders and shooing them away from the stairs, telling them to get to class. Only one or two followed the frumpy man's instructions before he waved over a hulky campus security guard in a rumpled blue uniform. The older man shouted and wagged his finger in the guard's face, instructing the man to make them leave and get back to class. The guard flicked away the professor's menacing finger with his forearm and sneered. The professor stepped back and stood there, his mouth agape.

Students pressed against her from behind as the protesters climbed the stairs, chanting, "The Qur'an will not free you. This was *not* God's will. Criminals will be punished."

Men from the cafés across the street lined up on the sidewalk and watched, and passersby stopped. A bricklayer, in worn coveralls and a grimy baseball hat, dropped his awl on one of the steps and joined the marchers. A great interview subject, but how could she get to him?

Amid the commotion, the crowd behind Perin gave way. She turned around and coming toward her were a pack of bearded men brandishing cudgels, running across the quadrant. She froze for a moment until she realized what was about to ensue. Wrangling free of the students around her, she took picture after picture as the fundamentalist students shoved the others away and formed a line across the top stair.

A fight broke out and a fist grazed Perin, nearly striking her temple. She scrambled toward a pillar and propped her arm against it to hold the camera steady. Bodies swirled toward her. One careened into her and knocked her down. She tried to protect the camera, but it hit the pavement with a thud. She felt searing pain in her wrist. A man stumbled and nearly landed on top of her, trapping the edge of her knee-length tunic under him. She tugged it free and darted to the periphery of the square. With no visible sign of damage to the camera, she began circling the marchers as they tangled with their opponents in the middle of the square, capturing the melee on film.

Then shrill whistles from the back of campus pierced the air. From the passageway between the library and the social sciences building barreled the morals police and their armed militia, batons swinging. The protesters tried to use the ends of their banners as lances to keep them away, but the bearded men thrashed their backs and legs and kicked them. Students cowered as blow after blow rained down on them; some held books or bags over their heads to blunt the impact.

Their screams seared Perin's mind and reminded her of the cries of the young girls caught in the fire. She took pictures as people fell, one on top of the other, until there was a heap of bodies in front of her. A glint of metal on a militiaman's hand caught her eye. Brass knuckles. She started to feel lightheaded, like she was going to pass out. She willed herself to stay upright, fearing what would happen if she was no longer able to escape, her beating at the fringe of her memory.

And Zahara? What if she's hurt? As she looked around for her friend, a woman with blood running down her face stumbled into her. Perin stashed the camera into her bag and grabbed the woman around the waist. She led her onto the grass and yelled out for help. A doctor with a gash across his forehead veered toward Perin and led away the battered woman. As Perin took a picture of them fleeing, a gunshot ran out. People scattered in all directions.

"Ya Allah! Ya Allah!" a man said to Perin as he pushed her out of his way, thrusting her into a group of people trying to escape.

"I'm hurrying," she said, as they pressed against her like a human vise. Adrenaline rushing, her head spun. She felt she couldn't breathe as she struggled against the sea of bodies.

"Stop pushing," a woman yelled at her. "We can't move!"

Perin bent over and scrambled under flying fists and flailing arms and banners. She twisted and turned wherever she could get through, losing her orientation. Reaching a clearing, she straightened up and came eye to eye with a morals policeman, snarling like a hungry hyena.

Everything played in slow motion. She didn't hear a sound as she watched him raise his baton and start toward her. Shaking off her daze, she spun around and elbowed her way back into the center of the crowd. She toppled over someone on the ground and clambered over the prone body. People pushed her back in the direction of the policeman but she lurched ahead, until she was jerked back; the strap of her bag had caught on the pole of a banner. With an eye out for the policeman, she yanked at it. Leave it and go, a voice inside her said. *Please, Father, if you're watching down, help me,* she muttered aloud. *Angels and djinns, don't desert me now.*

She jerked on the strap again and flung off the banner, throwing her to the ground. *Get up, get up,* she told herself, *people get trampled to death—the girls at the school were trampled to death.* She clutched her bag under her arm and crawled on her hands and knees. She tussled to stand up and then thrashed through people, not certain where she was, and in what direction she was going. An opening appeared and she extracted herself from the throng. Without looking back to see if the policeman was still after her, she sprinted past the social sciences and law buildings, and made her way to the deserted soccer field at the back of campus. Her knees wobbly, she sat down on the bottom row of bleachers to catch her wits. Her skirt and tunic were covered with dirt and one of the pockets on her tunic was half ripped. She tore it off and tried to spit on it to make it wet so as to wipe the sweat and grime from her face. But she couldn't get enough to clean her scraped and cut hands.

It was 8:40 a.m. She had to get to work. With little or no traffic, Mohammed could get her there before most of the staff arrived and she could wash off. And if Mohammed asked about her appearance, she'd say she turned her ankle and fell down on one of the dirt paths. It seemed plausible and it was all she could think of at the moment. And she'd tell him she got the report she needed at the university and her appointment at the gardens was cancelled. She'd have to trust his discretion and hope he wouldn't say anything to her mother, or to Nabil.

All day at work she couldn't concentrate on the pieces she had to write, jumping whenever someone came up to her. She kept looking around as if she was being watched or chased, expecting a morals policeman to pop his head over the top of her cubicle at any moment and grab her. As she listened to reporters talk about the other demonstrations at the downtown bus terminal and the girls' school, she shivered thinking of how close she had come to being injured or carted off to jail. And she couldn't stop worrying about Zahara. Every time she called the doctor's office, no one answered.

Finally, Zahara called her. "I had to get away when the police showed up. I couldn't get caught and be taken away. The women depend on me too much. Have you started writing about it yet?"

Exasperated at Zahara's relentlessness, she answered, "I have to finish articles for work first, and I want to see if the photos— oh, the photos. How will I print them? It's an old film camera. I can't do it here, or at home, and I can't take them to a shop. What if I get caught with them—oh, this is a nightmare."

"You'll figure out a way."

Perin hurled her pen across the desk.

Sure. I'll figure out a way. And to think I was so worried about you.

A few moments later, she calmed down and began to think.

Leave of Absence

*Why should I grieve because of a thorn? Once it had made
laughter known to me. Whatever you lost through the stroke of destiny,
know it was to save you from adversity. One small affliction keeps
greater afflictions; one small loss prevents greater losses. —Rumi*

The headlines the next morning read, *Grief and Rage Mark
Protests*. The paper was riddled with coverage of the memo-
rial services held throughout the city. It also covered the protests
against the fire, principally the ones at the school and at the
main bus terminal. Only token mention was given to the one at
the university.

Perin was convinced she could compose a riveting story
about what she experienced, especially with photos reinforcing
her words. But she hesitated to mention it to Ghazi. He might
accuse her of usurping *his* metro reporters. And even more
important, it wouldn't be wise to have her byline in print again.
She'd have to be content to send her piece to Eva and get it to
another outlet.

She hovered around the photography section until the technician
was alone. "Wafi, could you print some photos for me?"

"Fill out one of the forms by the door so I can log it in."

"You know, first I really want to see if the photos fit the piece
I'm writing. Maybe I won't use them after I see what I have."
Wafi stopped organizing negatives in a binder and tilted his head
to one side. She knew she wasn't making sense. "Listen, the truth
is I need you to do it without anyone knowing."

"Qadi has to approve everything. If he sees them, he'll ask what they are."

"Don't you have other photos to print?" Wafi nodded. "Then you could mix mine in with the others and he'll never know."

Wafi fiddled with a negative and then slid it into a slot. "What are they of?"

"Yesterday's protest at the university. It's a follow-up to the article I wrote on the fire."

He scrunched up one side of his mouth and hissed air out of his nostrils.

"I'll understand if you can't. But I'd really appreciate it." Perin twiddled the film canister around inside her pocket; the moisture from her hand made it slippery.

"You've been nice to me," he said in a tone so soft that Perin strained to hear. He placed the binder under shelves of digital cameras and stock film. With an eye on the open door, he took the film and stuck it in his shirt pocket.

Several hours later, as she was wrapping up an article, Wafi handed her a manila envelope. She slid it under a stack of papers and handed him a small leather-bound book, a collection of poems by Nizar Qabbani. "He's a Syrian poet I like. I hope you will, too." Wafi's eyes lit up as his fingertip traced the graceful curves of the embossed Arabic script adorning the cover. He muttered a "thank you" and went back to his workstation.

Perin cautiously opened the envelope. Some of the first photos were blurred, the ones she'd taken with the camera above her head. But the ones of the men beating their fists in the air, and wide angles of the marchers coming down the street, were in focus. Before she could look at more, Andrea came up beside her. "Do you think the police are here to complain about the fire coverage?"

Perin gasped and pressed the photos against her chest. She shot out of her seat and looked over the top of her cubicle. Andrea yanked on her jacket. "Your head isn't covered."

Perin sat down and stuffed the photos in her bag. She put on her scarf and tunic and slowly raised up again until she could just see over the top of her cubicle wall. Ali was directing the police to his office. Andrea swatted the air, gesturing for her to stay down.

Perin pulled her scarf out over her head so it covered her face from the side. "Andrea, I need to use the ladies' room," she said, pointing in the direction of the bathrooms.

As she scooted down their row of cubicles and then down the corridor that separated the newsroom from the reception area, the newsroom din lessened. The other reporters pretended to work while keeping an eye on the visitors.

She ducked into an unoccupied cubicle with a good sight line into Ali's office. He stood arms crossed, facing the two gray-robed men. In spite of it being quieter than usual, Perin couldn't make out what they were saying.

One of the men held up what looked like a photo. Ali looked at it and picked up the phone. A minute later, Qadi approached the office. Perin's stomach hit the floor—she'd left the photos sticking out of her bag. She slipped out of the cubicle and sped back to her desk. The envelope hadn't been touched. She stuffed it into her bag and rushed off again. Inside a restroom stall, she stuck the envelope under her blouse, flat against her abdomen, one end tucked into the waistband of her slacks. She buttoned her jacket and tunic over them.

After splashing cold water on her face and running her wrists under the faucet, she looked at herself in the mirror. The color had drained out of her face; she was nearly as white as her scarf.

She rang Zahara. "I need to see you straightaway. Can your driver collect me at the paper?"

"Be outside in fifteen minutes."

On her way out of the ladies' room, she glanced over at Ali's office. The *mise en scène*, with the addition of Qadi, had not changed.

Zahara's office at the hospital was a plain medium-sized room. It was unadorned except for diplomas on the wall; shelves lined with medical books; an abstract painting; and photos of her two children, both girls, around nine and eleven. Perin remembered what Lyes, the attending physician she interviewed at the demonstration, had said, and she guessed her daughters were one reason Zahara wanted to help the women.

"I just know the police were there because of the article I wrote on the fire," Perin said as Zahara looked at the photos. "And I'm probably on that watch list of people who lived in the West."

"Others wrote about the fire, too. The photos are excellent. You did a good job."

For a moment, a faint smile crept up Perin's face.

Zahara put down the photos and leaned across the desk. "Aren't you giving them too much credit? They're not all that smart. Just thugs with power. They were probably there to give the paper a warning. Until you know for certain, stop worrying—in the end, most of what you're concerned about will never happen, and you're stressing out for nothing. Not to mention keeping yourself from doing other things."

"Like writing your article on the demonstration," she added with a touch of bitters.

Zahara shrugged off her remark.

"But what was the photo they showed Ali and why did he call in Qadi? I never should have given the photos to Wafi."

"It was the best solution." Zahara sat back and scratched her forehead. "I don't know if—yes, you have a right to know." She handed Perin a piece of paper. "I found this note under my front door this morning."

Perin looked at the message's childlike scrawl, written in pencil. *We know what you're doing. You are infidels. We will tell the police and they'll put you in jail. We are watching.*

"I don't know who it's from. Someone in the building with a grudge, a relative of one of the women. Or it's a hoax to frighten me."

"Why did they warn you instead of just going to the police?" As the word "police" crossed her lips, Perin's skin crawled.

Zahara came to the other side of the desk and sat next to Perin. "It doesn't matter who did it or why. I have to close the apartment. I can't take the chance that one or more of the women will be harmed."

"Where will the women go?"

"Fatma will stay with me; she still needs counseling. A few of my friends and colleagues are taking in the others, except for Ummee, the older woman with arthritis. My friends are afraid that because she's older and can't do much, it would be difficult to tell their families she was a new maid. They also think she might need too much care and medical attention." Zahara paused. "I need you to help me find a place for Ummee and I was thinking you could take Imene."

"I'd love ... oh, no, I can't right now." Perin looked away and let out a sigh. "My father just died. My mother won't want someone she doesn't know in the house."

Zahara gazed steadily at Perin. The intensity of her silent stare made Perin uncomfortable. There was nothing she'd like better than having Imene with her, but it was impossible. Nabil would ask a lot of questions and he'd never agree. Besides, after almost being injured at the demonstration and seeing the morals police at the office, she was too wound up and on edge to take responsibility for the life of another. Perin sighed again. "I'll try and think of someone, but I can't promise anything." She rubbed the scar in the palm of her hand. "Please stop trying to draw me further into your web."

"When spider webs unite, they can tie up a lion," Zahara said.

At work the next morning, Perin found a note on her desk from Ali, asking to see her. Her stomach flipped. But it was better to get it over with and find out what he wanted. She walked slowly to his office, every step filled with dread.

"You left early the other day. Is everything all right?"

"Ah, my mother. But she's fine now." Perin's right leg jiggled up and down as if manipulated by a nervous puppeteer.

Ali nodded and shifted in his chair. "The police were here." Perin's breath backed up in her throat. "They filed a complaint about our coverage of the edicts. They accused us of bias, putting a negative spin on things." Ali flipped the corner of a piece of paper. "I told them we stand by our coverage."

She started to breathe a little easier.

"But there's something else."

Perin suddenly felt as if she were suspended in midair, waiting for a trapeze artist to hold out his hand and catch her.

"They brought up your article on the fire and said you shouldn't have been there." Perin started to say something, but Ali held up his hand. "There's more. They showed me photos of the demonstration at the university. You were in them."

Perin felt as if a sword had been plunged into her forehead. "It's simple. A friend asked me to go with her and I thought I could get something for a follow-up article—"

"They pointed to a camera you had in your hands and asked if we had the pictures. I checked it out and told them we didn't." Ali took off his glasses and rubbed the inside corners of his eyes. "They want me to fire you."

Perin's hand flung up to cover her open mouth.

"I told them no," he said, with enough conviction that Perin believed him. "I decide who's on my staff. But I assured them you'd only do what you were hired to do."

Perin exhaled with a long sigh.

"But later I thought it over. They don't want you working here and they might do something to harm you." Ali looked down at some papers on his desk and flipped the edges again. "I think it's best for you to take a leave of absence."

She moved to the edge of her seat, unable to believe what he'd said.

"Six weeks, two months." Ali straightened his bow tie. "If one of my staff is in danger, I have to do whatever I can to protect him or her."

"You and the paper will not be responsible. I'll sign a paper absolving you of all liability. Please, I don't want to go on leave."

Ali fixed his eyes on the furthest corner of the ceiling. "There are some risks I'm not willing to take. Trust me on this."

Perin watched Ali for a long, uncomfortable moment; many emotions passed across his face. What was she going to do? It would be near impossible to find another job. She placed both hands on the edge of the chair and leaned forward. "I know you're doing what you think is best for me, but *this* isn't it."

"It hasn't been an easy decision for me, but my overriding concern is for your safety."

As Perin packed up her desk, she fumed. Ali did not let her decide whether to stay or leave. It should have been her choice. He wouldn't have done it if she was a man. Maybe he really did want to protect her, but she was tired of people deciding what they thought was best for her. Even though she loved her family and country more than anything in the world, she started to realize that no matter how long she lived here, the two in unison would keep her a child-woman, meals prepared, room and clothes cleaned, errands run. Nabil would give her money, if she needed it, and her mother would be only too willing to plan social activities. If she'd let them, they'd probably even do her thinking for her.

If she had one consolation, it was that Wafi hadn't said a word about the photos.

Tie Up Your Camel

Silence is the sea, and speech is like the river. The sea is seeking you: don't seek the river. Don't turn your head away from the signs offered by the sea. —Rumi

To avoid going home early and having to make up a story, Perin met Zahara and they strolled around the park behind University Hospital while children, under the watchful eyes of mothers and family maids, played tag around the dried-up fountain and among the patches of arid, parched earth. Apart from their boisterous cavorting, a midday air of somnolence hung over the grounds, noon being too hot for patients.

"He should have let me decide—it should have been my choice," Perin said as she watched two boys scramble up a scraggly palm tree. A young girl stood near the boys, desire written all over her face. Perin wanted to tell her to her climb, too—and now; wait too long and your chance will pass, never to come again.

Zahara led Perin to an empty bench at the far end of the garden, catty-corner from a man stretched out on a bench, napping with one arm over his eyes to shield him from the sun. She tried to melt into the quiet rhythms of the park, hoping to ease her anguish at being put on leave. But the *djinns* did not oblige; it was still raw and gnawed at her. She looked at Zahara's dowdy and worn clothing. Were it not for her confidence and audacious manner, one would think her an average housewife, and not the forceful advocate for women's rights she was. Perin was convinced Zahara was fearless; she'd do anything, even risk her family and her livelihood, to stand up for what she believed in.

Zahara touched Perin's arm. "We'll have to find a place for Ummee in the next day or two." Perin winced and squeezed her eyes tight, wanting to escape into the quiet rhythms of the park, if only for a moment longer. "Have you thought more about taking Imene?" Zahara played with the frayed leather strap of her handbag.

"Don't you think I'm trying to help?" Perin chipped away pieces of buckled paint on the bench. "I'd love to take her home, but there's no way."

"It's really better if Imene leaves the country," Zahara said. "It's the only way she'll be safe. Here, her family will track her down. We can't let them commit an honor killing."

"Do you think Imene's family wrote you that note?"

Zahara shrugged. "Not important who did it. It's done. We have to concentrate on the women."

"How can you possibly get Imene out of the country?"

"The borders are guarded, so that's no good." Zahara slid her simple gold wedding band up and down her finger. "Boat is risky, especially with all the other refugees fleeing and they're planting people in the coastal villages to report suspicious activity. Besides, too many boats go off course and people drown or starve to death."

"That leaves the desert."

"It has no mercy. If you don't know its ways, it can kill you."

"What if Imene goes with someone who knows it, like the Bedouin?"

"I don't have connections there. Maybe someone at your paper does. Can you check?"

Perin weighed her response. Becoming involved would entail more than calling around to see if someone could take in a woman. "Perhaps there is someone. *Tawakilt Ala Allah.*"

"Trust in God, but tie your camel tight," Zahara added, with a smile.

Euphoria, the pleasant feeling of fright Perin felt whenever she contemplated something marginally dangerous, sprang up inside her. It was becoming addictive. Maybe her family was wrong and she really was immune from danger. Hadn't she gotten through everything so far? This thought of infallibility was tempered by her father's last words to her, *What if I'm not around to help you?* But realizing she'd already committed to helping Zahara, she'd just have to ask her angels to work a little overtime.

Zahara took Perin's hand and squeezed it. "Know that we're following Mohammed's example by caring for our fellow women. Certain events happen in our lives as a test of our faith."

Perin was in no mood to be lectured and she merely nodded, her eyes lingering on two elderly men sitting on a bench. One, wearing a beige turban with a feather jauntily stuck in its folds, twirled worry beads. His companion, a rangy man with white whiskers, rested his hands on his cane made from the limb of a tree. She wished her father had had the chance to know the simple pleasures of old age—and play with his grandchildren in the sea.

"Remember me telling you I wanted to set up a sewing co-op for women? Well, a friend is making patterns for bags, aprons, and tablecloths. Could you get me some fabric from your family's mill?"

Perin sighed. Zahara was incorrigible and seductive at the same time, unafraid to ask for anything. Perin stopped—she saw herself in Zahara; she often did the same thing. She glanced at her watch. "My brother has soccer practice today. He won't be there. Drop me off at the factory and I'll see what I can find. One of the drivers there will take me home."

"Don't forget to check on the desert."

"Let me check something now." She walked a few meters away and rang Yousef on her mobile. She could almost hear him jumping up and down as he told her about a new strain of beetle they found. She invited him for lunch the coming Friday, saying her father had always intended to invite him home, adding that

Huda had bouillabaisse on the menu. She hung up and smiled. She was going to wage her own little war against the clerics.

It was nearly five o'clock when Perin arrived at the factory. The armed guard in front of the large metal gates signaled the man in the nearby booth to unlock the small side door for her. Inside the compound, one of the company cars was parked alongside Nabil's Porsche. *How strange*, she thought, *he hasn't left for practice.*

As she entered the vestibule of the main building, Boulus jumped up from his desk. He bowed and opened the door leading to the darkened administrative offices. Only an engineer and the skeletal evening shift of weavers were on duty. To avoid Nabil, she took a roundabout route along the back hallways to reach the storage area where they kept samples of designs they produced, as well as fabrics they bought to study for construction, weave effects, and pattern. With the door ajar, the light from the hallway gave form to the racks of full-length fabric bolts and boards with folded cloth. She spied some multicolored yarn dyes and jewel-toned piece dyes she thought would be perfect for what Zahara needed. As she searched for scissors to cut off lengths, she heard Nabil's voice. "I'm over here. What is it?"

Rooted like a petrified tree stump, Perin held her breath and listened as his footsteps grew louder. She crouched down and moved behind the table. He stopped right outside the room. Her mouth went dry and it seemed as if her heartbeats were careening off the walls; it was difficult to swallow.

"Where are they?" Nabil asked.

The answer was indiscernible to Perin. His voice trailed off and she heaved a few breaths and told herself she was acting silly; the mill belonged to the family and she had every right to be there. And once Nabil found out she wasn't working, perhaps he'd be less critical of her.

She remembered the gold-plated scissors Hoerscht had given her father to commemorate the opening of one of their dyestuff facilities, the ones she used when doing her homework at her father's desk. The muted rhythmic clacking of looms—almost like the sounds of women pounding millet with wooden pestles in wooden mortars—echoed through the hall as she walked to her father's office—Nabil's in reality, but she was not able to cede it to him yet.

She flung open the office door and life suspended as she came face to face with Nabil and two men with full-length beards and gray robes—the morals police. She gasped. Nabil's eyes widened when he saw her and he snapped his pencil in half; the splitting of wood was magnified tenfold in the stunned silence. Out of the corner of her eye, she saw a newspaper lying on the table between the two guest chairs. It was the edition that covered the fire in the girls' school—the one with her article on the front page.

"Excuse me. I … I … I didn't know anyone was here." She backed out of the room, closed the door, and ran down the darkened hallway. She rounded a corner and turned to see if anyone was following her. But the only things trailing her were the men's raised voices.

She was about to start for the exit when she remembered the fabric. She gathered the bolts, three under each arm, and dragged them along the floor like alien appendages. She felt like she was running in taffy. Boulus bounced out of his chair when he saw her and took the tubes. She asked him to cut five meters from each roll, and to call one of the drivers to take her home.

"They're gone. I thought you were going with Mr. Nabil."

She paced the small room for a few moments and then as if a surge of intravenous tranquilizers had taken effect, she stopped and told Boulus that she would wait for Nabil in the conference room.

In the unlit room, she sat at the head of the long table and rested her head on the back of the chair; coolness from the day's air conditioning lingered. Perhaps it was good that Nabil knew about the article. It was time to clear the air. And it meant one less secret to keep.

Fifteen minutes later, she got in the car with Nabil and put the folded fabric in her lap. Nabil pulled up to the gate and waited for the guard to open it; twisting his hands around the steering wheel, his only communication was the anger misting from his pores. He dove into traffic, cutting off a car whose driver blasted his horn. "Why are you here and why did you barge into my office like that?"

"If I'd known, do you think—"

"Do you know why they were there?"

"I saw," she said with a measure of calm that surprised her.

"No, you only see what you want to see." Nabil rubbed the back of his neck. "They said you were inciting demonstrations—that they'd have to look more closely at the books to see if there were any irregularities. Irregularities! Do you know what that means? It means they'll find whatever they want and close us down."

"Nabil, I—oh, stop it. They're just trying to scare you. Can't you see it's a tactic? And if you give in, they'll think they can manipulate you."

"Every day you're like a tabula rasa. You don't get it." Nabil's eyes took on a steely look.

"I do get it. But I also get that you can't give in to them. Capitulate and they own the country." Perin thought of Ali and his decision to put her on leave of absence. Exactly what the morals police wanted. They only had to threaten and the parties themselves would follow through, ensuring the desired result.

"I agree with them. Jeopardizing the family with your article and taking pictures at a demonstration. You're crazy." Nabil hit the steering wheel with the palm of his hand. "It's that trivial job of yours that caused all the problems."

"It's not trivial. And stop deluding yourself that there's only one reality."

Nabil pressed his lips together. "You forced me to make a pact with—"

"Pact? What do you mean pact?"

"You're quitting your job right now. You have no choice."

Perin sat back. Now she didn't have to make up a story to tell her family about why she wasn't going to work. It was better this way. Nabil would think he'd won and she was finally listening to him. Maybe it was her *maktub* not to work. He kept turning to look at her, seemingly bewildered that she didn't protest.

"I'll do it for the family." Perin started to touch Nabil's arm, but pulled back before he noticed.

"Finally coming to your senses," he said in a lower register. "Things were fine until you came home. You should go back to New York."

Words sticking in her throat, she said, "I ... I can't believe you said that. Were things ... were they really fine? You delude yourself and find an easy scapegoat in me."

During the rest of the silent ride home, his words stung like red ant bites. She wondered if he meant what he said about her leaving. In spite of all the opportunities, openness, and freedoms the States offered, she knew she didn't want to go back. No problem could erode the bonds she had with her family, her home, her country, and her sea. Yes, it was her sea—a place that resonated deep within. Her deep connections to the land overrode any desire to live a life of her own abroad. Eva was right; she was fortunate and she didn't want to become a foreigner again.

The Dinner Guest

A basket full of bread sits on your head; yet you go from door to door begging for crusts. Attend to your own head. Knock on your heart's door. —Rumi

Assia and Rashid were playing cards on the verandah when Perin and Nabil arrived home. Before she could go upstairs, Nabil stopped her. "I want to talk to everyone right now."

"I need a few minutes. I'll be right back."

In her bathroom, she splashed water on her face and ran a comb through her hair, her stomach twisting as she thought of the pending family caucus. She tried to tell herself Nabil was just rattled and he'd calm down. She also remembered what Huda said about all men having nightmares; now Nabil would have new ones. Before leaving her room, she glanced at the photo of her father. *If only you'd stayed longer. You would have understood.*

Nabil was standing behind the large overstuffed leather chair when Perin returned. "I told them what happened and that you agreed to stop working." Assia's and Rashid's faces registered disbelief; Perin's silence confirmed it. "I also made it clear that I have to know what's going on. No more surprises. Mother, you'll be responsible for Perin."

"She's not a child. What do you want me to do? Lock her up like those—"

"Who said anything about locking her up?" Nabil looked to the side and shook his head. "This family has to exaggerate everything. All I'm saying is that she can't do anything that will put her—and us—in danger."

"Don't put Mother in this position," Perin said, her voice turning to steel. "I'm responsible for my actions, no one else." Imene and Ummee popped into her mind. Now more than ever it was crucial to figure out a way to help both of them that had no trace of her involvement, and wouldn't compromise her family.

Breathing air through his teeth, Nabil opened the cabinet opposite the sofa. "Where's the scotch?"

"I hid it," Assia said, "in case the police raided the house."

"Rashid, go get it."

Rashid's face went slack and he went to get the bottle, returning a few minutes later.

Nabil filled a shot glass and gulped it down. "Perin has to get married."

She felt she'd been kicked in the stomach. "Married? Me? Just like that?"

"Single women are targets. If you're married, there'll be less pressure on you."

"You mean less on you. You want to get rid of me so I'm someone else's problem and not yours."

"You're nearly twenty-five—"

"And what, Nabil? You're twenty-six and I don't see you running out and finding a wife."

"I can't stand your arguing," Assia said.

"It's different for a man. He can marry when he likes." Nabil poured another drink. "All the good men will be taken. And if you're barren, no one will want you."

"You're going at each other like a pair of hyenas," Rashid said.

Perin chafed at Nabil's words. "You want me to have children. Okay, but I won't get married."

Nabil turned red, the look on his face a mixture of rage and horror.

"Don't even say that joking," Assia said, shaking her head at Perin.

"That's enough," Rashid said, standing up. "You're upsetting Mother."

"I'd like to think there are men who marry for love," Perin answered, ignoring Rashid's plea. "Men who don't base marriage on fertility and cooking."

"You'd be surprised," Nabil countered.

"Really? You'll marry someone only because she's can make a moist couscous and has good pelvic structure? I doubt it." Perin smirked and looked away.

"Oh, merciful One, help us," Assia wailed.

"Are you going to wait until you're old and the skin hangs off your arms?"

Rashid pushed Nabil against the cabinet, knocking the glass from his hand onto the floor. He pinned his arms back. "She got the message. Stop it."

Assia gasped as Rashid's words circulated in the air. Perin held her breath and waited for Nabil's reaction. She'd never seen Rashid take a stand against Nabil and she worried Nabil's wrath would target Rashid now.

Sweat poured down Nabil's brow as he glared at Rashid. He shook Rashid's hands off and stooped to pick up the glass. He poured another drink, emptied the glass, and slammed it down on the cabinet. His slightly glazed eyes were still filled with rage. "She may not have a choice," he said, leaving the room.

Back in her room, Perin held her hands out in front of her; they were trembling. She balled them up into fists and hit the pillow on her bed; everything was crumbling around her. On the verge of tears, she wanted to let go and have a good sob, but she refused to indulge herself. She remembered what Zahara said about forgetting your troubles if you helped someone less fortunate. She needed to find a place for Ummee. She rang up Shereen.

"I need you to do just one favor for me—to let a lady stay with you for a short while. Less than a week. There's so much room at the ranch and none of your family's out there all the time. She won't be a problem."

"Hakim and his family are coming soon … the staff has a lot to do. We can't have anyone else around even if you say she won't be any trouble. Who is this woman?"

"Forget it," Perin said, jerking her head. "I have to go."

"Don't be upset with me," Shereen said before Perin hung up.

What a waste of time, Perin thought. And equally tormenting was that she had been too emotionally exhausted and upset to commiserate with Shereen about Nabil wanting her to get married. Humph, she thought, I'll find my own husband before I'll let him arrange a marriage for me.

The following morning, Perin stayed in her room and wrote about the demonstration, fulfilling one of her promises to Zahara. Every time the events of yesterday afternoon popped into her mind, she exiled them to "another time."

Finished, she e-mailed her article to Eva along with a note. Her pride wouldn't allow her to say she'd been put on leave. Nor did she mention that Nabil wanted to marry her off; she might not understand anyway.

Next, she opened the atlas she'd brought up from the study and pored over a map of the country. The desert seemed wider and longer than she remembered. She measured distances and tried to imagine pitfalls that might hinder the use of each possible route. Every time she thought of Imene, she felt nauseous: *I have this woman to get out of the country and I have to do it without jeopardizing my family.*

Dressed for dinner in black linen slacks and a vintage Pucci print blouse she'd picked up in one of the secondhand stores in New York, she went downstairs, hoping Nabil's ire had dissipated, and there'd be no more discussion of marriage. She had said explosive things she didn't mean, things that were hurtful for her mother to hear; it was never part of her plan to have children out of wedlock.

In the dining room, she noticed an additional place setting next to hers, and in the kitchen, there was a roasted lamb that the family usually reserved for special occasions. Perin put an olive in her mouth and asked Huda who was coming to dinner.

"Don't mess up my dishes," Huda said. "Nabil invited a friend."

She choked and a piece of olive fell out of her mouth. She collapsed into a chair and shook her foot; the daisy on top of her black flip-flop bounced up and down.

"You aren't wearing that tonight, are you?" Nabil said as he came into the room.

"Aren't I presentable for your guest?"

"We're having company," Nabil said. "Change clothes. I'm asking you nicely."

Eyes averted, Perin sat there silently for a few moments. Then without a word she got up and went back to her room, changing into her green, gold, and aqua print caftan. As she raised her hands to put up her hair, she saw the fleshy underside of her arms in the mirror and remembered Nabil's words: *You'll wait until the skin on your arm hangs before you marry.* Her shoulders slumped. She stroked the smooth turquoise stones around her neck. Father would never have told me I had to get married. Nabil can't force me to do anything I don't want ... but he could make things difficult.

When Perin saw Kamal enter the living room, she narrowed her eyes and figured his peacock-like aura was no doubt inflated by some sub-rosa pact with her brother. Kamal handed Assia a box. Inside was a candleholder encircled by entwined filigree branches of maize and green cut-crystal leaves. Assia thanked him and Kamal said, "Swarovski crystal."

Rashid leaned over and whispered in Perin's ear, "If you want to marry, give your presents to the mother." Perin swatted his arm, but she had to admit Kamal had good taste.

"Nabil tells me you helped prepare tonight's dinner," Kamal said, taking the dish of eggplant.

"She made the lamb," Nabil said. "It's one of her specialties."

Perin glared at Nabil; his glower willed her into compliance.

"You're no longer at the paper," Kamal said. "I suppose it doesn't matter much."

Nabil and Rashid looked at Perin. But before she could respond, Assia straightened up in her chair and said, "She wrote many good articles. Even Fuad said she made the column interesting enough for him to read."

"That's a father for you," Kamal said. Assia's smile faded. "From what I've observed, most women only work until they find a husband—even women in the States."

"You haven't been keeping up," Perin said as pleasantly as she could muster. "In many households there, the woman works and the man stays home. Having a family and a career are not mutually exclusive."

"Have some of Huda's hummus," Nabil said to Kamal as he handed him the bowl.

"That's the problem with their society. Emasculated men. How can a society function if men are relegated to a secondary position?" He scooped up hummus with an olive pierced with a toothpick.

"You're missing the point," Perin said, straining to keep her voice even. "People there are free to decide. Society doesn't dictate arbitrary standards."

"You're right. This hummus is great," Kamal said. "Things are like they are here, and in the rest of the world, because they make sense. Everyone knows the Americans are crazy."

Perin thought back to years ago when she traveled abroad with her family. The Europeans criticized the Americans for wearing hideous jogging suits and tennis shoes, and for running all over as if in a race. They also made fun of their aversion to tobacco. But now, even fashion-conscious Italians and French wore sweatsuits, and some European governments had enacted non-smoking regulations. She recalled an article in *The Economist* that said something along the lines of, "to criticize the United States, is to criticize your future."

"We tend to be late adopters," Perin said, sweet coating the acid in her voice.

"We were pleased to hear of Shereen's engagement," Assia said. As soon as she uttered the last word, she looked at Perin.

"He's suitable. Not very ambitious."

Perin sneered at Kamal. How dare he say he was "suitable" with his dictatorial air, and who gave him the right to grant a verdict? Shereen loved Hakim. Perin's anger percolated. He and Nabil were supposed to be the enlightened ones; they'd been brought up with Western traditions, they'd traveled abroad extensively, they had foreign friends. But deep down they were just as controlling as tribal chieftains.

Nadira announced dinner was ready. Kamal escorted Assia into the dining room, and after she was seated, he pulled out Perin's chair. As she scooted it nearer the table, he leaned over and whispered, "I hope my being here doesn't make you nervous."

Head tilted to one side, Perin looked up and cooed, "I'm quite immune to your allures."

"I've heard my reputation precedes me. But I can assure you there's a lot more water in the wine now," he said, trying to sound seductive.

Perin let out a sigh. She doubted age would mellow Kamal. Only a few more hours, she told herself, and then she could concentrate on truly important things—she had to get Imene out of the country and find a home for Ummee.

Nadira placed the lit crystal candleholder in the center of the table; its flame flickered off the facets of the candleholder's leaves like a stellar nursery, and its swirling masses of stars made a dappled effect on the tablecloth. Soon Nadira returned with the first course—a salad of hearts of palm and celery, tossed with salt, lemon, and olive oil.

As Kamal and Nabil bantered about their upcoming soccer match and Kamal's horses, Perin pretended to listen. She was forced to rejoin the conversation when Kamal said, "I heard your paper, or the one you used to work for, is under scrutiny. They say Zayer doesn't know what he's doing."

Perin felt the veins in her neck bulge. In spite of being predisposed to defend him, she couldn't think of one major criticism of her boss. "That's not true."

Kamal laughed. "They just took him because his father was friends with the owner."

"My husband liked Ali," Assia said, "and Omer said he's fair in his reporting."

Perin started to say something, but told herself to hold back, to go along—she had bigger things at stake, but Kamal rankled her. How could Nabil think she'd consider him for a husband? As Nadira cleared away the salad dishes and put out the dinner plates, her anger got the better of her. "I'll bring in the main course," she said, glancing at Nabil, "the one I helped make."

Nadira looked at Assia for approval. Assia nodded and the maid followed Perin into the kitchen, where Huda was wiping grease off the rim of the meat platter. After Perin told Huda she would take in the lamb and Nadira could bring the vegetables, she snatched the salt shaker and a bottle of *harissa* from the counter.

"What do you want those for?" Huda asked. "The food's fine. I tasted it."

Perin unscrewed the top of the shaker and moved toward the meat platter. Huda slid her bulk in front of it and grappled for the condiments. But Perin managed to wedge herself between Huda and the lamb, thrusting Huda off balance in the process.

"Merciful Allah, help me. I'm going to tell your mother."

"No, you're not!" Perin said, pushing away Huda's hand. "Like cures like. Isn't that what you told me? Be cruel to the cruel, kind to the kind."

Huda wrapped her veil over her face. "I don't want to know anything."

Nadira grimaced as Perin dumped the white crystals on a piece of lamb near end of the platter and rubbed the grains into the grease until they disappeared. Then she slathered on hot sauce, demarcating the laced piece with slices of roasted red pepper. Huda, her face still covered, swayed back and forth. Perin told her not to worry; they'd know she wasn't the one who did it. Huda broke out of her shroud and gazed up to the heavens, her hands in prayer pose.

Perin held the platter high as she walked into the dining room. Nadira followed, cowering in the corner with the vegetables. After Perin placed a piece of meat on Assia's plate, Nabil gestured for her to serve Kamal next, and Assia motioned for Nadira to serve the vegetables; as she put green beans and fried zucchini flowers on Assia's plate, her hands shook.

Kamal looked up at Perin, a sly glint in his eyes, and reached for the serving utensils.

"No, let me," she said, serving him before passing the platter to Nabil.

"This is very good, Perin," Assia said. "Seasoned perfectly."

"The best you've made," Nabil said. "Don't you think so?" he asked his friend. "Kamal, what is it?"

Hunkered over his plate, Kamal was trying to chew. The skin between his brows crinkled up and his mouth puckered. His cheeks inflated and deflated like bellows and his Adam's apple bulged as he tried to swallow. Then he put his napkin to his mouth and bolted from the room.

"Where's he going?" Assia asked.

"So help me, Perin, if you did something," Nabil said as he ran after Kamal.

"Maybe his colitis flared up," Perin said. "Or maybe he thought the food was *haram*."

"There's no prohibited food in this house," Assia countered.

Rashid chuckled. It was enough to crack Perin's seemingly placid façade, and she let out a nervous laugh. "Or maybe he suspected vanilla," she said with a flip of her hand.

"I don't find this amusing. Kamal's our guest. What did you do?" Assia said.

Perin turned serious. "You knew about this. You helped Nabil set me up with Kamal."

"I did no such thing. I only found out this afternoon he was coming. Don't you accuse me of such things."

Tears welled up in Assia's eyes; Perin reached out to her. Why hadn't she heeded her own advice and gone along with everything? "I'm sorry, Mother."

Nabil returned, eyes flashing reproachfully at Perin. "Are you some silly teenager with your stupid tricks? You and your childish pranks. I'm warning you—"

"About what?" Perin stared down her brother. "That I'll have to quit my job? That I'll have to marry?" Perin threw down her napkin. "That I'll have to go back to New York?"

"You think you're so clever. But men talk. He'll tell everyone. They'll know you're trouble."

"He'll think I haven't raised you properly," Assia said, cradling her head in her hands. "'*Mal éduqué, mal élevé*,' he'll say. Badly educated."

"You insulted Kamal, Mother, and me," Nabil hurled out.

"And not me?" Rashid said, with a forlorn look. Nabil gave Rashid a dismissive look that only served to fire up Rashid. "He deserved it," Rashid said. "You should have asked Perin before—"

"Stay out of this," he snarled at Rashid.

"Allah, help us," Assia wailed, her hands over her ears. "Your father would hate how you are treating each other."

"Okay, I was wrong," Perin said, "it was childish, but I don't like being manipulated—and you only want me to like your friend so you can feel better."

"You're a curse on this family," Nabil said. "You've dishonored father's memory."

Stunned, Perin sat back and stared at the wall.

"That man you invited for lunch," Assia said, "the one you met in the desert and he came to your father's funeral—"

"Yousef," Perin said.

"Well, I hope you don't act this way when he's here," Assia said.

The expression on Nabil's face changed and he was quiet for a few moments. "I don't trust her. We'll take him to the club. She can't tamper with the food there."

"But he's expecting a home—" Perin stopped. She needed to speak to Yousef and it dawned on her that it might be easier to speak to him alone at the club than at home. In a public place, with others around, her mother and Nabil would be less inclined to keep an eye on her. "Whatever you want," she said, lacing her words with as much humility as was possible.

That night, Perin was racked with nightmares. Her mother's face kept appearing, fraught with disappointment, and Nabil hurled insults at her: *You'll be old and barren and no one will want you; You're acting like a silly teenager; You're a curse on this family.*

As dawn was barely chasing away the night shadows, she showered to try and wash away her thoughts. As water cascaded over her, she watched rivulets run down her dark hair and heard Nabil's voice echo off the tiles of the shower stall. There was no escape.

Hoping to avoid the family, she went down early for breakfast. Huda was arranging a vase of papyrus stalks and lavender-blue irises on the dining room table. When Huda saw her, she scowled and headed back to the kitchen.

"It was harmless," Perin said, her lips twitching. "You read Kamal's face. You know how he is. And you also know I could never be with him."

"Eat your breakfast," Huda said, aiming her index finger at Perin's place setting.

"The fly cannot be driven away by getting angry at it. Isn't that what you say?"

Huda shook her head and went into the kitchen, returning a moment later with a pitcher of steaming milk and a pot of coffee. She plopped them down in front of Perin, and marched out of the room again.

Looking at the flowers, Perin wished she could be whisked away to a secluded garden. But the rite of nothingness would have to wait until Imene out was out of the country. If Huda was this grumpy, she could just imagine how Nabil and her mother would be.

As she was spreading jam on a piece of bread, Rashid walked in. "That was some performance last night." She winced. "Hey,

I'm on your side." Rashid sat down and poured coffee and milk into his oversized cup.

"I was so angry," she said, picking up breadcrumbs from her plate with the tip of her finger. "I have more important things to worry about than getting married."

Rashid stopped sipping his coffee. "What do you mean, more important things?" Perin licked her finger and didn't answer. "Are you forgetting who took you to that doctor's apartment?"

It was useless trying to fool Rashid; she had to give him something. "If you must know, I told Zahara I'd help her find a home for that older woman I told you about. I asked Shereen—"

"Forget it, she's a ninny. That whole family is selfish."

"They can be generous. They treat their staff well. And Shereen's a loyal friend."

"Whatever." Rashid put another spoonful of sugar in his coffee. "Call Aunt Safina. She'll do it. Someone to fuss over now that Tariq's in Paris."

Perin smiled, thinking of Ummee participating in one of Aunt Safina's *Stimbali* nights.

Friday at the Club

If you have no eyes, do not walk blindly; take a staff in your hand. If you have no staff of insight, do not walk without a guide. —Rumi

The gardens lining the perimeter of the club's grounds were ablaze with amethyst and dusty blue hydrangeas. Bougainvillea, the colors of curry, wine, and raspberry, crept up and over the walls. As she escorted Yousef around, Perin looked over at her mother, elegant in a coral linen suit, sitting with a group of her women friends at one of the umbrella-covered tables that spilled out onto the terrace from the open glass doors of the dining room.

"Your mother seems to be doing better," Yousef said. "It's good she has you and your brothers. Your father was proud of all of you. He said you'd become the people he'd hoped you would be."

Perin smiled. She knew her father was proud of them, but that he expressed this to others gave it special meaning.

"Ah, sea air," Yousef said, taking a deep breath. "If you grow up around water, you never feel complete unless you're near it."

"I call it *my* sea."

"I do the same. My desert. My bugs." Yousef let out a throaty chortle as he put his hand under water running from the turquoise tile fountain built into the sandstone wall. "Do you think it's about possession?"

"More of a connection," she said, watching the bugs and flies flapping their wings in the fountain, the weight of the water preventing them from taking flight. And then Kamal came to mind; he would certainly consider any woman he married a possession, in spite of his trying to project the contrary. She was glad she made certain Nabil understood she'd never consent to an arranged marriage, even one with his best friend.

Several boys in wet bathing suits shrieked past, splashing water. Perin wiped drops from her cheek and started to doubt whether she should ask Yousef about Imene. But she had no other option. He'd told her on the phone that he'd be leaving the country soon, so it had to be today.

"What did you miss most when you were away?" he asked.

"My family, Huda's food, my aunt's laughter, going to the baths with friends, doing things with Nabil—we used to do a lot together."

"Not anymore?"

"Maybe I was away too long. Can't keep our childhood forever."

"It's woven into our being," he said. "It just gets lost in our everyday lives." Yousef picked a leaf from a mint plant, rubbed it between his fingers and put it under Perin's nose. "Natural deodorizers. Good to have in your pocket for the city."

As Perin sniffed the crushed leaf, she saw Nabil walking over to Assia; he'd finished his tennis game and changed into slacks and a linen jacket. "Yousef, I have to ask you something. Would you mind if we go over there?" she said, pointing to an empty bench near the wall.

Seated, she looked around at the stylishly dressed women having lunch, others still in tennis whites, and another group in swimsuits at the edge of the pool watching their children frolic in the water. In this enclave they shed their body armor. It was if they were living two lives—one inside walls and the other outside.

She told Yousef about Imene.

He grew quiet and unrolled his shirtsleeves; sand fell out of the folds. "Occupational hazard," he said brushing off the golden grains.

"I could tell the people in the village like and trust you," she said. "If you asked, couldn't they find a trustworthy desert safari guide to take Imene to the border—the kind tourists use."

Yousef twirled the mint leaf in his fingers; the corner of his mouth seemed to have disappeared in the folds of his fleshy face. His silence filled the air with uncertainty. She looked at the deep scar on his lower arm and wondered if the war or his work caused it. It would seem too familiar for her to ask.

"I know it's risky," she said, again doubting her decision to ask him. "I don't want you to feel put upon. If you'd prefer not to do it, it's okay, but I remember you saying that things here reminded you of what went on in Lebanon during the war," she said. "I thought you'd understand."

Yousef leaned forward and rested his elbows on his knees, his face cupped in his hands.

Perin was wondering if her entire plan to escape through the desert was ridiculous when he said, "A Tuareg camel train. One goes to Mauritania every week. They have a measure of autonomy. The soldiers don't mess with them," he said, looking at Perin, his eyes a little too small for his head. "I've heard people in the village say the Tuaregs would just as soon slit a throat than listen to anyone."

"Can we trust them?" Perin asked.

"As much as anyone else. And the others wouldn't talk. *Whoever tells the truth is chased out of a village,*" he said, quoting a familiar saying about people in the countryside. "How much money does your friend have for this?"

Perin shrugged. "Do you think it'll be expensive?"

"Possibly, but let's assume she has enough. I'll make inquiries. Someone in the village will have a connection and if it's people they trust and work with, we should be fine."

Perin liked that Yousef used "we" when he described the plan. Any misgivings she had about asking Yousef disappeared. "When will you know something? She can't stay where she is much longer."

"Depends. I'll try and go there for lunch tomorrow and check around."

"Will this put you in danger?" she said, wanting to give Yousef one more chance to change his mind.

"What can they do? Deport me? I go home in two weeks."

Nabil motioned for Perin and Yousef to join him and Assia in the restaurant.

"Please don't mention this to my family," she said, smiling.

Yousef winked at her and looked up at the cloudless sky. "Lovely day. *Bien sur*. Shouldn't complain. Just give thanks for all I have."

"Yes, be grateful for all we have."

In the park behind the hospital the next day, Perin gazed at the late afternoon shadows that cast angular shapes around the trees whose branches spliced the waning light into beacon-like blades that bounced off the surface of the walkway. She picked up gravel from the walkway and tossed pebbles at the base of a stone urn while waiting for Zahara to agree to Yousef's plan. Zahara had wanted to meet Yousef, but he wouldn't be back in the city before she closed the apartment. She'd have to take Perin's word that he was trustworthy.

"You've certainly painted him as the most marvelous man," Zahara said, turning up one of the corners of her mouth. "And he thinks we can trust the Tuaregs?"

Perin's voice took on an urgency to underscore her point. "Who do you think smuggles in all the cigarettes and liquor? And weapons? That's why their price is so high."

"Five thousand euros. And it has to be in euros," Zahara mumbled to herself as she looked beyond the trees toward the medical-office complex. "I have some extra money in my daughters' college fund."

"You don't want to take it from that."

"There's no time to get it elsewhere."

A boy ran past, unfurling his kite, trying to catch a breeze that would send it soaring. It teetered on the brink of lifting, and then rose to the boy's delight.

"I'll give you half from my savings," Perin said.

Zahara placed her hand on Perin's. "I'm not convinced the plan will work."

A honking horn startled Perin. Trying to keep her voice calm, she asked Zahara if she had another idea. Zahara didn't answer; her face betrayed a flicker of exhaustion. "We should plan for this coming Thursday, Zahara. People will be at mosque. We really have to make a decision at once."

"All right. I'll have to trust you—and *your* Yousef."

Instead of the lightness Perin expected to feel with Zahara's approval of the plan, she felt the muscles in her neck tighten. The responsibility for the plan's successful completion rested firmly on her shoulders.

That evening, Perin updated Yousef and confirmed they had the money. Yousef said his contact assured him the Tuaregs would keep their end of the bargain. He'd try and arrange it for Thursday night. When she thanked Yousef again for his help, he said, "Damsels in distress and wounded birds are my soft spots."

Relieved Yousef was confident the plan would work, Perin tried to think of any loose ends that might have escaped her. The wait was going to be agonizing; she'd go over the plan ad nauseum until it was a *fait accompli*. She jumped when her phone rang.

"I should have explained better why we can't help that woman," Shereen said on the other end of the line, "but with Hakim com—"

"Don't worry. My aunt's going to take her."

"That's good. I was wondering if you'd like to go to the ranch with me tomorrow. We can ride on the beach again," Shereen said, her tone of voice making amends.

Thinking she'd be distracted in the country, Perin agreed to go.

Perin let sand run through her fingers as she watched the rippling waves scoot across the sea and crash on the beach, creating a frothy meringue.

"Can you imagine me married to your brother?" she said to Shereen. "We would end up killing each other."

"It must have put a dent in his ego—he didn't mention a thing," Shereen said with a laugh.

"It was in bad taste. My mother was so upset and Nabil went crazy."

"You had every reason to be angry. Pity though. I always wanted you as my sister. And I'm sorry Nabil made you quit."

Perin purposely did not mention that Ali had put her on a leave before Nabil forbade her to work; Shereen might let it slip to Kamal.

"Now you can help with the wedding and spend time with Hakim and me when he comes," Shereen said, feelings entering her voice with the mention of her fiancé.

Perin wished she could be enthusiastic about the wedding for Shereen's sake. But she was disappointed her friend failed to grasp how important it had been for her to work.

Back at the ranch, while Shereen went to tell the cook they'd returned, Perin stayed in the white clapboard stable, stroking a mare's mane. Sunlight cast a web of light and shadow through openings in the wooded slats as a worker put fresh hay in the stalls. Another entered with a stallion that was snorting and stomping; he put the steed into the stall across from her. On his way out, Perin asked, "Why are there so many empty stalls?"

"Mr. Kamal sold six horses and we won't get new ones for a month or longer."

Perin started thinking—there was limited access to the ranch and Nabil said the clerics left Kamal and his family alone; they were too powerful with their mining and agriculture businesses, and she also suspected they paid off people. When Shereen returned, Perin asked, "Does anyone besides Kamal and the workers come into the stables?"

"Me when I ride. And the vet occasionally. Why?"

"Someone could hide here quite easily, no?"

"You're not thinking of hiding from the police here, are you?" Shereen said, raising her eyebrows. "They can't be after you now that Nabil said you won't work anymore."

"Not me. Another woman who needs a place to stay for a day or two."

"I thought you said she's staying with your aunt."

"Not that woman. This is a younger one who had a terrible experience and needs to get away from her family."

"I can't put my family in danger. Absolutely not." Shereen shook her head. "If Kamal found out I even discussed such a—"

"Strangers pass this way all the time on the way into town—they could assume she was from the mountains, was exhausted, saw the stable and stopped for the night. We can tell Imene, that's her name, to say exactly that, if someone comes."

Shereen kicked at small stones in the dirt, a distressed look on her face. Perin realized she was badgering her, just like Zahara badgered her, and she did not like it any better than Perin did. "Trust me on this," Perin said, remembering a second later that *trust me on this* was what Ali said when he put her on leave.

She had to convince Shereen now, as there was little time left to arrange everything properly as it was, and if she agreed, Imene could leave the apartment in time.

Shereen was still feeling guilty about not helping to find a place for Ummee; she'd have to use that to her advantage. "I understand you didn't want someone living in the house, but this is different and it will be only one night, or two."

"You're sure nothing—oh, no, I don't like it. You make me so angry sometimes." Shereen kicked another stone across the gravel and looked off into space. "Okay," she said in a half voice. "*Tawakilt Ala Allah.*"

Follow Your Destiny

*At midnight say, "I am near you: be not afraid of the night, for I am
your protecting friend." Last night in your dream you saw One with a prayer-rug.
That was I, and what I told you in that dream about the meaning of the
prophesy: make those words of Mine your mind's guide. —Rumi*

Perin paced her room as she waited for Yousef's call. He and
Zahara agreed to use the ranch as a hideout, and Zahara arranged to have Imene brought there. Now Perin needed confir-
mation that the transfer would take place on Thursday. Remembering Shereen's agitation, she worried she'd asked too much of
her friend.

It was mid-morning when Yousef finally called. "My contact in
the village said the men coming for Imene would try for this
Thursday. But it isn't certain. They want an extra day or two, in
case they have trouble getting there. I don't know what the man
meant by trouble, and I can't pressure them because there are
risks on their side, too."

Perin tried not to let on how nervous she was, but if Imene
had to stay through the weekend, Kamal might be around, and
she dreaded thinking what would happen if he found her.

She decided to tell Zahara later that Imene might have to
wait longer at the ranch. She didn't want to quibble over details
now, and tomorrow it would be too late to change anything. The
possible delay added to the feeling Perin had of being perched on

a slender limb, and that any extra pressure, even a slight breeze, could mean collapse and disaster.

Now that everything was set, all she could do was wait. She answered Eva's last e-mail, still unable to tell her she'd been put on leave.

> Hi Eva,
>
> I still think of the times we had together here and I wish you could have stayed longer. But now is not the best time as the dry, dusty, stifling sirocco winds from the Sahara are coming this way. Did I ever tell you how people blame the winds for everything? If they forget to do something, if the food was rotten, and some men have said that the winds drove them so crazy that they killed their wives.
>
> I enjoyed the last article you sent me, especially the one you wrote on the Brooklyn Museum exhibit. Wish I had been there to see it with you. I miss you, dear friend.
>
> XoXo, Perin

After she sent the e-mail, she went downstairs. Channel surfing, she bypassed a Pakistani sitcom and a documentary on the cultivation of frankincense in Yemen. None of the programs held her interest, and she wasn't in the mood for Al-Jazeera. On the last channel she flipped to, a cleric lectured: "You cannot escape Allah's judgment. The day of judgment is coming. Repent your sins."

Sin. Eva told her someone said it stood for "self-inflicted nonsense." Sounds about right, she said to herself as she turned off the TV.

"I don't like to see you mope around," Assia said, coming into the room. "Safina needs some cookbooks. I put them on the kitchen table. Have Mohammed drive you over there."

Perin thanked the *djinns* that her mother interpreted her nervousness for sulking.

Aunt Safina stood on a stepstool in one of the guest bedrooms and held the sheer white fabric up to the open window, its shutters splayed out against the wall of the villa. "You can leave the windows open during the day and these will cut the glare," she said to Ummee. Sea breezes lifted the white gossamer and it billowed out into the room.

"Aunt, the room is fine." Perin watched Ummee twist one arthritic hand with the other as she sat on the edge of the bed, her taut legs stuck out in front of her.

"Don't you love the yellow color I painted the room? It matches that lovely Chinese design." Safina pointed to a small chair covered in a block-print fabric of pagodas, rickshaws, and cherry red chrysanthemums. "And it goes nicely with the turquoise bowls. Dina needs to sprinkle some more bergamot in the room. I can barely smell it."

Aunt Safina was the perfect one to care for Ummee; Perin was surprised she hadn't thought of her first. And Omer had not objected. He said having someone in the house made it less lonely.

"Was it hard to see Tariq leave for Paris?" Perin asked her aunt as they went downstairs.

"Terribly. But it was for the best. He refused to change that awful spiked hair and he was always playing foreign music. Sometimes it was so loud, I was sure they could hear it down on the beach or at the villa next door. Sooner or later he would have been reported." She fanned herself with her hand. "Let's go in the sitting room. It's too hot on the terrace."

As they sat on one of the divans lining the walls, Safina asked, "Are you getting used to not working?"

"Not yet. But maybe now Nabil won't worry so much." *Stick with the party line*, she told herself—*at least until Imene is safely away.*

Dina placed glasses of sweetened tea and a dish of almond biscuits on the coffee table.

"Such a shame he made you quit. Your mother felt bad for you. I know you young women all want careers. But the best career is to have a family."

Her words reminded Perin of what the editor of *The Gazette* said to her in the interview. But coming from her aunt, she didn't mind. "You worked before you met Uncle."

"It was different then. Most women didn't want careers— well, maybe your mother. She wanted to be an artist. That's why she went off to Paris." Aunt Safina paused and took one of the thin wafers. "Well, one of the reasons."

"There's another reason?"

"Oh, not really." Before Perin could ask again, Safina continued, "Then she met your father and changed her mind. I met Omer when I was working at my first job at the cultural center." Perin had heard this story many times. But her aunt enjoyed telling it and she listened as if hearing it for the first time.

"When I came back with the family after our August holiday, Omer told me I was much calmer, more fun. He said women should never work—it changes their personalities. I agreed."

Dina returned with a bowl of burning sandalwood. Its sweet scent filled the room.

"Didn't you miss the independence you had when you were working?"

"What independence? Having to be in an office at a certain time, having to do what other people told me to do?"

Perin laughed. "How did you know Uncle was the one you wanted to marry?"

"He thought I was the most wonderful creature. It was like I was floating on air around him, that I could do anything. And he didn't want to be the center of attention. No domineering dictates, no spoiled baby wanting another mother. It's marvelous to be someone's entire life." Aunt Safina stopped and looked at Perin. "Why all the questions?"

"Just wondering." Perin pondered what it would be like to be in Aunt Safina's shoes. Outwardly, she never seemed to have a care in the world, and yet she'd had her share of heartbreak, especially with her miscarriages.

Safina picked up one of Perin's hands. "Biting your nails. Your cuticles are a mess, too."

Perin pulled her hand away and picked up her tea. "Nervous habit."

"What are you nervous about?" Perin shrugged and gazed at the carved Moorish vault on the opposite wall. "I heard about that dinner with Kamal. You never thought of marrying him, did you? He's always struck me as pompous."

"He is, and no, I'd never marry him."

"What about Yousef? I heard you invited him to the club."

"Oh, no. He's a friend. He kept in contact with Father after we went to the desert. Father liked him."

"He's too old for you. Personally, I find Ali Zayer attractive."

Her stomach aflutter, Perin stroked her necklace and fixed her eyes on the antique brass pot on a shelf across the room. "He's engaged."

"Oh, engagements are broken all the time. As far as I'm concerned, until he's married, he's free. Does he know you like him?"

"I didn't say I did."

"Don't pretend with me. I saw you on the terrace, telling us about your interview with him, trying to sound professional. But the way your eyes lit up gave you away."

With a soft laugh, Perin said, "You're imagining things."

"Let's invite him to dinner here when Omer gets home from his trip."

"No, I don't want any setups."

"Sometimes you have to help fate and it seems like a good plan to me."

I can't handle another plan right now, Perin thought, as once again Imene popped into her mind. "I'm beginning to feel you're in cahoots with Nabil to get me married."

"Why are you acting like it's a fate worse than death? But just to set the record straight, I'd do a better job than Nabil."

Two days later, on Thursday, after the baths and their hair appointments, Perin and Shereen arrived at the ranch as the sun was setting. Its waning light cast a reddish-orange glow over the house and the surrounding pastures.

Shereen unbuttoned her tunic as she strode across the verandah to the patio, exposing her ripped-knee jeans. She plopped down on one of the lounge chairs and let out a sigh.

Perin sat next to her and cradled the knapsack she'd brought for Imene. The queasiness she'd felt all day intensified to the point of nausea. She told herself she had to appear calm for Shereen's sake.

When she'd told Shereen Imene might have to hide at the ranch a day or two longer than originally planned, Shereen had exploded, saying she never should have let Perin talk her into hiding a fugitive on her family's property.

Perin had corrected her, saying she didn't like the word fugitive for someone whose family wanted to kill her because they thought she'd dishonored the family name. She'd been forced to tell Shereen Imene's story so she'd understand the urgency.

"I just can't sit here," Shereen said. "We can at least hide the food and water while we're waiting."

"You're certain the orchard and stable staffs are gone?"

"Have you seen anyone?" Shereen said, her voice tight.

So far everything was going as planned. Darkness would soon fall, making it difficult to see figures moving around. And they had an hour until the night watchman started his shift.

As they entered the main stable, the horses stirred and shifted in their stalls. "Don't turn on the lights," Shereen said. "I don't want to take a chance that someone sees us." She pointed to the rafters filled with stacks of hay. "It's better if she stays up there."

"But we agreed she could hide in one of the empty stalls."

"I'll decide what's best," Shereen said with a tone of resentment that was unlike her.

Perin took a flashlight from Shereen and climbed up. She hid the knapsack in the corner, under a bale of straw. On her way back down, her foot on the last rung of the ladder, she heard a car drive up. "Zahara's early."

Shereen dropped her head to her chest as if she no longer possessed the strength to hold it up.

The car stopped and flicked its headlights twice. Perin started toward it and then froze. "That's not Zahara's car."

"Oh, great," Shereen muttered as she clung to the doorframe.

"But it has to be." Perin's heart thumped wildly. "That's the signal. Maybe she drove a different car."

"I'm going to be sick." Shereen put her arms around her waist and doubled over.

A woman got out of the passenger side carrying a small cloth bag. Her scarf was pulled down on her head. It was too dark for Perin to make out her features.

After the car turned around and headed back down the driveway, the woman came closer and Perin recognized Imene's deep-set eyes and pointed chin.

"I thought Dr. Zahara was bringing you," Perin said. "Who was that?"

"Her husband. She had to see a patient. She said to wait for her."

An unplanned change. Waves of heat rolled over Perin. Of course, Zahara would want to check on things before Perin left, to ensure all was in order.

Imene bowed her head and thanked Shereen for letting her stay. "… you are so kind."

Shereen sprang to life. "Have you eaten? We didn't leave you much. I can see what cook has left in the kitchen."

"I ate a large meal before coming."

"It's terrible what's happening to you." Shereen furrowed her brows and shook her head. "I can't imagine my—if there's anything you need, let me know."

Perin marveled at her friend's newfound fervor and could just see how eager she'd be to tell someone how she helped save a woman's life, if she dared.

Leading Imene into the stable, Perin asked, "You know the Tuaregs might not be able to come as planned."

Imene nodded. "I can wait."

"Do you have the money?" Imene tapped her diaphragm.

Perin could not believe how calm Imene seemed, calmer than her and Shereen. She was so changed from when Perin first met her. While still shy, it was like something in her core had stiffened, giving the young woman the fearlessness to follow her path.

Imene had just hid in the rafters when Perin heard another car coming up the driveway; it had to be Zahara. She stepped outside with Shereen as the car came closer without stopping. Its headlights blinded Perin for a moment before it turned into the parking area. The driver didn't flick the lights.

"It's Kamal," Shereen said. "What'll we do?"

Perin ran back inside and told Imene to be quiet and not move until he left. She went back out and grabbed Shereen's arm as Kamal walked toward them. Out of the side of her mouth, she told Shereen to act natural and say something. Standing shoulder to shoulder, Perin felt Shereen's body shake.

"Well, I, umm, I didn't think—" Shereen said, her voice cracking.

Kamal asked Shereen what she was doing out in the dark before staring at Perin for a long uncomfortable moment, his look a mixture of pride and scorn.

"We were … well, we thought we'd come and see the stars." Shereen pointed up and tried to smile, her brows scrunched together. "You can't see them in the city with all the lights."

Listening to Shereen's halting voice, Perin wished she could say something to encourage her, to let her know she was doing fine.

"Why are you here?" Shereen asked Kamal.

"The foreman called. Said one of the horses was anxious, kicking its abdomen and lying down more than usual."

Kamal walked into the stable and turned on the light. A yellowish glow poured out of the stable like a beacon, beckoning bugs and night creatures. The strong light and visitors unsettled the horses more than before; a cacophony of snorts, mixed with the thrashing of hoofs, filled the air. Perin was glad for the noise; it would mask any unexpected sounds.

In one of the front stalls, Kamal stroked the hindquarters of a thoroughbred with a white splotch on his forehead; the horse kept pawing at the ground and curling its upper lip. Next, Kamal looked into the horse's mouth. While he was busy feeling its underbelly, Perin looked around to see if they'd accidentally left anything out, or if Imene was visible in any way. Everything looked fine.

Perin kept an ear open for Zahara's car, and for the first time that evening, she noticed the chirping of crickets. The wind picked up and she made out the sound of waves crashing on the nearby shores.

Perin heard Shereen's voice straining to mask her fear as she asked Kamal what was wrong with the horse. "Probably colic. Maybe he ate something an infected rodent or beetle or something left in the hay," Kamal said. "Why are you acting so strange?" The metallic chill of his voice left Shereen at a loss for words.

"It's because of me." Perin stepped forward. "I told Shereen what happened at dinner. If I'd known you'd be here, I wouldn't have come."

Kamal's body tensed. "You both have to leave. I want the stables cleaned out now." Perin and Shereen looked at each other. Kamal's words hung in the air until Shereen said, "It's the weekend. The workers are gone."

"They'll have to come back. I don't want my horses twisting their guts."

Shereen, her face chalky, whispered to Perin that Imene had to leave.

Perin knew there was no choice. Kamal was suspicious, watching their every move. She wondered if Imene could hide in the nearby fields or orchards. But it was August—too hot during the day, and a farmhand might see her and chase her off. She had to be stationary so the Tuaregs could find her. As she was trying to think of what to do, Perin again heard the sound of tires on gravel.

Kamal walked to the center of the stable and looked out at the driveway.

"It's my ride," Perin said. *Please Allah let it be Zahara. Angels and djinns, please help Shereen and me through this. Don't let Imene be discovered.*

The car stopped before it reached the stable and its lights flicked.

With Kamal's back to her, Perin whispered in Shereen's ear, "I'll pretend to leave, but I'll wait at the end of the driveway. Have Imene meet me there."

Zahara started to get out of the car. Perin waved her back inside and popped her head in the passenger side window. "We can't stay here. The brother came home, a horse is sick, and they're cleaning out the stables. We'll wait for Imene down the road."

"I knew this wasn't a good idea." Zahara's voice was flat and dry.

"Stop. I don't want to hear it."

Kamal was watching them. "Thanks, Shereen, for a night of stars. I'll call you later." She tossed her bag on the car's seat and got in.

Kamal turned off the stable lights and said something to Shereen. As soon as Zahara turned the car around and started down the driveway, Kamal headed toward the house. Perin watched out the back window until he was out of sight. Zahara stopped the car and waited. A few minutes later Imene emerged with the bags; she got in and lay down across the backseat.

"Why didn't you know about this?" Zahara's words were sharp.

"It was just decided. Stop being unreasonable," Perin said.

Zahara turned off the headlights and in a raised voice, said, "Hurry, think of something."

"You can leave me here," Imene said. "I'll find a way to hide."

Again, Perin was amazed to hear the confidence in Imene's voice. *Necessity changes us*, she thought to herself.

In the distance, Perin again heard waves slamming upon the sands. "Wait. My father has a plot of land on the shore not far from here. I've never seen it, but he told me about it and I think I can find it. There's supposed to be a shack where Imene could stay." As soon as the words came out of her mouth, Perin regretted it. If she couldn't find the shack, Zahara would blame her.

"We have no choice, unless you can come up with something else in the next few minutes."

"I don't see you thinking of—no, wait. We can't do anything yet. What if the Tuaregs are already on their way here?"

Zahara tapped her fingers on the steering wheel. "Well, find out."

Perin reached Yousef on his mobile phone.

"I just spoke to the men and tonight's off, but they'll come tomorrow. I have to have the exact location of the new place. And, Perin, no more surprises."

"I promise. No more." She closed her mobile and turned to look out the back window. "We can't stay here. Kamal—he might leave soon. Quick, turn right."

Zahara turned on the lights and drove east on the highway. "Maybe it's best she didn't stay there. Your friend could have blurted out something."

Yes, thought Perin, perhaps it was best. It had pained her to see Shereen so tormented.

There was little traffic on the coastal highway. With the new moon, Perin had to rely on the headlights of Zahara's car to keep track of the route markers that counted the kilometers from the center of town. The Tuaregs had to have the exact number so they could find Imene.

After passing the second village, the countryside along the shore became desolate. Prime real estate for international developers, Perin thought. As much as she hated to admit it, there might be some advantage to having the fundamentalists in power—foreigners would be wary to invest and the coastline wouldn't be snatched up for gaudy resorts and vacation condos.

Perin strained to watch the road and finally saw the outline of a crane hovering over partially built walls. Her father had said a villa was being built next door. "It has to be right after that construction." They had just passed kilometer forty-seven.

Forty-seven. I'm too rattled to remember what Huda told me that number means.

Zahara turned into the lot. The car's lights illuminated a rustic wooden shed near a clump of palm trees. Its tin roof was covered in fronds.

"Get the flashlight from the glove compartment," Zahara said.

The sky was awash in stars. In the distance, the lights of the city glimmered and formed a halo against the dark velvety sky. Seashells and small pebbles crunched under Perin's feet as she followed Zahara around the shack. There was a window in the back of it and another in the front. Both panes were broken. Zahara shined the flashlight through the front one and commented that it looked as if it had been empty a while. "Not cozy, but it'll do."

Perin turned the doorknob, but the door wouldn't budge. She put her weight against it and flung it open. A loud creak rang out and a dog started barking. Zahara said it was probably the watchdog next door and nudged Perin inside.

The first thing Perin saw was a cot in the corner. Tufts of horsehair stuffing spilled out of its lumpy mattress and next to it was a darkened spot where a cooking brazier had been placed. She walked around, careful not to step on the trash: wads of crumbled paper, a single plastic shoe with its sides split open, a dried-up apple core, and a plastic jug with the top third cut off.

"Get Imene," Zahara said. "Let's see what else is around here."

Perin bristled at Zahara ordering her around again. But tensions were high enough and this was no time to argue.

As they walked along the water's edge, Perin tried to focus on the sounds of the wind rustling through the trees and the water lapping on the shore. A few meters away, they found a small cove. "You could hide here also, if necessary," Zahara told Imene. "Let me know when you're out of the country." Zahara kissed Imene on both cheeks. "I hope we can count on you, if we need help in the future."

Perin shuddered. *Why was she saying this to Imene? Even though she seems stronger, all this had to be trying for her.* And it was too emotionally and physically draining for her to contemplate doing again—at least not until sometime far in the future. And until she was certain their methods were fail-safe.

Taking leave of Imene at the shack, Zahara told the young woman, "*Allah Yisallmak.*"

"May Allah guide your journey," Perin said. She embraced the young woman, holding her tight, not wanting to let go. She had developed a deep fondness for the young woman and felt responsible for her safety; she prayed that she'd reach her destination without harm. She was hesitant to leave until Zahara grabbed her arm and pulled her toward the car.

As they drove back to the city, Zahara said, "I have to stop at the apartment. With everything going on, I forgot to take some papers."

"Can't you do it another time? I need to get home. Mother thinks I went to Shereen's for a quick dinner."

"Yes, I have to go now. Remember the landlord takes the apartment back tomorrow. It's on the way." Zahara patted Perin's shoulder. "Stop worrying. You'll be home before you know it. And you'll sleep well tonight knowing you helped save someone's life."

All the way to Satellite Village, Perin had a nagging feeling that she should go straight home. But she couldn't let Zahara go alone.

Hidden Lives

When your heart is dark as iron, steadily polish yourself that the heart may become a mirror, a beautiful shine reflecting from within. Although iron is dark and dismal, polishing clears the darkness away. —Rumi

Zahara crept down the narrow streets devoid of traffic, knuckles taut as she gripped the wheel of the car. Men stood idly in front of metal-shuttered storefronts, and gathered around falafel carts festooned with carnival-colored lights. A makeshift light atop a car illuminated boys in tattered clothing as they played marbles in the middle of the road. A man stepped out from behind the raised hood and held up his hand. Zahara stopped. The man yanked a boy by the neck of his shirt and pulled him back while the other boys scattered. Zahara drove on and turned at the next street. She pulled into a parking place a few houses down from her building and told Perin she couldn't stay alone in the car; she'd have to accompany her.

Perin tucked a stray strand of hair inside her headscarf and took the flashlight Zahara handed her, placing it in the pocket of her tunic. She stared at the open entryway and hesitated, unable to move, as if stopped by an invisible wall. "What are you waiting for?" Zahara said, tugging on her sleeve.

The pungent aroma of stale cooking oil and onions saturated Perin's senses as she entered the apartment complex. The lone bulb still dangled from the hallway ceiling, a silent witness to the scrapes, stains, and marks along the peeling walls. Muted adult voices seeped out from doorways. It was after ten o'clock.

Zahara's leather-soled heels clicked up the cement steps. Perin, her tennis shoes muffling her footsteps, tensed every time Zahara's shoe hit the hard surface. When they reached the third-floor landing, a lock turned and Zahara stopped and looked both ways. Perin held her breath and waited. No one appeared. Zahara took out her keys and opened the door to apartment 3B.

The light from the hallway leapt into the front room, highlighting the cracked tile floor. The room was empty except for the battered sofa and tie-dyed Indian curtains over the windows. Perin dashed over the doorway and Zahara bolted the door. "The electricity's off," Zahara said. "We can use the flashlight when we're away from the windows."

Perin's heart thumped in her throat. "Do you think someone's watching?"

"Better not take chances." Zahara started down the dark hallway. The bedroom doors on each side were closed.

Except for a faint hissing noise that oozed up from the street, it was eerily quiet in the apartment. Zahara entered the last door on the right, the side of the building facing the back alley, and inside the small windowless space, a musk-like smell assaulted Perin; she plugged her nose. Strewn on the floor were yellowed newspaper clippings, a magazine, a blouse with a sleeve ripped off, and an empty cup on its side, its trail of coffee grinds looking as if awaiting a fortune teller's gaze.

Zahara went to the far corner. "Hold the flashlight here, at this spot where I'm pointing." On her knees, Zahara took a metal nail file from her bag and pried up a section of the floorboard, coaxing up pieces of wood until she had a cavity large enough to accommodate her hand. She pulled out papers with curled, dirty edges.

"What are they?

"Contact information for the women, their relatives, their histories." Zahara opened her tunic and stuffed the papers inside her blouse. "I can't let anyone find them. I'll bury them in my backyard."

She replaced the slats of wood and motioned for Perin to go out of the room first. They were almost to the living room when Perin heard a car pull up in front of the building. Doors slammed, followed by loud voices. Perin froze and looked at Zahara.

"Turn off the light," Zahara said before putting her index finger to her lips.

Footsteps trudged up the outside walkway. Perin tracked them into the downstairs hall, then up the first flight of stairs—plodding, lumbering steps weighted down with menace. Her nervousness amplified every sound she heard, and the dampness in her armpits prickled.

Zahara pulled Perin back down the hallway and into the last bedroom facing the street. The light outside shone through the curtains, setting the room ablaze in blood-red hues. Zahara hovered at the door. "Look out and tell me what you see."

Perin cracked open the curtain, the gauze-like fabric fluttering in her hand. Steam hissed from an open manhole and cast a fog over a black car, double-parked in front of the building; a bearded man in a gray robe and black turban stood next to it. He gestured and another car pulled up alongside him.

"It's the police," Perin gasped, her body rigid with fear.

"Get away from the window."

As Perin rushed toward Zahara, the flashlight slipped from her hand and landed with a thud, nailing her to the spot. Zahara grabbed her by the arm, pushed her into the corner near the door, and placed herself in front of Perin.

The footsteps grew louder. They were on the second floor. Perin, her voice quivering, asked if there was another place they could hide.

"Quiet." Zahara cocked her ear against the door.

The footsteps grew closer and then stopped. There was a loud thwack. "Open up. Police."

Perin felt a pressure striking her chest, beating in-sync with each bash on the door. How did they know they were inside? *Were they followed, or had there been a stakeout, awaiting their return?*

Sweat spread across Perin's back as they continued to whack the door. The sound of wood splintering made her close her eyes, and her mother and father appeared in a vision. She ran her fingers over the turquoise stones of her necklace for a few seconds, and remembered her father's words—*what if I'm not there to protect you.* She pushed Zahara toward the window. "Jump. It's our only chance."

"We'll kill ourselves," Zahara said as she pinned Perin back against the wall.

The door crashed down and a voice cried out, "Search the rooms. You—in there. You, come with me."

Perin gripped Zahara's arm as heavy footsteps bounced off the floor and resounded into the hallway. She stared at the knot in the back of Zahara's scarf and remembered what the family cook Huda taught her as a child: "Call on the angels when you need help." *Please, oh please, dear angels, help us. I swear … I swear I'll never do this again.* She called on the good *djinns* for help.

The footsteps came closer, pounding in Perin's head like a clapper hitting the inside of a bell.

The men entered the room next door.

Perin's head started to spin. She lowered her chin to her chest to try and stop the lightheadedness.

The door swung open and nearly hit Zahara in the face. One thin plank of wood separated them from the intruders. Zahara squashed Perin against the wall and the pressure on Perin's chest made it difficult to breathe.

One of the men walked into the room and Perin caught a glimpse of a bearish man in combat boots, a rifle running parallel to his leg—one of the religious police's militia escorts. As he walked toward the window, his foot hit the flashlight Perin had dropped.

Zahara's body tensed and she pushed Perin flush against the wall.

"What is it?" the man by the door asked as he shuffled into the room. The light from the street silhouetted the religious policeman's short, plump figure, his nose shaped like the beak of a hawk.

The man with the rifle picked up the flashlight and turned it on, running its light along the back wall and toward the corner where they were hiding. It caught the edge of Zahara's shoulder. "There they are!" the militiaman said.

He slammed shut the door and grabbed Zahara by the arm, flinging her into the middle of the room, where she landed on her hands and knees. He raised his rifle and thrust its butt down on her back. Her screams echoed against the walls.

Instinctively, Perin lurched out and tried to catch hold of the rifle but it was moving too fast. Zahara raised her arms over her head as he struck her shoulder. Before Perin could intervene again, the religious policeman caught hold of Perin's necklace and pulled her toward him. She jerked back and the necklace broke, its stones bouncing and pinging on the wooden floorboards.

Perin stumbled against the wall and her balance faltered. The man grabbed her by the wrist and twisted it until she fell to her knees. She shrieked as his baton landed on her back. Dazed, she struggled to her feet. As she staggered around, she heard something shatter.

The policeman pounced on her. His hands encircled her throat and she started to choke.

She grabbed at his scraggly beard. He blocked her hands with his arms. She was woozy. Flailing, she reached around his arm and jabbed her thumb into his eyeball. He pitched back and doubled over, his hands covering his eye. Before she could check on Zahara, he was standing up again. Whipped into a frenzy, he threw Perin to the floor. As she scrambled to get away, something fell on top of her and pinned her to the floor. Sprawled out, she gasped for air while strike after strike came down from above, vibrating through the object on top of her.

Perin thought she vaguely heard one of the men say *make sure they're dead*. And then a hand fell in front of her face and she felt excruciating pain at the back of her head, as if a searing blade had been thrust into her cranium.

Everything went black.

Afloat at Sea

This world is full of remedies. But you have no remedy until God opens a window for you. You may not be aware of that remedy just now. In the hour of need it will be made clear to you. The Prophet said God made a remedy for every pain. —Rumi

Perin struggled to free herself. She was adrift on an ocean and the shore was close, but she couldn't reach it. She yelled for someone to help, but no one heard or saw her and tides took her farther away. Her father put out his hand and she tried to grasp it. "Don't give up. Don't give up," he said before gliding away.

Hushed tones pranced and leaped around her and she tried to let them know that she was all right, that she just needed them to pull her out of this sea, but she was powerless, incapable of responding, paralyzed within the current that pulled her down deeper and deeper.

"… consciousness … gradual. We … don't … months … effects … every case…."

Perin heard the words *young and healthy*. She wondered who they were talking about.

"… injuries … kidneys…."

Kidneys. Huda's cooking one of my favorite dishes. I can help her cut the onions.

Perin ebbed away for a moment and then the voices continued. "… spleen and liver don't … damaged."

Huda doesn't cook kidney with liver. I don't think I'll like it.

"Talk … unconscious can hear. Comforting words … medicine…."

Medicine—she forgot to tell her father to take his medicine. He would have been all right, if she had reminded him.

She sensed something brush against the side of her face.

"Good, Rashid ... speak ... left ear."

Rashid can help me. He always helps me.

She tried to clutch onto her younger brother, to tell him she was sinking again to the bottom of the sea. She struggled to kick her legs, to propel herself to the surface, but they wouldn't move. For a split second, she lifted her eyelids a fraction and saw a dimly lit room, and though the blurry haze, she thought she made out figures. She closed her eyes and their voices swirled overhead, the figures flitting from one side of her head to the other before gradually growing softer as the wind on her ocean blew them away. A wave came up and she floated out to sea again.

The next time Perin opened her eyes, early morning light was scattered around the room, sneaking through the metal slats of the shutters, and skirting out from the small space where the shutters met the windowsill. Nearby, she heard a clicking sound and someone mumbling.

She fought to emerge from the void and little by little, her eyes stayed open longer. Huda was hunched over next to her, hands in prayer pose, prayer beads intertwined in her fingers. "Merciful One, please grant us this blessing. We are but your servants."

Perin tried to move her hands but they were too heavy; there was something stiff under her left arm. "Imene," Perin muttered. "Did she—"

Huda leaned closer. "Oh, child, you're awake. Merciful One, we give You praise."

"Did she get away?"

"*Habibti*, I don't know what you're talking about. Don't say another word. I'll get someone." Perin felt Huda's kiss on her forehead, one kiss, then another, and another.

"Where am I?" she asked. But Huda had already left.

The back of her head throbbed with pain and an intense tiredness overcame her. She succumbed to its beckoning and closed her eyes, once again descending into blackness.

Sometime later she heard a voice, asking her to open her eyes. This time it was easier to force her eyelids open and she saw their family doctor. "Perin, it's Dr. Kareem. You've been unconscious for two days. You were found in an apartment in Satellite Village. Do you remember what you were doing there?"

She tried to shake her head, but it hurt too much. *Why did she go to Zahara's?* Zahara closed up the apartment. She couldn't tell anyone about the apartment or the women could get hurt. "Am I going to be all right?"

"With time. Your mother and brothers are outside. I'll let you see them after I examine you." Dr. Kareem put his index finger in front of her face and had her follow it as he moved it from right to left and back again. Next he asked her to look up and down, diagonally, and straight ahead.

The nurse moved the board under Perin's arm that held the I.V., and the doctor pushed her onto her side. Pain shot through her body like arrows guided by the wind. She bit her lower lip and held her screams inside. The doctor peeled down the bandage at the back of her head; she flinched when he stretched the skin around the injury. "There's still bruising, but you're healing nicely." He replaced the bandage and opened the back of her hospital gown. As he gently tapped up and down her back, he said, "Tell me where it hurts."

"All over." A tear rolled down her cheek.

"You were hit hard, so I expect it to be sore. Now come back this way."

Perin yelped as the back of her head touched the pillow.

"The neurologist will run some tests later and he and I will monitor you in hospital for a few more days. Once we release you, you'll have to stay in bed until I give permission for you to get up. Complete bed rest I'm talking about. You can see only your family now, and afterward, if I'm pleased with your progress, your friends can visit." Dr. Kareem smiled. "You're one of the fortunate ones."

Perin frowned. "This is lucky?"

Assia rushed into the room, kissed Perin on the forehead, and stroked her cheek. Perin saw the sorrow etched on her face. "Mother, I'm sorry—"

"Hush. You're safe and that's all that matters."

Nabil came in and stood behind Assia, his head drooping as if burdened by a bag of rocks hanging from the back of his neck. Rashid put his arm around Nabil and said, "Good to see you back with the living." Assia turned around and swatted his arm.

"Is everything going to be all right?" she asked her mother.

"It will be once you're home. Don't think about anything now, just rest and get better."

Dr. Kareem asked her brothers to step out into the hallway. After they left, Assia moistened a handkerchief with lavender water and placed it on Perin's forehead, just like she used to do when Perin was little and couldn't sleep.

Perin touched her throat. "My necklace. Where's my necklace?"

Assia turned to the nurse. "Can you see if you can find it? It's important to her."

The nurse rummaged through the cupboard and the corner cabinet. "Someone must have put it somewhere for safekeeping. I'll ask around."

Dr. Kareem walked back into the room with Nabil and Rashid. "Enough stimulation. They can visit again this evening."

After they left, Perin wondered what Dr. Kareem told her brothers outside the room. She sensed they were not telling her everything. As she was imagining what could be wrong with her, Imene's image appeared in her mind. She had to call Zahara. She might know by now if Imene reached the border safely and Zahara could tell her why she went to Satellite Village.

As quickly as the thoughts came, they disappeared, and Perin fell into slumber with only the good *djinns* guiding her dreams.

Perin's first week home from hospital the days melded, one into another. Her family flitted in and out as she alternated between deep sleep, dozing, and wakefulness. Pain and the headaches Dr. Kareem warned her about were constant companions, and it also hurt to use her eyes so she didn't try to read, and resigned herself to the prescribed rest.

In her listlessness, she participated in the life of the house through its sounds: Arabia yelped and scratched at the tree outside her window to chase away the birds that alit there in the morning; Mohammed tuned the cars' engines, and later, when he washed them, she charted the tin bucket's journey as it scraped across the driveway; the gardener clipped the bushes that had grown tall with the summer rains; and Huda clanged pots and pans as she prepared meals. But what especially comforted her was the sound of voices—muted, laughing, serious, hushed—each one reminding her she was alive.

She often tried to remember what had happened, but she'd only see Imene's face, and she kept telling herself it would come to her later, she had to be patient and let it go for now.

Before Dr. Kareem's visit on her eighth day home, some of Perin's energy returned and she was able to push herself upright in bed. Her eyes followed the golden sheen that emanated from the partially open shutters, streaking across the foot of her bed, highlighting the wood grain on her armoire and the painting of the scribe on the maize wall. She trailed it across to her desk and her eyes rested on the photo of her father; she longed for him to be there to comfort her, even though she knew it would have distressed him to see her injured.

She glanced at the picture next to his. There she was with Eva, standing against the railing at Battery Park in New York, the Statue of Liberty in the background, when they'd line-bladed half the length of Manhattan, months ago, the day after graduating. They'd wanted to breathe in the city one more time before they left to start their new careers, full of hopes to make a difference, to make their marks.

She fingered the blue embroidery on her handkerchief-linen nightgown and grew sad for those dreams that had tarnished like silverware left out on the beach.

Then an image flashed in front of her eyes. It was the woman she and Eva had seen beaten on the ride from the airport. She flinched and felt an imaginary blow to her shoulder, then her eyes suddenly filled with tears. But she didn't know why.

Longings

*Sometimes in order to help He makes us cry. Happy the eye
that sheds tears for His sake. Fortunate the heart that burns for His sake.
Laughter always follows tears. Blessed are those who understand. Life blossoms
wherever water flows. Where tears are shed divine mercy is shown. —Rumi*

The following day, as Perin struggled to adjust the pillows on her bed, her head started pulsating. She laid back and gazed at the photo of her father, her hand stroking her throat; the nurse had not found her necklace.

Her eyes settled on her laptop, which was next to her father's picture. Eva had to be wondering why she hadn't written. She wanted to write, but it remained a nascent thought, one she was unable to infuse with energy.

She still had no recollection of what happened to her and it was making her anxious. Zahara and Imene were always present in her mind; she had to find out why she'd gone to Zahara's apartment, and if Imene had escaped. After that, she wanted to thank Shereen for helping.

Nadira was in the hallway, running a dust mop over the landing, occasionally hitting it against the walls. "Nadira," Perin called out, "please come here. I need you to look for my phone." Perin heard the mop handle hit the floor with a thud, and then the housekeeper's small frame hovered at the door before entering Perin's room with measured steps. She could not find the phone.

"Please ask my mother if she's seen it."

Nadira nearly stumbled over her own feet in a rush to get out of the room, no doubt attributing Perin's injury to bad *djinns* lurking around.

A few minutes later, Assia came into her room. "I haven't seen your phone. Did you have it the night you were hurt?"

"I can't remember. My memory's buried. I only get fragments … sounds and thoughts—you said my friends called."

"Shereen wants to know when she can visit, some of your school friends, Mr. Zayer, and Safina and Omer, of course."

Perin wondered what Ali felt when he heard she'd been injured. He'd wanted to protect her by putting her on leave of absence and yet that very act propelled her into danger. There was no chance now of her going back to work. While sad about it, she also sensed a strange liberation, and at the same time, she knew she'd have to find something meaningful to do to fill the void, something she'd figure out later when she was healed.

"Zahara … didn't she call?"

"Who's Zahara?"

"She's … she's the doctor I was helping … with the used clothing."

Assia shook her head and straightened the top sheet on Perin's bed. "Huda didn't mention her either." Perin winced. Assia placed her hand on Perin's forehead as if feeling for a fever. "See what happens when you try to do too much. Rest now. You'll have plenty of time to talk to people later."

Perin didn't have the energy to argue. She closed her eyes and welcomed the whirl of white clouds that lifted her up and glided her away.

Later, Huda brought her bouillon and fresh baked bread, placing the tray on the bedside table as Perin tried to sit up. "Wait. I'll help you."

Perin shook her head. "I have to start doing things myself."

"Tomorrow. Today I'm still taking care of you." Huda put her arms around Perin and hoisted her up. "The three best doctors are: trust in Allah, time, and patience—and maybe there's a fourth." Huda let out a chuckle. "Me."

Huda tucked a napkin into Perin's nightgown and opened a vial of turmeric, placing a dab of the spice in the middle of Perin's forehead to keep her safe. As curlicues of steam spiraled upward from the soup, Huda cut off a slice of bread and handed it to Perin. "I want to ask you something," Perin said. Huda nodded as she blew on a spoonful of broth. "I know everyone's worried about me. You hear them talking. What are they saying?"

Huda kept her eyes on the spoon. "They're worried. They talk about what the doctor says. What we should do for you."

Perin wondered if she really was going to be all right. Perhaps to encourage her, Dr. Kareem had given an overly optimistic prognosis and only later she'd find out she couldn't walk well, or she would have memory lapses.

Huda brought the spoon to Perin's mouth and Perin swallowed the salty liquid. "If there's more—tell me. I won't say you told me."

Huda paused and puckered her mouth the way she did when she was debating something. "Nabil blames himself. He thinks he should have done more to protect you."

It pained Perin to hear this. She'd told the family several times that she alone was responsible for what had happened to her. "Anything else?" Her hand trembling slightly, Huda fed Perin another spoonful of soup. "You seem nervous."

"And why not? Terrible shock. Your mother and Nabil were very angry at you. Even Rashid. And me, worrying sick that you were going to die." Huda shook her head. "Just like when you were a child, always asking questions, always wanting to know everything. A person gets no peace around you." She stopped and her tone became plaintive. "Eat now so you'll get strong."

A profound sense of guilt overcame Perin as she realized how she'd worried and distressed the people she loved most. She apologized to Huda. "Hush," Huda said, "I want to forget how my heart hurt."

Dr. Kareem had good news after he examined Perin that evening. "You can get up for short periods, thirty minutes at a time, and start by sitting in the garden and taking meals in the dining room."

"Can I see my friends?"

"As long as you don't overdo it. You'd be surprised how exhausted you can get just talking to people, and don't talk to anyone who might upset you."

Perin thought the only thing that could upset her further now was if Imene hadn't got away. Whatever happened to Imene, she had to find out. Not knowing was agonizing.

She thanked the doctor and asked her mother to bring her a phone. A few minutes later, Rashid came into her room. "Before you call anyone, we need to talk. Why were you at Satellite Village with Zahara?"

"I can't remember. Give me the phone and I'll find out."

"First you listen. A woman also was brought into the hospital with you that night. She was beat up, too, and the doctors recognized her—she worked at University Hospital. It was Zahara."

"Oh, no. Is she all right?"

"They tried to revive her, but she was already dead."

After his words slowly sunk in, Perin felt woozy. She leaned over the bed and started to vomit. Rashid grabbed the wastepaper basket and put it under her until dry heaves left her exhausted. Every muscle in her body ached again and her head throbbed.

"The neighbors saw the police raid the apartment around the time it happened, and they heard noises, but waited until it was quiet to check. The door was ajar and they found both of you on the floor." Rashid let out an exhalation through his mouth. "You were probably saved because Zahara was on top of you. She took most of the blows."

Tears welled up in Perin's eyes. "It's my fault. They were watching me."

"If they'd wanted you, they would have come for you here and not at Zahara's"

"They followed me." Perin clutched her head. "She died trying to save me."

"Huda said you asked about Imene. Isn't she one of the women Zahara was helping?"

The room started to spin and Perin turned her face into the pillow. "Not now, not now."

"Damn it, Perin, look at me! No one's going to tell you this, but you almost died." He emphasized the words with a punishing hoarseness.

Fighting back another wave of nausea, Perin said, "Please don't yell." Rashid look down and shuffled his foot. "Yes, she was one the women. She needed to escape because her family was going to kill her." Perin laid back on the pillow. "Please don't tell anyone."

"Maybe you'll realize you can't do this superhero stuff. Good thing you didn't end up like Zahara, because it would have killed mother. And to think I helped you." He slammed the mobile phone down on the bedside table and left.

The next morning, still weighed down with guilt, Perin couldn't piece together what happened and she invited Shereen over for afternoon tea, hoping her friend would shed some light on what took place.

Seated in the courtyard, Shereen gave Perin an encouraging smile and said, "You don't look bad, just a little pale, and some bruising." It didn't matter to Perin what she looked like. At least she was alive.

Nadira placed a pitcher of fresh lemonade on the table between them and as soon as she left to go back inside the house, Perin asked if Imene got away. "But, Perin, you took her away." Shereen told her what happened that night at the ranch, but it was not enough to trigger Perin's memory. "The next thing I knew, you were in hospital and your mother was asking me questions. Don't worry, I only told her a friend I didn't know picked you up." Shereen stopped. "You look like you're in pain; can I get you something?"

"The physical pain's nothing. Shereen, Zahara was killed."

"I know. Terrible." Shereen let out a laugh between gasps and waved her hand in front of her face as if trying to shake tears away and then blurted out, "I can't think about that any more. I still have nightmares. Ever since you left the ranch, I haven't been able to sleep, and I keep thinking someone is going to ask me about Imene and I see that doctor lying dead. It could have been you."

Perin was alarmed to see the terrified look on Shereen's face, like a puppy caught in a snare trap with wolves nipping at its heels. After she asked for Shereen's forgiveness, she tried to assure her that the nightmares would go away, even though she wasn't certain that Shereen's, or hers for that matter, would disappear any time soon.

As soon as Shereen seemed calmer, Perin said, "This is my first time out of bed and I'm feeling weak. Maybe you can come again in a few days."

"Oh, yes, certainly." Shereen fumbled with her tunic and bag and then stood up. "Let me know if you need anything."

"Your company would be nice," Perin said out of politeness, knowing their relationship had changed, like a chasm time would only erode more. Perin had always thought of Shereen as a kindred spirit—from the same background with similar experiences growing up, same value systems, but then Perin went away, returned home, and met Zahara—forever altering her path. Shereen, like many others, would follow tradition and marry, devote herself to her husband and children, never questioning the justices and injustices of the world, as long as she and her family were all right. It saddened Perin to realize this, and she wished she could be more accepting of Shereen. Isn't that what friendship is about, to accept the entire person, not just the parts you like? Maybe she was too hard on Shereen, expecting her to have the same standards. Was it fair to judge her in the light of whether she measured up to Perin's subjective criteria? Probably not, Perin decided. Perhaps one day she could be more generous toward Shereen, but for now a door had closed—it was the end of their friendship as she had known it.

She had to speak to Yousef. Perhaps he could tell her what happened. She reached him as he was packing to return home to Lebanon.

"Remember, we changed the pickup location. There was a lot with a shack on the coastal highway at kilometer forty something—forty-seven I believe it was."

My father's place?

"They took her to a mountain village for a few days, where she waited until the camel train was ready to leave."

Perin imagined Imene stepping across an invisible line in the sand. *I am not willing*, she mumbled. *We did it, Zahara, we did it.*

The next day, Perin took lunch in the dining room, hardly able to eat and fighting back tears, as the burden of what had happened to Zahara weighed upon her. Nadira handed her a package wrapped in paper from a bookstore in the colonial part of town. It was a tome of poems by Rumi. She randomly opened it. *"I want to sing like the birds sing, not worrying about who hears or what they think."*

An ecru notecard fell out of the book; it was from Andrea.

Dear Perin, Your mother told me you were doing much better and that you could have visitors now. I was hoping to come over but with so much going on at work, I need to be here. You probably heard that Ali was jailed.

Perin blinked a few times and brought her head closer to the note as she reread the last paragraph. Her world was truly falling apart.

The police trumped up vague charges about him undermining national security. The rumor is that he'll be in prison for a while and he won't return to the paper. I don't know if that's his decision or the publishers. We're all hoping we'll have jobs. It's very tense around here, as you can imagine. Ghazi's acting editor.

That was why Ali hadn't called again to see how she was doing.

Take good care. Call me when you feel up to it. With affection, Andrea.

Perin placed the note back inside the book and returned to bed. The next three days she ate little and refused to leave her room. Concerned, Assia asked Dr. Kareem to stop over. After he examined Perin, he said, "You're healing well physically. It's not unusual to see depression in patients who have suffered major traumas, and even some surgeries." Perin didn't have it in her to tell him that it wasn't the injuries that were making her feel so alienated.

"I'll prescribe a mild antidepressant for you to take for a few weeks."

"I don't want any medication."

"Do as he says," Assia said, her face sagging. "It hurts me to see you like this."

For her mother's sake, Perin agreed and took the first dose later that afternoon; it helped her relax a little. As she was about to doze off, Nabil knocked on her door and came in. His slanted eyebrows gave his face a weary look, and she could tell he had something on his mind. He averted his eyes and clasped one hand inside the other. "Since father's death, I'm the one responsible for the family. I should have been firmer with you and set more boundaries, then you might not have been injured."

"And if it didn't snow in Switzerland in January—Nabil, please. I already told you I'm accountable for my actions. Stop blaming yourself."

"The woman they found you with, was she a friend?"

"I interviewed her for a story once," Perin said, not willing to open any doors for further questioning. With the precision of a surgeon, Nabil began asking questions—quick, decisive, antiseptic—about the night she was found in Zahara's apartment. She feigned she couldn't remember and brushed away the tear that crept down her cheek.

Nabil stopped asking and hesitated; his eyes fixed on the carpet. "I'm very sorry this happened to you." Nabil's chin quivered. "I wouldn't want anything to happen to you."

Two days later, it was women's day at the mosque and Assia told Perin she wanted them to go together. Remembering Dr. Kareem's instructions, Perin agreed, hoping the holy site would give her some peace. As she entered the courtyard with her mother, the sun struck the tops of the minarets and sent blazes of light against the outer walls. She put her shoes in one of the wooden bins while Assia dropped a donation into the metal slot on the outside wall. She didn't have to ask what blessing her mother prayed for—she, too, wished for a complete recovery, and guidance in how to still make a difference without endangering those she loved.

Women sat on carpets in the middle of the mosque, talking to friends and watching their children play. Perin and Assia walked around them before heading to the rear, where Perin leaned against the cool marble wall, and Assia placed several pieces of amber in her onyx bowl and set them aflame. Aromatic smoke rose as Assia walked to the *mihrab*, raised the bowl, and said a prayer. Sadness and love intermingled inside Perin as she watched her mother.

Assia returned and knelt beside Perin, placing the bowl in front of them and bowing down. As Perin lowered her body, her shoulder grazed her mother's; she reflected on her relationship with her mother and felt the bond of their womanhood.

"I'm sorry, Mother, for all I've put you through."

Assia touched Perin's cheek and smiled, a hint of sadness etched around the corners of her eyes. "*Habibti.*"

The Secret

*It is love that brings happiness to people. It is love that
gives joy to happiness. My mother didn't give birth to me, that love did.
A hundred blessings and praises to that love. —Rumi*

Several days after Perin visited the mosque with her mother, Ali called. He'd been released from jail and asked to see her. She suggested he come for tea the next afternoon, assuming his visit was a courtesy call to see how she was doing. But she also had to wonder if it signaled more. In spite of evidence to the contrary she still held hope she was more than a work colleague to him.

Wanting to look her best, she tried on several outfits, finally deciding on a long gauzy melon-colored skirt and matching geometric-swirl print blouse in chartreuse, pink, and buttercup yellow, an outfit Eva had convinced her to buy in New York's Soho: *Every girl should have something like this. It's perfect for when you're down in the dumps.* Innocent days, innocent wiles, Perin thought.

The first thing Perin noticed when Ali arrived was how gaunt he looked, with pronounced circles under his eyes.

He told her how he got through the ordeal of prison, stuck in a small cell with five other men, by writing about it on scraps of paper, wanting to remember what it felt like to be deprived of freedom. He confirmed that the owners of the paper wanted him out; they feared the police would use any pretext to arrest him again. "They let me tender my resignation so it didn't appear as if they were firing me."

Perin's eyes wandered over his handsome gray, brown, and rust tweed linen jacket. His shirt was open at the neck and it was the first time she'd seen him without a bow tie.

Wary of the answer, she asked, "What do you plan to do now?"

"I applied for an op-ed position at the *Cairo Times* and I'm waiting to hear from the Middle East News Agency."

The back of her head started to throb. "Won't it be hard on your mother if you're away?" she asked, really wanting to know about his fiancée. Fearing she'd overstepped polite decorum, she added, "I don't mean to pry, but you are her only son here, aren't you?"

Ali put a sugar cube in his tea and twirled it around with a demitasse spoon. "She'll probably come with me. I told her I'll need someone to take care of me."

Perin picked up her cup; it rattled against the saucer and she put it back down. "I thought I heard Andrea say you were engaged." Her heart beat wildly as she braced herself for Ali's answer.

Ali tilted his head heavenward and lowered his voice. "She must have been referring to a distant cousin." He faced Perin and smiled. "Our families had hoped we'd get together and we went through the motions for their sakes. But we both knew it wouldn't work."

She thought back to the day Ali had touched her hand. Her instincts had been correct. He did care, and now he was going away.

Placing a biscuit on a small dessert plate, he asked. "What are you going to do?"

Perin shook her head. She knew Nabil would never allow her to work again, at least not for a long time, and unless it was with children, or something she could do from home. He might also try to marry her off again, but she took comfort knowing few men would consider her eligible, as she was no doubt labeled a headstrong troublemaker.

"One day it'll just hit you over the head—oh, terrible choice of words." A pained look crossed Ali's face.

"I'm not that sensitive." Perin looked out the window at a barren shrub, dry from the summer heat.

Ali continued, "My mother always says if things don't go right, it means you're supposed to change directions."

Perin nodded. *Did it mean she wasn't supposed to be here? No, she told herself, running away never works. Once you start, how do you know when to stop? And wasn't part of life to learn to overcome hardships?* She'd stay and face whatever fate brought her.

"You did a wonderful job reporting on the fire at the school," Ali said, picking up the teapot to refill Perin's cup. "With time, you'd have been a terrific reporter. I had hoped to give you something more challenging in a year or so."

She smiled. It meant a lot to hear Ali's words, but it was useless to dwell on what could have been.

"I don't know how much of a career you can expect to have here now. Have you considered searching opportunities abroad?"

"I've thought about it and I prefer to stay here. I'll find something to do."

"I wasn't going to mention this, especially since I'm leaving, but I did a lot of thinking in jail … I wish we'd been able to see more of each other. But I was your boss." Ali put his hand on top of hers and she felt color rise in her face. In his subtle way, he was telling her he cared.

She noticed how elegant his wrist was, as if sculpted for playing the violin, and she remembered Aunt Safina suggesting they invite Ali to dinner. Why had she been reluctant? And now Ali was joining the list of those forced out of her world. "Don't go. If you leave, they win." She dabbed at the tear in the corner of her eye with a bent knuckle. "The country needs people like you; it needs to hear your voice."

Ali looked away and rubbed his hands together, and then turned back and looked directly at her. "I know what you're saying, but I think I can be more effective abroad. If I am wrong, I'll reconsider."

Before leaving, he told her he'd like to keep in touch and offered to help should she decide to pursue a career elsewhere.

She spent the rest of the afternoon replaying the moments they shared and pondering all the things that had been said between them over the months, as well as all that remained unspoken— wondering if she should have insisted more that he not leave. But what opportunities remained here for him? Deep down, she couldn't help but feel disappointed. He'd decided to leave instead of staying and fighting, while she was sticking it out.

Needing to be alone, she took dinner in her room. Later, before turning in to bed, she was restless and craved something sweet; her favorite nougat with pistachios, stored in a jar in the kitchen, called to her.

At the top of the stairs, she tied her robe around her waist and watched Huda hovering near the entrance to the living room. She tiptoed down and whispered in her ear, "What's so interesting that you have to eavesdrop?"

Huda jumped, then put her index finger to her lips and pushed back Perin.

"She says she's responsible for her actions," Perin heard Nabil say. "So, she'll have to face the consequences."

Perin ignored Huda's tugs and moved closer to the doorway.

"Dr. Kareem can't keep convincing them she's still recovering," Nabil said. "They're going to demand that one of their doctors examine her."

"We can't let her go to prison," Assia said, her voice quavering. "She could be tortured or worse."

Perin's mind reeled and she felt lightheaded. Her breath caught as she tried to brace herself against the wall, while Huda yanked on the back of her bathrobe.

"I can't keep bribing them," Nabil said.

Perin swatted Huda away.

"Can't we find a hiding place?" Assia said.

"Where?" Nabil asked. "For how long? A month? A year?"

"Maybe we can get her out of the country," Rashid said.

"You want all of us to be jailed?" Nabil said. "I won't let that happen to Mother."

"I could do it," Assia said. "Better me than her."

"I warned her, Father warned her," Nabil said, his voice raised. "And she did whatever she wanted. I told you this would happen." Nabil didn't speak for a few moments and then said, his voice cracking, "I'm as upset by this as you are. Don't think it doesn't torment me. I want nothing bad to happen to her. She's my sister, too."

Perin felt a pang in her chest and it was becoming harder to breathe.

"She has to go. No other option," Nabil continued, defeat edging his words.

"You're willing to sacrifice your own sister," Rashid said in a disgusted tone that distance could not diminish, "just to make your life easier, so you don't have to—"

"Keep your voices down," Assia said.

"They've already tried to kill her," Rashid said in a lower register. "What'll stop them if they have her in custody where no one knows what's going on?"

"Aiyee, don't say that," Assia wailed.

Something shifted inside Perin; it was too maddening and painful to just hide there, listening, without having a voice in what was to be her future. She entered the room and the conversation stopped. Her mother and siblings looked frantically at each other. Nabil shifted in his seat, Rashid looked up at the ceiling, and Assia put her hand to her mouth.

"I'm going to prison?"

Nabil looked first at Assia, and then Perin. He paused for a moment before saying, "The police issued a warrant for your arrest. The charge is subversive acts and carries a minimum sentence of three months for you. Uncle Omer got them to reduce it from six."

It was as if she were floating above her body, watching someone other than herself mouth her words. "I'll go. I've hurt you enough already. I don't want them to harm you. I'm so sorry. Please forgive me."

"No, you can't," Assia cried out. She went to Perin and hugged her. "Terrible things happen there."

Perin saw no way out; she'd only be exchanging one prison for another. "If I don't, you're all at risk. *Maktub.*"

"It's not destined. How can you say that?" Assia hugged Perin tighter.

As her mother and brothers all started talking at once, Perin blinked several times, and started to sway. She grabbed the back of a chair. Assia struggled to hold her up until Rashid rushed over and put his arm around her waist, helping her upstairs. Once again, sleep became her escape and solace.

Early the next morning, Assia and Rashid came into Perin's room. She feigned sleep, wanting a reprieve, if only for a few moments, from the inevitable and dreaded discussion of her imprisonment.

Assia shook her. "Rashid and I worked out a plan last night with Omer and Safina. Tell her, Rashid." Assia sat on the bed next to Perin.

"As you know, they're making it difficult for a woman to leave the country without the accompaniment of a male relative. But there's a way around it—for medical treatment that's not available locally. She'd need a letter from a physician testifying to the necessity of the treatment, and another letter from the head of her household, granting her permission to leave."

Perin pushed herself upright.

"Dr. Kareem has agreed to write a letter for you. He'll say you had a serious contusion—which is true—and it requires calibrated tests that can only be done abroad with special equipment."

Perin's thoughts swirled as she tried to digest what her brother had just told her. "Nabil will never agree."

"Don't worry," Assia said. "Nabil won't know until after you're gone. Omer found your name on a watch list and he thinks he can get you and Rashid new passports and identity cards with different names; Rashid's card will say he's head of household."

"Omer's friend at the French Embassy agreed to give you a visa," Rashid said.

"If I get caught—you heard Nabil, you could all be jailed." Perin shook her head. "No. It's too dangerous."

"Dangerous but not impossible," Rashid said.

"Tell her the rest," Assia told Rashid

"I take Dr. Kareem's and my letter, saying I'm head of household, to the magistrate's office and get them authorized. Omer will bribe the magistrate to get it done straightaway. Then I get the airline ticket."

"You have to do it, *habibti*, I won't allow my daughter go to jail."

Perin was taken aback by the force of her mother's words. She didn't want to go to jail and there was no other recourse now that she was on a state enemies list. "Only if I have to."

After her mother and brother left, she tried to imagine the possible scenarios: What would happen if she went to jail? What would happen to her family if she escaped? The enormity of what lay ahead weighed heavily on her. She really didn't care about herself any longer. She wanted assurance that her family would be fine.

She took out her prayer rug and knelt down, facing Mecca. *All Merciful One, protect me and my family. Father, what should I do? Please give me a sign.*

She heard a soft tap on her door. Assia walked in, saw the prayer rug, and turned to leave.

"Stay, I'm finished," Perin said, standing up. "I don't know what to think any more, Mother. I don't want to leave."

"You can't go to prison. Trust that we'll be fine. The plan may seem a bit—"

"I can't leave you like this." Perin rolled up the rug and sat on her bed.

"I'll be heartbroken, but ... Perin, there's something I've never told you. I don't know why, foolish pride, I guess. I made everyone in the family swear they would never tell you or your brothers." Perin looked up at her mother and prayed it wasn't any more bad news. "Everyone thought I went to Paris to study, and I did. But that wasn't the whole story."

As Perin watched her mother's lips, everything else faded into the background.

"My parents promised me in marriage to their friends' son when I finished school. He was nine years older, an arrogant, spoiled brat and on the chubby side. Oh, why not say it—he was fat. Anyway, I refused to marry him. It was terrible; I fought with my mother every day."

"Was she the one behind it?"

Assia nodded. "There was no way they were going to make me do it, so I devised a plan the summer after I graduated. A friend of mine was going to Morocco on holiday with her family and I talked her into insisting that I come, too, and my parents agreed."

Perin hung on her mother's every word. This had to be what Aunt Safina referred to as her trump card.

Assia explained how before they left for Morocco, she started collecting money for an airline ticket and a little extra to live on. She took her savings and Safina's, and her friend gave her what she had. Then one night, when everyone was asleep, she slipped out of the hotel and caught the first morning flight to Paris.

Perin looked at her mother as if seeing her anew.

"My parents were furious and they disowned me and cut off all communication. You always thought that I wanted to study and work in Paris, but initially I worked because I had to support myself. Later, I grew to love the work and my own independence, so you see, I understand you, although I'd hoped you would not be so independent and I could keep you near me." Perin smiled and sympathized with her mother, imaging how difficult it must be to lose a daughter.

"Anyway, I met your father and it wasn't long before we planned to marry. He wanted to have a big wedding here, but I persuaded him to marry in Paris, hoping my parents would welcome me back when they found out I was married to him, coming from such a respected family. But they still wouldn't have anything to do with me. When people asked them about me, they'd say they had only one daughter, Safina."

"How did you finally reconcile?"

"After Nabil was born, they wanted to see their first grandson and we slowly reconnected."

"You must have recognized yourself when I wanted nothing to do with Kamal."

"I should have stood up for you." Assia looked down and added in a wistful tone, "I feel better telling you." She took from her pocket the turquoise necklace Fuad had given her. "I want you to have this to accompany you and help you understand that even though you may not want to go away, sometimes you have to. *Maktub*."

It is destined.

Two days later, Perin, Assia, and Rashid sat in the courtyard with Safina and Omer as the last rays of the sun faded from the sky. Rashid had all the papers and Perin's flight was booked for that Wednesday, when Nabil would be at work. Rashid would accompany her to the airport as head of household and Aunt Safina suggested she go with them to divert anyone who might ask too many questions. Assia said she should be the one; she was Perin's mother. But Perin told her although she'd love to have her come along, it would make it even harder for her to leave. In the end, Assia, enveloped in a veil of sadness, agreed.

"You'll love living in Paris again, dear," Aunt Safina said. "Stay in the apartment with Tariq as long as you want."

"*Absolute* secrecy," Omer said. "Don't even tell Huda."

Perin's heart felt heavy. How could she leave without saying goodbye to Huda? And in spite of all their differences, she wanted to say goodbye to Nabil. And Shereen—she wished she could explain to her in person why she wouldn't attend her wedding. She thought of Ali and how she'd been disappointed in his leaving, and now she, too, was being forced, exiled from her homeland. She should not have been so quick to judge.

"I'd like to visit father's grave before I leave."

"You can't be seen in public," Rashid said. "If they think you look healed—"

"We'll find a way to take you tomorrow," Omer said.

Perin looked around as the day's waning light reflected off the water in the fountain, wanting to remember the palm trees outside her bedroom, rustling in the breeze; how the rose petals rode the fountain's gurgling waters; and how insects scurried across the patio while Arabia lounged, his breathing loud and rhythmic. And the aroma of Huda's vegetables roasting on the grill, mingled with the nectar of garden flowers.

Mourning had descended on the family. Perin watched them, reading in their eyes something she hadn't wanted to admit to herself—it might be a very long time before they could be together again.

Late afternoon sun hit the whitewashed tombstones and cast shadows around the cemetery. Construction workers, covered with a chalky residue, rested their backs against the gravestones and smoked. Assia handed Perin the silver shaker filled with rosewater before walking with Safina and Omer back to the car to leave her alone.

Perin bowed her head and sprinkled the water over her father's grave.

Baba, I miss you so much. I wish you were here to help me, to let me know if I'm doing the right thing. I don't want to go but Mother insists I leave. It hurts so much to think of not being with the family and I don't know when I'll see them again. Only the unknown lies ahead and it scares me. But I remember you used to tell us when we got lost on trips that the unknown is the most exciting voyage of all. I hope that's the way it turns out for me. Watch over everyone. Please don't let my leaving harm them. I love you so much.

Perin pressed her fingers to her lips and then placed them on the tombstone. The sun dipped behind the hills as she started back to the car. She'd only gone a few steps when a blue speck on the ground caught her eye. She reached down and picked up a chip of turquoise. Then looking up at the sky and smiling, she recalled a passage from the Qur'an: *"Allah has laid out the earth for you like a carpet that you may journey its limitless roads."*

Endings/Beginnings

We honored man by the gift of free will. Half of him is
honeybee, the other half snake. True believers are stores of honey.
Stores of poison are those who do not believe. —Rumi

A northeast wind rattled the palm fronds against Perin's window as she sat silently on her bed with Assia, her two suitcases near the door. As they waited for Rashid, someone knocked. Assia motioned Perin back and opened the door a crack. Huda, trying to poke her head through the small opening, said, "Is everything all right?"

Assia blocked her view. "Everything's fine. Did Nadira clean the patio?"

Perin got off the bed. "Mother, please, I want to say goodbye."

Assia sighed and let Huda in. When Huda saw the suitcases, she raised her hands in prayer position and started swaying back and forth. Assia clutched her wrists and forced her arms down. "Stop it —it's no longer safe for her here. Don't make it any harder than it is."

"O Merciful One, no." Grief and fear etched lines on Huda's face.

"Did you hear what I said?" Assia demanded. "There's great danger here and Nabil must not know. If you have any love for Perin—for this family—for my beloved Fuad—you must swear to tell no one."

Perin threw herself into Huda's arms, tears streaming down her face, heaving in tandem with Huda's body, their sobs muffled in each other's shoulders.

"Wipe your eyes," Assia said to Huda, herself tearing up, "and go see what's keeping Rashid."

Huda wiped her eyes with her apron and left. Assia put her arms around Perin and they remained rooted there wordlessly until Huda rushed back into the room with a bowl of ground henna leaves and a bottle of rosewater. "Nabil's here," she said, nearly out of breath.

"Here? Now?" Assia put her hand to her head and looked away for a moment. "Go downstairs and keep him from Perin." Huda stood there, mouth agape, shaking her head. "Go. You'll think of something." Assia's voice had an unfamiliar harshness. "Tell him the kitchen sink is clogged—or a toilet's backed up."

"But I must do this—to keep her safe," Huda said, holding up the bowl and the bottle.

Assia told her to hurry. Huda's hands shook as she made a paste and put a dab of it on the inside of each of Perin's wrists. Just as she finished, Rashid burst into the room, stopping when he saw Huda. Assia told him to not ask questions. Rashid shook his head, a non-verbal scolding for having included Huda. "Nabil's here," he said.

"We know. Huda will distract him." Assia nudged Huda out of the room.

"We have to go *now*." Rashid propped the door open with his foot.

"I don't know if I can do this," Perin said. "If Nabil sees me, he'll blame you and make me stay. It'll be worse—"

"You have to go. Trust in Allah," Assia said, pain coloring her words. She held Perin's face in her hands and kissed her cheeks and forehead, and then hugged her for a few brief moments. "I'll go help Huda."

Perin stepped out into the hallway and then turned and looked into her room. She caught her reflection in her grandmother's antique mirror and ran back and grabbed the embroidered slippers her grandfather had given her on her third birthday, sticking them into her carryon.

Perin clutched her tunic at the spot over her heart and trailed her brother down the stairs and into the hallway that led to the back of the house. Tiptoeing past the kitchen, she heard Nabil's and Huda's muted voices. Rashid was at the back door, motioning to her to hurry.

Her eyes brimmed with tears. There would be no lingering embrace, no last kiss, no farewell blessing to send her on her way from either her mother or Huda. *Blessed Allah*, Perin thought, *why this final cruelty?*

A block from the house, Aunt Safina was waiting in her car with her driver. When Rashid pulled up alongside them, she jumped out and got in the backseat with Perin, cradling her in her arms. All the way to the airport, scenes from the past months flitted through Perin's mind like reels of old films. She saw herself recently arrived, full of optimism and hope, coming home to begin her life, believing she could accomplish much—and in the end all she'd done was hurt the people she loved most in the world, and been forced to leave them. The future seemed bleak and barren. But she reminded herself, she'd saved a life.

As they left the airport parking lot, Safina pulled Perin's scarf out over her head like a visor, shielding her profile. Scurrying to keep up with Rashid, Perin, in her black tunic and scarf, kept her eyes planted on the ground—an anonymous black figure like so many others.

Rashid sprinted past the armed soldiers at the entrance to the international terminal, and threaded his way through the crowd of departing passengers and their entourages of family and friends; Perin and Safina followed directly behind. In the crowd were two morals policemen and their militia escorts. One stopped and pointed to the hem of a woman's red dress that peeked out from the bottom of her coat, while his cohort inspected the hands of the other women, checking for nail polish.

Rashid skirted around the policemen and made his way to the Air France ticket counter, where there was a line for the Paris flight. Perin, rounded shoulders and head down, queued up behind Rashid, his body erect as he looked ahead without moving. The air was stifling and it smelled stale; there was no air-conditioning. Perin stealthily wiped the top of her lip as streams of sweat poured down her back. She looked at the dried spots of henna on her wrists and tried to think of what she'd do when she reached Paris—assuming she did reach it. Her emotions a tangle of dissonance, and all her senses attuned to every sound and movement, she couldn't keep a coherent thought in her mind.

Trying to make herself small, she followed Rashid to the check-in counter. Rashid handed the agent Perin's passport, permission-to-leave letters, and their new identity cards. The agent checked the documents and asked, "You're head of household? You're very young."

"Our father just died and I'm the only son."

Perin reached behind and grabbed Aunt Safina's hand, starting to breathe easier only when Rashid put her suitcase on the scale.

The agent handed Rashid the boarding pass and the baggage tickets and directed them to Gate 11, telling him to go to Immigration Control straightaway as there was often a line.

"You handled that well," Aunt Safina said as they walked away.

"Only the first hurdle," he whispered over his shoulder, his words reinforcing that the greatest peril lay ahead.

As they neared Immigration, Aunt Safina tapped his arm. "Omer said to look for an older man. No young men. They have too much to prove."

Only young men manned the four booths. Rashid shrugged his shoulders. Safina then told him to find one who looked sympathetic. He shook his head and got in the shortest line.

When they were nearly to the front of the line, a man at the booth next to theirs started yelling. "What do you mean? These are the papers I always use. What's missing?"

"A letter from your reserve unit." The official slid his passport back across the counter and waved up the next person in line.

The man protested, saying he had a meeting and could not miss the flight. The officer stared at him expressionless. The man said he would not leave unless his passport was stamped.

The official nodded at the armed guards manning the electronic doorway to the departure lounges. They slung their rifles across their backs and each man took one of the passenger's arms. "You have no right to do this," the man yelled as he was carted away.

Rashid didn't flinch as he watched the encounter, but Perin was unsteady and leaned into her aunt. Safina pushed her back upright and kept a hand on her waist.

Fear, mingling with the hot airport air, made Perin's head throb, especially where she'd been beaten. Everything was happening too fast. She clutched at memories of her father and Zahara, trying to derive strength from them. She heard a voice in her head whisper to her—it sounded like her father: *Stand firm. You'll be fine. Everything is as it should be.*

Rashid stepped forward and presented the documents to the official. The man opened the passport and read the letters. "Why does she have to go abroad for treatment?"

"She injured her spine and neck, was in a coma, and now needs tests done with equipment that's not available here."

The official scrutinized Perin. "She looks fine to me."

Perin's nausea and the pain at the back of her head grew worse; her knees wobbled.

With his hands behind his back, Rashid's thumb nervously rubbed the thumb of the other hand. "Her injuries are internal and can't be seen with the naked eye."

"How long will she be gone?"

"Three weeks. You can see it there on her return ticket," Rashid said, pointing to the ticket the man held.

The official glared at Rashid and then opened a binder, flipping the pages and skimming his finger down a list, no doubt looking for Perin's new name on the wanted list. "You're certain she'll return?"

"Yes, she has only enough money for necessities, and she's staying with family friends who don't have room for her to stay long."

"How do I know she's not faking her illness so she can leave?"

Perin felt slashes of pain in her back and on her kidneys, where she'd taken the worst blows. It was getting harder to stand up.

"Our family doctor said it's serious," Rashid said without hesitation. "She's still having difficulty thinking and remembering."

Perin fiddled with the top button on her tunic and tried to control the rolling feeling in her stomach.

"Young man." Aunt Safina stepped forward. "I ran into a woman who has a son with your name." She pointed to his nametag. "Never stopped talking about him, she was so proud. Said he was an immigration officer but she was worried because he wasn't married."

Perin glanced up to see if the man wore a ring.

"Who's she?"

"Our neighbor. Her driver brought us here today."

The immigration officer put out his hand for Safina's identity card. "In fact," Aunt Safina continued, ignoring his outstretched hand, "she asked if I knew any women who I could introduce to him, and I said I'd think of someone. You have to be the one, she described you perfectly. Handsome like that singer heartthrob everyone talks about."

If Perin hadn't been staring at the man, she'd have missed seeing the corners of his mouth turn up. He stamped Perin's passport, ticket, and boarding pass. "Stay with her in the transit lounge until she boards the plane," he said, handing the documents back to Rashid.

"I'll tell your mother I saw you," Aunt Safina said, raising her eyebrows.

Perin, still shaking, silently pleaded with her aunt to not overdo it.

It was forty minutes before takeoff and at the gate several male passengers congregated near the jet bridge. Rashid led Perin to a far corner and sat her down between him and Safina. Little by little, the lounge filled up with more men and a few families; a couple with their young son sat across from them. Aunt Safina moved to the edge of her seat, angling her body in front of Perin's to block her from view.

A cacophony of conversations filled the room and then there was a hush. A morals policeman had entered the departure area. Perin gripped the plastic arms of the chair and Rashid whispered, "Relax. It's normal. They check everyone before departure."

The policeman went from row to row, occasionally stopping to ask for papers. Waves of nausea came over Perin again, her nerves stretched taut like threads on a loom. Head down, she pretended to doze until she heard someone's labored breathing through the mouth—the person was standing in front of her. A scream rose in her chest when she opened her eyes and saw scaly, callused feet in dirty sandals.

Rashid handed him the documents and the inspection process played out again. As she listened to the rustling paper, Perin felt the man's eyes on her.

"She isn't married?"

"She's engaged," Rashid said.

"When is she getting married?"

"The end of the year, if her health improves. *Inshallah*."

Terror gripped Perin as she gazed up at the policeman's round hooded eyes that seemed to bulge out of their sockets. Her sweat-dampened hands tingled. She told herself to hold on a few minutes more, a few minutes more.

The policeman took out a notepad and wrote something in it. "She'd better come back. I'll be watching for her." For a few seconds he stared at Perin, seconds that passed glacially, weighted as they were with his menace and her fear. Perin's alarm turned to fury and she wanted to yell out that what they were doing was a travesty to Islam. Even though she wanted to lash out, she was tired of this fight, fearing she was nearing the point where it would kill her spirit; she wanted it to end, if only temporarily.

The policeman walked away and she saw in Safina's eyes all she could not say aloud. Her aunt kissed her on the forehead. "Omer will take care of everything, so don't worry."

The boarding was announced and Rashid handed Perin the travel documents. Passengers swarmed toward the jet bridge to the plane while Perin stepped gingerly, expecting an alarm to go off, signaling a violation, but there was none.

Wrapped in sadness and regret, she hesitated and thought of all she was leaving behind, and of all she hadn't said, knowing she could never adequately express all her love and gratitude. She just looked into Rashid's and Safina's eyes and hoped hers communicated all she wanted to tell them.

Numbly, she made her way inside the plane, not daring to turn around again to glimpse everything she was losing. Sitting alone in the in back row, she felt her isolation. Again, there would be no one at her side to encourage and comfort her.

She kept an eye on the door and prayed it would not open again, trying to dispel visions of the morals police rushing the plane, stopping the pilot from taking off, and yanking her off to prison. Only after they were airborne was she able to breathe normally.

Like a slide projector, her mind flashed pictures against her lids. Her mother. Rashid. Aunt Safina. Huda. Ali. Shereen. Zahara, Imene—would she ever know what eventually happened to the young woman? She hoped she was safe and would be able to make a life for herself. And Nabil, how would he react when he found out she'd left; she hoped he would not take it out on her mother and Rashid. And Eva—she still had to tell her all that had happened. She wondered if Eva would be sympathetic or chastise her for not heeding her warning, of making another bad decision. And Ali—she'd keep an eye out for his byline, and scan the internet for his whereabouts; just maybe they might meet again.

She was certain the authorities would discover she'd disappeared, no matter what Uncle Omer did and how careful he was. But all that mattered was that he, possibly in jeopardy himself for helping in her escape, would be able to protect her family. She asked Allah's and her family's forgiveness for putting them in danger and tried to console herself with the Prophet's words: *Those who seek forgiveness will find that Allah helps them out of every difficulty, and provides for them from His limitless bounty.*

Swells of sadness washed over her as her father came to mind; he'd have been devastated to see her leave this way and yet, he'd have insisted she embrace her destiny and create new meaning for her life abroad since none was possible at home. She thought she'd have it all—a noted career where she'd make a difference and give back to her country, while encircled by cherished traditions and her loving family. In the end, she was exiled from all.

On the curb outside Charles de Gaulle Airport, Perin breathed in the late August day as soufflé clouds shuttled across a cobalt blue sky. A multitude of languages swirled around her as arriving and departing passengers made their ways in and out of the terminal. Mostly tourists, she surmised, the French not yet back from their annual holidays. Lost in thought, she didn't notice her cousin jump out of the cab that stopped in front of her.

"Traffic was terrible. Hope you haven't been waiting long." Tariq took her bags and handed them to the driver before opening the door for her. He scooted in next to her and said to the driver, "*Avenue de Ségur, s'il vous plaît. 7th Arrondissement.*" As the driver swerved into the traffic circulating in front of the airport, Tariq discussed the bottlenecks up ahead with him.

Perin looked at the people waiting in front of the other terminals. How many had also left home not knowing if they'd ever see their families again? Her exile weighed heavily upon her, especially because of the potential impact it would have on her family.

"I almost forgot," Tariq said. "Mother called and said to tell you that the weather back home is fine. Don't know why she wanted me to tell you that." Perin allowed herself a smile.

Before turning onto the expressway, she saw three women in headscarves. By choice or dictate, she wondered. And along with their scarves, did they carry the extra baggage of what it meant to be a woman in their homeland? I am not unique, she thought. I am not alone.

She caressed her turquoise necklace and then tugged at the ends of her scarf. It fell on her shoulders before floating down onto the seat beside her, where it rested until a gust of wind picked it up, and swirled it around until it finally flew out the open window.

CPSIA information can be obtained
at www.ICGtesting.com
Printed in the USA
LVHW041224210820
663783LV00006B/496